SO GLAD TO MEET YOU

LISA SUPER

DIVERSION
BOOKS

Diversion Books
A Division of Diversion Publishing Corp.
443 Park Avenue South, Suite 1008
New York, New York 10016
www.DiversionBooks.com

For more information, email info@diversionbooks.com

First Diversion Books edition July 2018.
Paperback ISBN: 978-1-63576-397-3
eBook ISBN: 978-1-63576-396-6

Printed in the U.S.A.
SDB/1807
1 3 5 7 9 10 8 6 4 2

In memory of Bernice and Charlene,
my grandmothers of middle names.

TUESDAY

THE FINAL BELL RANG A DECIBEL LOWER THAN USUAL. OR the pitch was a half note sharp or flat. Daphne didn't have the musical ear to distinguish exactly what it was, but something sounded different. Maybe because it was Tuesday, and Tuesdays had a tendency to sound that way. She twisted her neck to the surrounding desks. The other students either hadn't noticed the fluctuation in the bell tone, or they didn't care. They gathered their books and waited at the door to funnel out of the classroom. Daphne cleared her desk and joined the mob formation.

The student body drained into the hallway like pipes connecting to a festive, heavily perfumed sewer. Homecoming banners dangled from the walls, one gust of wind away from being trampled on the floor. Senior year was in full swing. Three classrooms down, Daphne saw Janine whack a rogue balloon into the air. Even in maximum exertion mode, her best friend's face rested in its standard quasi-sour state. Daphne leaned against the lockers and waited for Janine to catch up.

"Yo, yo, yo," Janine said.

"Did the final bell sound different?" Daphne asked.

"Maybe a little louder," Janine said. "Probably psychological, though. Or both our speakers are on the fritz. Did you see that balloon assault my face?"

Daphne smiled at Janine's talent for switching subjects in the same breath. "No, I only saw you teaching it a lesson. You should've popped it."

"It will be the greatest regret of my life." Janine grumbled, but her brown eyes twinkled under the thick, dark brows that intimidated everyone but Daphne.

The two girls plodded down the school hallways, together and alone. Their thrift store attire, with mismatched buttons, vintage threads worn thin, and patches covering the tears, set them apart from the other students clustered against the lockers in assembly line sweaters and knockoff denim. Plus, the secondhand wardrobe was cost effective.

Daphne dialed her locker combination. "Want to go to the game on Friday?" She left out the sarcasm to mess with Janine's head.

"Why? Do you want to watch a bunch of dudes in spandex concuss themselves?" Distressed, Janine flipped the part of her long, wiry black hair to the other side.

Daphne continued feigning innocence. "I don't know. I like the sound their helmets make when they collide. It's so raw and animalistic."

The tan skin on Janine's forehead furrowed at this revelation.

Mission accomplished.

Daphne's voice went dreamy, and she slung her bookbag over her shoulder. "It's the sound I imagine hearing on my deathbed when I'm taking my last breaths. That heavenly sound ushering me into the afterlife."

Janine groaned, embarrassed that she'd fallen for the ruse. "I thought you'd gone and caught school spirit or something. You know, I'd have to take you out back and put you out of your misery." They reached Janine's locker.

"You have my permission," Daphne said. They'd been doing their best to ease each other's suffering since fifth grade.

Gazing past Janine, Daphne spied a girl walking away. The hair on Daphne's arms tingled and pointed straight to the ceiling. From the back, the girl could be Emily. Except that, of course, she couldn't. The blonde hair swishing at the girl's shoulders couldn't be her sister's. Neither could the slopes and valleys where her ribs and hips became her waist. But Daphne grabbed these seconds, the ticks of time when she reclaimed her sister, when history was rewritten. She held them tight, fingernails digging into her palms, so she was ready to let go when Janine slammed her locker and blocked her view.

"You saw the library was closed, right?" Janine asked.

Daphne flinched, and the raven ends of her asymmetrical bob flopped against her neck and shoulder. "What?"

"I drove by and the sign said it was closed for repairs."

"What does that mean?"

"The library broke." Janine shrugged.

"What the hell, L.A.?" Daphne slumped against a locker. "Get your public services together."

"Use the school's library."

"That's crazy talk."

"You're crazy talk."

"Can I come over?" Daphne pleaded.

"I'm still grounded for flunking my Spanish quiz."

Daphne scolded Janine. "You already speak two languages. Seems like it shouldn't be such a struggle to learn a third." She smirked.

Janine snickered. "What's your excuse, monolingual?"

Daphne tilted her head up to the ceiling, pretended to think, and lowered her chin with the obvious answer. "White privilege."

"Damn skippy. If this stupid school offered Armenian, I'd be aces. I mean, I wouldn't get an A, but I wouldn't be grounded."

"Janine, ace of the B-. It's an art form."

"Put it up." Janine raised her arm, and Daphne high-wristed her, joining the fragile bones where arm meets palm.

They'd been doing this in place of high fives since sophomore year. One Saturday, after a fruitful haul from Buffalo Exchange, Janine had dressed for a family reunion in a faded pair of overalls and a black turtleneck with a hole at the wrist.

Janine's mom wasn't impressed with their thriftiness. "I can deal with the overalls, but you shouldn't buy damaged clothes."

Janine picked up a pair of scissors, cut a hole in the turtleneck's other wrist, and stuck her thumbs through the holes. "Better?"

Daphne giggled.

Janine's mom shook her head. "You two are literally wearing your teen angst on your sleeves."

Janine held up her arm. "High five with wrists."

Daphne bumped her wrist against Janine's. An inside joke was born.

Two years later, they were still wearing their literal teen angst on their sleeves. Daphne tapped Janine's wrist twice for emphasis. "See you tomorrow." She grinned down the hallway.

• • •

Daphne weighed the cost against the sacrifice. If she went to a coffee shop to do her homework she'd spend three dollars. No, four dollars with the tip. Three dollars hurt. Four dollars hurt a dollar more.

If she went home, she might have to talk to her dad. That would be painful. Hurt versus pain was a tough choice. Even after she spent the four dollars, her dad might be awake when she walked through the front door. And then she'd be in pain *and* hurt. She was economical, fiscally and emotionally. Going home offered less potential for spiritual and financial rug burn.

She dawdled the three-quarters of a mile to her home, taking the long way around the park, adding another mile, another half hour toward sunset, until there was nowhere left to go except up her driveway. She ignored the garage door. The past tried to crawl up her legs from the concrete, but she shook her knees and kicked the memories away.

The extra mileage on the journey home paid off. When Daphne slipped the key into the knob and turned, demonstrating mastery of the silent unlock and door open, her dad was asleep on the La-Z-Boy. The light from the TV reflected off his balding head, and his overgrown blond hair splayed with static electricity against the cushions. She could see his eyelids twitching, which meant he was gone for the night. Tiptoeing down the hallway, she silently praised herself for not choosing the coffee shop.

It was only when she crossed her bedroom threshold and closed the door with a miniscule click that she could breathe again. She plopped down in the chair and adjusted her laptop to her body. In moving the computer, she inadvertently knocked the nickel she had propped against it. The coin tumbled to the ground with a mocking, spinning chime. Daphne sighed. The perfect end to another perfect Tuesday.

Daphne scanned the floor, under the chair, under her feet. The nickel was nowhere. She knelt and, on further inspection, detected a flash of silver between two floorboards. There was barely enough room to stuff the tops of her fingers down into the crack. The sensation of her cuticles scraping against the wood ran down her spine, and the pain shot up her neck and into her molars. She gritted her teeth and shoved her hands down further, until a loose plank shifted.

Daphne pried up the floorboard. The nickel fell for a final time, resting next to a carelessly folded piece of notebook paper and a small bottle of perfume or cologne, Daphne wasn't sure which.

She picked up the bottle. "FLAME" was printed across the barrel. The "A" was a lick of fire. She sniffed the nozzle but could only smell cold metal. She sprayed a fine mist into the air. The essence of Jason Pagano rushed into her mind through her nose—his shadowy figure slinking behind Emily everywhere she went, always disappearing behind a closed door. Daphne had liked his scent. It evoked the embers of summer camp and winter fireplaces.

Her jittery hands smoothed the paper open, cautious to not damage the relic, an archeologist discovering a Pharaoh's tomb. Small pen doodles, like hieroglyphics, spread across the page. The horned head of a bull. A mountain. The Eiffel Tower. A parachute. A waterfall. A cactus. A brick wall. Stars in all the open spaces of the page, framing the words. It was a list, written with two different hands, one more legible than the other.

EMILY & JASON'S TOP TEN

1. The Great Wall of China
2. Jim Morrison's grave
3. Climb Mount Everest
4. Skydive
5. The Sahara Desert
6. Own a pair of designer shoes
7. Niagara Falls
8. Running with the Bulls
9. Go To Outer Space
10.

The list trembled in her hands. For seven years, she had listened for the clue and this was her reward. Instead of finding treasure, she had found a map.

• • •

"Whoa. Whoa. Whoa." The immensity of the situation had reduced Janine to a malfunctioning AI.

"I need some sentences," Daphne said into the phone.

"My thoughts are all in Armenian. That only happens in dreams."

"Well, I'm glad my sister's bucket list is such a cultural experience for you."

"When do you think they wrote it?"

"Seven years ago."

There was a pause before Janine chuckled, and Daphne was pleased with herself. "That's dark, dude," Janine said.

Daphne shrugged. "Yeah, well." She propped the fallen nickel on the desk against the spine of *The Catcher in the Rye*, making sure Jefferson's head was perfectly centered.

"You could tell your mom?"

Daphne let the silence hang until Janine apologized.

"Good point." Janine said. "So, what're you going to do with it?"

"I don't know. But I should do something, right?"

"Yeah, probably. But what...?" Janine trailed off and came back with a frantic whisper. "Oh, my mom's coming!"

Janine hung up, another abrupt ending Daphne could associate with Emily and Jason.

All evening, Daphne's brain was a magnet stuck on the list. Calculus homework wasn't happening. Daphne did something that she never did: copied the answers from the back of the book. Not showing her work would earn her a "C." Fine. She moved on to half-assing her English assignment, skimming *Lord of the Flies* and using loose tangents to fake her way through the essay. Between paragraphs, she read the Top Ten list over and over again.

What could she do with a list about dream places scattered across the world? The universe, even. What did it mean? Why had she found it? And now, after all this time?

That night, the minutes ticked away as Daphne lie half-asleep. Visions of Emily spun around her head: the gold strands of her hair catching the sunlight, the constellations of freckles on her nose linking directly back to the Sun, everything in orbit, the Earth frozen but still spinning.

Daphne woke up groggy and depleted. No sleep, no solace. Apparently, that would be her motto until she figured out what to do with the piece of paper weighing down her pocket.

She couldn't tell her parents. Bringing up Emily's name sucked them into the vortex of that Tuesday night. The way their skin tightened and the air chilled and sparked with electricity was enough to warn Daphne away from asking any more questions. They would freak out and ask the same questions she couldn't answer. Her parents might even accuse her of being an accomplice in burying the relics and take away the list and Flame. She whipped out her cell, snapped a photo, and backed it up in five places.

Daphne's dad was still asleep when she made breakfast. She pulled out a box of Bran Flakes, careful not to bang the cabinet. She sprinkled raisins in her bowl, facing the two converging counters against the opposite wall. Standing in the same place, she remembered them.

Emily sits on the counter. Jason stands next to her. Their heads are close, mouths in a whisper. Emily looks up at Daphne, who's pouring a box of Lucky Charms, but her smile never leaves Jason.

"Let's go." Emily vaults off the counter toward the door.

Jason follows. He reaches for Emily's hand, grabs and holds tight, speaking through their palms. He gives Daphne a shy smile, twice the acknowledgment that Emily gave her.

"I promised my brother we'd play catch," Jason mumbles to Emily as they disappear through the doorway.

Daphne's Bran Flakes hit the bowl, and the ceramic jingle woke her with the force of five espresso shots. Her earlobes went warm.

The brother.

Oliver.

He might be the key to getting a good night's sleep.

It was the longest morning of a school day in her twelve-plus years of education. If the bell had been an emergency siren, she still would've fled to the library at lunch without regard for her safety. She sat at a computer and searched his full name, "Oliver Pagano," on Facebook. She had no clue what he looked like because his profile photo was a man in a bird costume. They had ten mutual friends, but they weren't real friends. Daphne hadn't had an actual conversation with any of them. She scratched her nose. All his photos were private. His profile indicated that he went to Sacred Heart High School.

"Of course." Daphne's mouth pinched at the corners to form a sarcastic smile.

He was rich, after all. His family owned that furniture chain with all the annoying commercials that were intentionally cheap looking. Because if you had that much money, playing poor was a fun game.

She studied the profile photo of the bird-man. At least he had a sense of humor. She clicked on the "Send Friend Request" tab.

"Hi, Oliver. This may seem weird…" She immediately deleted it.

"Hi. My name is Daphne. Which you can already see because you're not blind. And you probably declined my Friend Request because you saw my last name." *And my face.*

"So, your brother and my sister. Barrel of laughs, right?" Delete, delete, delete.

Her first instinct was usually best. She typed and revised, doubting every keystroke. She hovered the mouse over "Send" and gulped. The bell rang, slightly muffled in the library speaker.

Click. She closed the window, message unsent. She'd send it tonight, after spending another five hours obsessing over the exact wording, commas, and balance of subtext. By the time she hit "Send," the message would be so built up that Oliver Pagano could only be a letdown.

OPPOSITE POSSUM

Oliver's phone buzzed on the coffee table. It was a Friend Request from a name he recognized, one that he hadn't thought about in years. He started to read the message: "Hi, Oliver. This may seem a little weird…" His stomach shifted. He knew it was because of Jason. Like most things concerning Jason, Oliver ignored it.

"Am I boring you?" Katrina asked. She was half joking, half possessive. Her eyelids were heavy with infatuation, and he felt extra good every time she gazed at him. Under those eyelids, her irises were weapons, green blades ready to slice him. With every blink, she'd been sneaking over his boundaries without him noticing. Oliver raised his guard. They needed to have the No Boyfriend conversation.

He tossed the phone aside. "Nope."

Kissing Katrina was heaven. She knew what she was doing, knew how to use her entire body, molding herself into precise positions against him. He wanted to see her naked, smell her skin as it rubbed against his. And this was exactly why he waited two minutes too long to give the No Boyfriend speech. She straddled him on her sofa and removed her navy Sacred Heart polo with such ease that he didn't realize what had happened until he was staring at a black, lacy bra filled with her small, lovely curves.

"Katrina, I like you…"

She gathered her hair over one shoulder, so the long, red waves cradled her neck and left her breastbone bare to run her fingers across. Oliver translated the deliberate move and pressed onward. "You know I like you."

"The feeling's mutual." She tugged at her bra strap and the release snapped against her shoulder.

"Yeah." He didn't know how to segue, so he didn't try. "I can't be your boyfriend."

"Why not?" She bit her lip, still playing the seductress.

"It's my thing."

"Well, my thing is I can't have sex with you unless you're my boyfriend."

An ultimatum. Oliver had never received an ultimatum this early into a nonrelationship. He nodded, impressed. "That's fair."

She crossed her arms under her chest. "How is it fair?"

"Uh, because you said it was."

"I never said it was fair. I want you to be my boyfriend."

She knew what she wanted and was saying it out loud. Oliver showed his gratitude by placing his hands on her thighs. "And I said I couldn't be your boyfriend, so you said we couldn't have sex, and I said that was fair."

"Thanks for the recap." She climbed off him and yanked her shirt back on.

"Why are you upset?" He genuinely wanted to know.

"You know why I'm upset."

"No, I don't."

In some ways, girls were still a science experiment to him. He wanted to understand the workings of their minds on a theoretical level. He wanted to become a master, a black belt in women. Earning that piece of cloth might be his key to figuring out the universe.

Katrina sighed and sank into the sofa facing him. "We should be together. As a couple. You should be mine. And I should be yours."

"But we can still be that. We're exclusive. I'm faithful to you and you alone."

"Then why can't you be my boyfriend?"

He scratched at a tingle in his chin. "Because it's a word I don't like. I have my reasons."

"What reasons?"

"Jason," he said.

"You don't have to explain. I get it," Katrina said.

The mere mention of *Jason* won every argument. When Oliver said his brother's name, he attached no emotion to it. Yet, for whoever listened, guilt and anguish always harmonized in its two syllables.

Oliver and Katrina nodded at each other in understanding. For the time being, they would both get what they wanted, until she needed more. Oliver stood up. "I should probably go."

"Okay." Katrina leaned over and kissed him, sucking on his lower lip as she pulled away.

He gathered himself, touched his quads to make sure his legs could carry him. "Pick you up before school?"

She grinned, breaking her seductress façade. Something even more stunning shined through the cracks. "Yeah. I'll see you tomorrow."

Oliver limped out the front door blue-balled, anxious, and pleased. He couldn't tell which sensation outweighed the other two. Driving home, the testosterone and pleasure faded, and only the anxiety remained. He'd thought about Jason twice in a single conversation without his parents' prompting. These statistics were troublesome.

At the dinner table half an hour later, the Jason percentage increased as predicted.

"I was going through Jason's box today, and I found a note that he left on our car one morning." Oliver's mom pulled out the crayon scrawl on green construction paper, cut into the points of a star. "Dear Mom, have a god day. A *god* day. He forgot an *o*," she cooed.

"Maybe he's hinting that we should go to Mass." Oliver's dad matched her tenderness and scratched a sentimental itch in his salt and pepper beard.

Jason had died when Oliver was eleven, but not a day passed that Jason wasn't mentioned in the Pagano household, revered as the most perfect son that ever existed. Jason, who had taken his first steps before any of the other children his age. Jason, who had gotten straight A's on every report card since kindergarten. Jason, who had written the most thoughtful Christmas and birthday cards every year and always delivered them early.

Oliver resented that his parents never once mentioned that this perfect child had also permanently wounded them, twisting the invisible knife so the hole would never heal. And Jason didn't even have to stick around to watch the suffering. Not that Oliver considered his brother to be lucky, but it wasn't fair that his parents only spoke of Jason's great accomplishments and his kind and beautiful and pure soul. The way Oliver saw it, Jason, a questionable soul, had made a series of unkind and not beautiful decisions that couldn't be undone. It would've gone a long way with Oliver for them to mention this, even once.

Oliver took a deep breath and opened his mouth, ready to enlighten his parents. But the bright tears ready to fall from his mother's eyes sabotaged him. He panned across the table to his father's flush of pride and twitching nose. The sadness was all right there under thin layers of skin and laughter. If this is what the happy memories did to them, what would the worst memory of their lives do? Oliver couldn't bear to inflict this upon them. If he did, he would be just like Jason. Except the intent would be worse because Oliver was alive.

He exhaled the tight balloon of air in his chest, stuffed his mouth full of mashed potatoes, and reminded himself that their pain was worse than his. And surely they knew that Jason wasn't Prince Perfect. But, seriously, couldn't they say it out loud?

"Cute," Oliver mustered for the green star, earning some good will.

Further validating that Jason wasn't Prince Perfect was the fact that Oliver's parents had taken an approach to raising him that he referred to as *Opposite Possum*. They played dead to the fact that Oliver was an actual individual with a distinct personality, that he held different inclinations than his older brother. Oliver had no intention of ending his life, especially before he'd reached the legal drinking age. Nevertheless, they steered him to be Jason's opposite in every aspect. Jason had gone to public school, so Oliver was enrolled at Sacred Heart. Jason hadn't been policed by a curfew, so Oliver was due home earlier than all of his friends. He'd discovered a workaround for the curfew situation, though. It was called lying, and Oliver was getting pretty good at it.

"Can I stay out until one on Friday?"

"A curfew is a curfew, not a malleable state." His dad trimmed the fat from his pork chop.

"I'm negotiating," Oliver said. "I know you don't want to hear this, but there's a party. My friends are going. I told them I'd be the DD."

His mom sighed. The distance between her thin brown eyebrows and pixie haircut left a lot of forehead to condemn him.

"I'm just being honest. And responsible."

"We didn't buy you that car so you could play chauffeur to your drunk friends," his dad said.

"They're gonna drink, Dad. And they won't be done by ten. I'm just making sure they get home without killing anyone."

Oliver's parents had a telepathic debate across the table. His dad wasn't easily convinced. A bite of pork chop was chewed long and slow in deliberation. His mother answered, "Midnight. And we appreciate your honesty. But maybe you should get a job to help supplement the gas and insurance for your valet service." His mom stabbed a broccoli floret with her fork.

Oliver accepted these terms.

Luckily or unluckily, Jason had been an employee at

Quickee Car Wash when he died. His parents wouldn't press Oliver further on the employment front as long as he didn't push the curfew extension limits.

When it came to dating, Oliver chose to apply the Opposite Possum strategy on himself without his parents' decree. Since Jason had a girlfriend at the time of his demise, Oliver would have no such thing. Thus, the No Boyfriend conversation. It wasn't malicious. It was merely full disclosure.

Some girls would immediately be turned off, and the dating would be over. Most took it as a challenge, thinking that he'd simply taken the stance because he wanted to keep playing the field. Like in all the movies, he just hadn't met the right girl to commit to, and each one thought she was *the* girl. She would be the one to awaken his soul at last.

They thought they could change him, and their efforts always failed. The girls eventually acknowledged that he would never be their boyfriend. More often than not, this conclusion led to feelings of deep, personal failure. This was the exact situation he'd tried to avoid, the whole reason he'd had the awkward No Boyfriend conversation in the first place. And still, his final encounters with the girls he'd been seeing usually involved flinging grenades of tears at him and/or showering him with expletives.

He wouldn't give Daphne Bowman or her Friend Request that chance, even if it was just platonic. There was too much history. She had all the baggage of an ex-girlfriend and he'd never even met her. She was more dangerous than Katrina. He took out his phone and contemplated her photo for the last time. Her weird haircut and ghostly white skin. Eyes big and blue enough he could practically swim in them.

Something in those eyes told him she was the smartest girl he'd ever met, and he was never going to know her. Oliver hit "Decline."

Keeping trouble out of his life was supposed to leave Oliver feeling cleansed. Instead, his skin drew tight, as if coated with dust. His whole body itched. Even though his brother had been gone for seven years, it was all Jason's fault.

SACRED HEARTS

SEVENTEEN. STUPID OLIVER PAGANO AND HIS STUPID BIRD face reminded her that she was very much seventeen.

Even before finding the list, Daphne had been thinking about her sister more than ever now that they shared the same age. Seventeen was the link to Emily that had been simmering in Daphne's veins for seven years, a curse to be revealed and a chance to break its spell. If Daphne could just make it through seventeen, the doors of life would open to her and she could walk through anything. Emily's list gave her a charm to counter this spell, but she didn't know how to use it.

She reached deep into the black nothing of her mind and grasped for any clue that Emily may have left. Her last memory of Emily was the most prominent, a few months before that infamous Tuesday, when Emily's mood had swung on a peaceful hammock blowing in the wind.

Daphne sits at her small desk, filling out a workbook for

spelling class. Emily knocks on the door, which is strange because Emily isn't a knocker. She's barged in and out of rooms as long as Daphne can remember with absolutely zero courtesy for the people on either side of the door. The knock validated her parents' whispers of medication and working, a quiet joy in their voices.

"Come in." Daphne's words come out as suspicion rather than instruction.

"How's it going?" Emily tiptoes in, as if reduced volume lessens the disruption. Daphne goes back to her writing.

"Doing homework?" Emily asks.

Daphne is no fool. Plenty of times Emily has asked Daphne about school only to ridicule her teacher's pet status. It's better to say nothing and just let Emily get frustrated with the lack of attention and storm out of the room. Daphne nods without looking up.

"Sorry you have Mrs. Morris. She's a huge bit..." Emily catches herself. "Big, nasty person."

"That's what I thought, too, before I had her. She seems really mean in the halls and at recess. But she's a really fun teacher and not mean at all."

"I don't know if I believe you."

"Why would I lie?" Daphne cocks her head, half innocent, half annoyed.

"Why would you tell the truth?"

Daphne gives this three seconds of thought. "Because I do."

Emily smiles at her, a smile Daphne hasn't seen in a long time. A real one.

"Yeah, you do." Emily exits louder than her entrance. The ground creaks and moans under her feet, and she takes extra, weighted steps to build the noise.

Daphne stares at Emily, at her rude feet.

"So serious. You need to get out of this room." Emily throws Daphne a wink as she saunters through the doorway.

This list was probably there the whole time—maybe that's what the wink was about. Daphne played the scene again and again in her mind. At the end of each wink through the doorway, her thoughts returned to Oliver. The other boy at another desk in the other house with another set of floorboards.

She'd given Oliver a full week. Rather, she'd given herself a full week to forget about him, and she'd failed. Basic cyberstalking showed that he'd "Liked" one of their mutual friend's photos. Deductive reasoning pointed to him having read her message. Still, she couldn't let it go. She didn't know what the list meant, but it meant something. He should have something, shouldn't he? The list had become a secret she was keeping from him. Whether he wanted to hear it or not, the universe owed it to him. And Daphne was the universe.

A quick Google search revealed that he'd scored a touchdown in football three years ago in a JV game. It was a start. The first place she'd look was the Sacred Heart football field.

After school, one block before her house, she passed the Sacred Heart campus as she'd done roughly twelve hundred times before. Striding by the elite prep school every morning, she fantasized rolling out of bed at the first bell and still making it to first period without a tardy. Daphne had the sensibility to keep her dreams feasible.

Though a block away in proximity, Sacred Heart levitated miles above her family's income bracket, even with her mom working eighty-hour weeks at the hospital, even before her dad lost his insurance job. Daphne shared the sidewalk with girls whose shoes cost more than her entire wardrobe, and the student parking lot could stand in for an Audi dealership.

The whole scene was pretty disgusting. Sweet-sixteen birthday presents could pay for entire college educations. Well, almost. Daphne always held her head high and slowed her pace when walking alongside the Sacred Hearters. The rich would suffer the sight of her ninety-eight-percentery as long as possible. She tugged on her vintage Harley Davidson T-shirt. The safety pins holding it together shimmered in the sun.

"Cool shirt." A blonde girl slipped in six dainty conch earrings, no mirror required. She gave Daphne a nod of approval and adorned her fingers with thick silver rings.

That's what Daphne got for trying to make a socioeconomical statement: a compliment.

"Thanks," Daphne mumbled. She also acknowledged that if she had the money, she'd buy the same pair of Alexander Wang ankle boots that No Mirror Girl was wearing, college education be damned.

Daphne wondered what the girl would wear if she wasn't hampered by the Sacred Heart's polos and knee-length skirts. And that's when Daphne realized the fatal flaw in her plan—the dress code. She couldn't blend in wearing all black in a world of navy blue and khaki.

She circled back, taking long, slow breaths to coax her stomach up the four inches it had fallen. In an effort to calm herself, she analyzed her findings from the initial Sacred Heart flyby. The main entrance had too much security to get through without a Student ID. All the other gates were locked, but the East Gate had a fair amount of foot traffic. That was her best chance of sneaking in. She just needed someone to open the door.

By the time she made it back to the East Gate, the stream of students had run dry. Daphne milled about the sidewalk for ten minutes, pretending to be on her phone, until someone finally came. The Chuck Taylors beneath the boy's khakis made him a solid prospect. They were decked out in rebel fashion with band logos reimagined as pro-Catholicism talking points. On one white toe cap, the squared NIИ of Nine Inch Nails now read "NIV." On the other toe cap, NOFX's logo now promoted "NOSEX." She walked to the gate, keeping her eyes on her phone, playing it cool. She moved to slide behind him, but he jerked the gate closed.

"Hey, you don't go here." He held her shoulder.

Daphne almost dropped her phone. "I…was…" She stuttered, unable to concoct a lie.

He scowled at her and walked away.

Entitled asshat. Trent Reznor would not approve.

Daphne leaned against the fence, ready to give up. Out of the corner of her eye, No Mirror Girl crossed into the parking lot from the main entrance. This was Daphne's last chance. She ran to the Alexander Wang boots.

"Hey!"

No Mirror Girl turned. "Hi?"

"I don't have a badge." The line came out smooth because it wasn't a lie. "Could you, please, let me in?"

No Mirror Girl gave Daphne's T-shirt a second look and pointed up and over the fence. "See those?"

Daphne followed her finger to three security cameras aimed in different angles at the gate.

"If you do anything illegal, it's my ass. And I like my ass just the way it is."

"Understood. No asses will be affected."

NMG ran her badge over the sensor. The gate unlocked.

"Thank you." Daphne hoped the wavering in her voice conveyed her gratitude and ran inside.

She didn't know where she was going, but a sweet-rich-exotic cloud of incense swarmed the sidewalk. She followed the scent, averting her trespassing eyes from any remaining students. The trail led her to the school chapel. Directly behind it were the football field bleachers. The entrance was right there! But between her and the fifty-yard line, two male faculty members with badges dangling on lanyards were headed straight toward her. One of the men spotted Daphne and nodded in her direction. Daphne couldn't turn around. They'd call her out for sure, and she'd be escorted out as soon as she'd arrived. The chapel was her only hope. *Don't panic.* She held her head high and marched the ten steps to the chapel. Not too fast, not too slow.

The chapel was filled with smoke from the incense. She froze in the doorway. Her own memories swirled in the exhaust.

The thick haze escapes as the garage door opens. Her mom throws open her car door, tries to jump out with her seatbelt still on. The yank of the seatbelt reaching the end of its give, like a noose snapping a neck.

PHLUGH-MEH-DUM! The brown flash in Daphne's peripheral vision brought her back to the chapel. A priest whipped a rug through the air, whooshing fresh air in and incense out. A nun waved a broom, trying to do the same, while an overachieving altar boy apologized profusely.

"It's fine, Wyatt. I know it won't happen again." The warmth in the priest's voice comforted the boy. The nun scowled, unconvinced Wyatt wouldn't repeat his sins.

Still flapping the rug, the priest spotted Daphne in the doorway. "Please, come in. If you don't mind a little incense. This might put you off the stuff for life."

It struck her that the last time she'd attended church was Emily's funeral. She considered turning around and running, but she liked the way the light blazed through the stained glass windows in the late afternoon. The vivid colors of the Virgin Mary and Jesus, mercifully not on the cross, energized her. At the same time, the listless eyes of shepherds and angels lent the room a sense of serenity. No worries, no happiness, no sorrow. She gave the priest a sheepish look and stepped inside.

The two faculty members were right behind her. "Everything alright, Father?" They said it referring to Daphne, not the smoke.

"Yes. This is a prospective student," the priest said. "We should be so lucky."

The faculty members smiled at Daphne and left.

"I'm Father George. Please don't tell me if you're not a prospective student. I like to consider myself an honest man."

Normally, there was something off-putting about the black and Roman-collared attire of priests, such formality for a religion based on a notoriously informal carpenter. Father George overcame her apprehension with an assertive handshake. She wasn't a delicate creature to him, nor a soul that needed to be saved.

"Daphne." She shouldn't have given her real name, but he was a priest. Lying to him was an express ticket to hell. Not that she believed in hell, but still.

"Welcome to Sacred Heart, Daphne." His kind eyes eased her nerves.

"I'm looking for someone. Oliver Pagano?"

Recognition lit up Father George's face. "I imagine he's on the field."

"Is it this way?" Daphne pointed to the back door.

"I'm sorry, Daphne. You're not a student here, so you can't go through there."

"Oh." Her knees turned to jelly. She struggled not to slump to the floor in defeat.

"But there's a home game Friday night."

"Oh," she said again. Her legs reconstituted, and she grew an inch while attempting to make more than vowel sounds. "Can I do my homework here?" *Every night*, she wanted to add.

"You're welcome here, anytime." Father George reached into his pocket and handed her a business card bearing his name, phone number, and the Sacred Heart emblem. "Call this number at the Main Gate." He pulled a pair of scissors from behind the pulpit and trimmed the wicks on the prayer candles. "Call every day, if you like. I'll be here."

Daphne swallowed and nodded, barely able to contain her smile. "Thank you."

Over the next hour, a few people stepped in and out to say a brief prayer. If Daphne was distracted by their entrance, they exited quietly without her notice. This place was a homework mecca, while her broken public library was a crowded and noisy substitution for a babysitter and a homeless shelter. She was going to study here tomorrow and next week and the week after. The idea made her head go fizzy. Even reading about the horrors of Gettysburg couldn't take away all of the carbonation.

• • •

She wanted to bring Janine along for moral support. But the merciless teasing—for a boy, much less—wasn't worth it. Friday night, Daphne arrived at Sacred Heart an hour before the game, paid the entry fee, and sat at the bottommost bleachers, prime real estate for reading names on jerseys. She knew she was in the right place because the bird head from Oliver's profile photo was cheering at her feet.

The stands filled up and screamers of all ages, all wearing red and white, packed in around her. By the end of the fourth quarter, Oliver Pagano hadn't made any passes, blocks, catches, tackles, or touchdowns. He hadn't incurred any penalties, and he wasn't sitting on the bench. The masses around her hadn't screamed his name.

He wasn't on the football team.

Sacred Heart was fourteen points ahead as the final seconds ticked down. Everyone in the bleachers stood and cheered. It was time to make her escape before everyone fled for the exits. She ran along the bottom bleacher, careful not to step on any toes.

"Oliver!" A female voice shouted.

Daphne halted and turned to the voice. Beneath her, right in front of the bleachers, most of the cheerleading squad ran and hugged the hawk mascot. She shuffled back to her seat, closer to the hawk, now pushing against the flow of bodies.

"We did it!" a short, buxom girl squealed, burying her boobs in the bird's feathers.

Daphne grimaced. Squealing girls were nails on chalkboards.

"Oly, are you coming out tonight?" Another cheerleader asked. The hawk head nodded.

Jason Pagano's little brother had been right in front of her the whole game, running back and forth as the Sacred Heart Hawk. She'd made a point not to watch him because she pitied the sticky, stinky person in the hawk costume. Her eyes stung imagining the sweat dripping into his eyes, the hot breath hitting the headpiece and blowing back in his face. Even more irritating was the realization that the profile photo wasn't a reflection of his sense of humor—it was realism.

The Hawk flapped his wings over to a redheaded cheerleader near the stands. His bird. Something resembling jealousy fluttered in Daphne's chest, but she blamed the cool night and shivered away the implausibility. She didn't know Oliver Pagano, and there was nothing to be jealous about. She hadn't even seen his face, which was probably vastly overrated since it was covered up all the time.

Facing Daphne, he took off the headpiece. Her suspicions were confirmed: Oliver Pagano was nothing special. The resemblance to Jason was there, but Oliver was taller, his hair lighter brown, and his jaw curved where Jason's had angled.

Oliver's cheeks were bright red, his eyebrows mashed

onto his forehead and pointed all directions of the compass, his hair damp and flattened in awkward cowlicks. He suddenly became aware of this and shook his head to reposition the clumps. The result was slightly better.

In his eyes, Daphne saw mischief, curiosity, and light. Only a tiny shadow of emptiness lurked in his brown irises. Could Jason Pagano's little brother's eyes look like this? Shouldn't they look more like her own tired, doubtful eyes?

In one way or another, she'd been searching for Oliver Pagano for seven years. Finally, he was right in front of her, laughing in a chicken costume. And Daphne wanted to fly the coop.

THE HAWK

AFTER THE VICTORY, HIGH FIVES WERE SLAPPED FROM EVERY direction. Half the cheerleaders rushed their boyfriends on the field, the other half rushed Oliver in celebration. He glanced at Katrina and watched her mouth curve from a smile to a scowl. But he didn't care. He was just a man in a costume handing out hugs. He wasn't going to discriminate because someone was attractive and wearing a short skirt.

The crowd dispersed, the cheerleaders scattered, and Oliver strolled over to Katrina. She was no longer attempting pleasantries, her arms crossed over the Sacred Heart emblem on her chest.

He opened his arms. "I'm a hugger, not a fighter."

Her pout cracked. The good thing about Katrina was she didn't know how to hold a grudge. Not yet, anyway. Oliver presumed she would soon learn.

His arms spread even wider. "Full wingspan." He hugged her, picking her up and swinging her in a circle.

She shrieked, "I'm flying!"

His prospects for seeing the black bra before midnight looked good.

Oliver headed toward the locker room with Katrina, Joe, and Mitch. Joe Valdivia and Mitch Bryant had succeeded where Oliver had failed, starters on the offensive line. He didn't regard Joe and Mitch to be his close friends, but they were the closest friends he had, and they always associated as a threesome. Their names combined to become one word, Mitch-Oly-Joe. It had a nice ring to it. They'd been friends as long as Oliver's mind went back, since T-ball when they were four. They'd sustained the longest friendship of anyone he could name, and Oliver respected tradition.

Mitch and Joe also continued to be valuable friends because they always knew where the parties were. "Party at Haggerty's tonight," Joe said, on cue.

"That's what she said." Mitch grinned. Last year someone had told him he looked like a tall Kevin Hart, and it had gone to his head. He'd been mangling jokes ever since.

Oliver and Joe exchanged their usual glance of amusement and pity, though Oliver was never sure if the pity was for Mitch or themselves.

"Because Mandie told us. See?" Mitch didn't understand that if you have to explain a joke, it's a failure. "A girl, a she, told us about the party. That's what *she said*."

"That's not…" Joe sighed and shook his head, giving up.

Oliver bit his cheek so he wouldn't laugh. He was in the mood for a few beers and checked with Katrina. "You want to go?"

By the enthusiasm of her nod, Oliver understood that she was in the mood for a few beers, too.

"Oliver!" An unfamiliar voice next to the bleachers called his name.

He turned around and saw a girl with dark hair standing behind the chain link fence. His stomach clenched. Even from fifty feet away, he recognized the girl from the Friend Request because of the odd haircut and dark makeup around her eyes. It wasn't his favorite look. Eyes were pretty enough on their own. And he was never supposed to see these eyes in person, these eyes that were now locked on his.

She gripped the triangles on top of the fence and balanced on her tiptoes. She raised her arm timidly and waved, every inch a struggle. With all they'd been through, it shouldn't be this hard to say hello. Oliver's urge to run melted into the turf beneath his feet. He crossed the track toward her. Katrina, Mitch, and Joe eagerly trailed behind him.

"Hey, that's Emily Bowman's little sister," Mitch said, loud enough for the girl to hear.

"You know her?" Oliver asked.

"Facebook," Mitch answered.

Oliver waited for an elaboration that never came. They reached the fence.

"Hey." She twisted her fingers around the fence as if bending metal would be easier than what she wanted to say. "Good game."

That was not what she had come to tell him. He smiled to try and break the tension.

"The boys in red, it's all them." Oliver nodded at Mitch and Joe.

"The guy in the chicken suit is no slouch." The Bowman girl's words were mean, but they didn't sound mean. Her mouth was straight, but her eyes were shining. She was a silent joker, and he liked her style.

"He's a hawk," Katrina snapped, defending his honor.

The Bowman girl remained stoic, but Oliver caught the condescending glint in her eye when she shifted her focus from Katrina and back to him. "Can we talk alone?"

Oliver turned to his friends. "You guys go ahead. I'll meet you at Haggerty's."

Katrina rolled her eyes and huffed before backtracking to the middle of the field with Mitch and Joe. She was too far away for him to see or hear it, but Oliver felt the gritting of her teeth. The image of the black bra drifted away, and he solemnly watched it go.

Oliver gestured toward the bleachers. After a quick scan, he didn't spot anyone who would spread salacious rumors about his involvement with a strange girl of unknown origins.

Daphne ascended three rows of bleachers and walked across a few paces. She seemed to be counting. Not too high up, not too low. Not too close to the end of the row, but not at the edge, either. She chose her seat with more care than Oliver used when selecting his prospective college. He settled next to her, slightly in awe, studying her face. Close-up, the eye makeup was an abstract painting. The dark, blurry lines blended into greens and blues and purples, but he could only see the colors when she blinked.

The girl held two folded pieces of paper. The first was frayed, the corners askew. She handed Oliver the second, its creases pristine and symmetrical. "That's your copy."

He chuckled. "Your name is Daphne, right?"

"Yeah. Sorry, I thought you knew."

"I'm Jason Pagano's little brother. You're Emily Bowman's little sister. Do we even have first names?"

He hoped to connect with her, but she lowered her eyes.

"Did you get my Friend Request?" she asked.

"No." A firm, cold lie. It was convincing.

"Oh."

His lie was rewarded when she almost cracked a smile.

"Well, I sent you one," she continued. "I wrote a message."

"Maybe I accidentally deleted it." He hadn't read the message, so this lie wasn't really a lie.

"It was about this." She nodded at the paper in his hand. "Open it," she prodded.

"I am. Geez. I'm getting scolded by the Pony Express." He unfolded the piece of paper. Pen drawings he immediately recognized as Jason's handiwork jumped from the page. Oliver moved on to the words, absorbing the puzzle before him, a list of places and experiences in boisterous and scrawled handwriting. He was still making sense of the pieces when Daphne interrupted him.

"It's a list of all the things they wanted to do. A list they made together. I found it last week."

His eyes were locked on the list, but she kept talking, saying something about the weird message she'd sent. He was so focused on the piece of paper in his hands that her words faded into the sound of crickets and distant traffic.

"Number ten is blank," he said.

"Seems fitting, doesn't it?"

For a split second, she looked right through him. Her blue eyes reduced him to a shadow, like he knew they would from her profile photo. He filled his lungs with air, but his body was still empty. She almost sounded…happy? Could anything involving Jason and Emily qualify as happy?

"Hope you weren't expecting closure," she added, tucking her chin.

"When do you think they wrote it?" he asked. Ten seconds hadn't been long enough to figure out a timeline. He doubted ten minutes, ten hours, or ten days would yield better results.

"Before they died." She crossed one ankle over the other and swung her foot back and forth, a nervous clock keeping time. "Sorry. Bad joke."

"Not really a joke, even."

She averted her eyes to the field. "Nope."

"It was kind of funny, though."

Daphne turned her head toward the parking lot—anything so she didn't have to look at him. "A few months before she…they…died, Emily was happy. I think she wrote it then. Or maybe I just want her to have written it then."

Oliver nodded. "Did you show it to your parents?"

"God, no."

He waited for an explanation, but her shoulders slumped without words. Oliver proposed a pact. "I won't show it to anyone, either."

"Okay." They locked eyes in agreement. "I just thought you should have it. It's…something."

He didn't know how to describe the list, either. He wasn't experiencing the usual displeasure that accompanied all things Jason. The sturdy angst he'd grown around his brother loosened at the roots. "That it is."

"You have your party to get to."

"No. I think I'm just going home tonight. Do you need a ride?" He shifted forward, preparing to stand.

Daphne hopped up, beating him to his feet. "No, I'll walk. Thanks."

He recognized her anxiety. A similar form resided in his own chest, the fear of getting left behind. "Well, I guess I'll see you around."

She called back from the bottom of the stands. "Yeah. I'll be in your chapel doing my homework. Just warning you." She shook her head, scolding herself for what she'd said before disappearing behind the bleachers.

Oliver sat back. He analyzed the list in his hands: the two pens that had written it, the haphazard spacing, the unreliable capitalization. He'd committed the numbers, their descriptions, their exact punctuation to memory by the time the stadium lights switched off above him.

• • •

He drove around for a long time, windows down, the dizzying orange of the Valley lights beneath him.

Katrina grilled him the next evening over pizza. He explained that Daphne had questions about her sister and his brother, and he would always be there to help answer them if he could. He left the door open for future collaboration, he told her.

When Katrina pressed for more specifics, he bowed his head and played the dead brother card. Katrina dropped the subject. Her curiosity wasn't daring enough to tempt negative emotion. Oliver was best when he was upbeat and carefree. Sad Oliver was pointless.

Like every night, she and Oliver made out for hours on every flat surface before her parents got home. Oliver determined that if a crime were committed in this house, he'd be the only suspect. He imagined the CSI agents shining their blue lights, his patchy fingerprints glowing white all over the walls like reverse spots on a Dalmatian.

"Are we going to homecoming together?" Katrina asked between kisses.

Girls and those silly dances. Oliver figured he could have saved up a few months of rent and moved out when he'd turned eighteen if he'd pocketed the money his parents had given him for the suits, tuxes, shoes, corsages, limos, and dinners that separated these dances from being just another Saturday night party. Jason had never attended high school dances, so Oliver's parents contributed generously to the Oliver Pagano Formal Fund. Not that Oliver minded the dances. Like any party, he always had a good time no matter how many beers were guzzled or tears were shed. What bothered him was the way Katrina had asked him to the dance.

Are we going to homecoming together? She had whispered it while pushing him against the kitchen counter and nibbling on his ear lobe. Did not being her boyfriend mean she couldn't ask him basic questions without trying to trick him into acceptance? He sucked in his breath, ready to push her back and make her face him. He would tell her that he wanted to go to the dance. She didn't need to turn him on to get a false positive that she could wave around as evidence. He would always answer with the truth no matter what was going on under his boxers. His words would be received with relief. Or they could be rejected with scorn. And he had a desperate yearning to see her black bra again.

He let the black bra win. "Yes."

• • •

For the next week, Oliver tried to ignore the list, stomping it down into the deep crevices of his mind. But Daphne Bowman kept climbing up the tunnels, setting the list afire. Flashes of her fingers gripping the fence, her legs keeping time in the wind, the jagged edges in her blue eyes struck him at all hours of the day. With this piece of paper, an unknown part of Jason had been resurrected. Finally, Oliver possessed a sliver of his brother he could relate to. Oliver owed it to this bond to breathe life into the list instead of burying it. The only person who would understand how to revive it would be Daphne.

He hated the chapel. All those eyes in the stained glass windows and paintings on the walls gave him the unease of a zoo animal. But it was his first and best idea for locating the girl with stained glass eyes of her own. And there she was, alone in the chapel, kneeled over a thick textbook, attacking a notebook with her pencil like she was committing the most important information ever to paper.

"Hey, Daphne," he said over her shoulder.

She startled at the interruption and brushed her hair out of her face. "Hello."

"Do you want to go somewhere? Maybe get a coffee?"

"Yes." She said it too quickly and packed her bag slowly, in penance.

Daphne and Oliver walked three blocks to Frank's

Diner, not knowing what to say but trusting that coffee would give them enough time to figure it out. It was a silence Oliver couldn't have with any of his friends. Katrina never stopped talking unless they were making out or watching TV. Sometimes he could hear the apprehension of boredom in her voice. Joe and Mitch were always quick to talk about sports or movies if the conversation lulled. The most comparable silence to this sidewalk sometimes came after Jason had been mentioned at the dinner table. All that needed to be said had been spoken, and all there was left to do was eat. His parents ate their food like it was a reward. They'd made it through another day; they'd earned this meal. That's what silence was for Oliver: a prize.

Oliver and Daphne sat in the farthest booth from the door, the place nearly empty except for two old men at the opposite end of the restaurant. Oliver's back faced the entrance, just in case anyone he knew came in. He'd been discreet about this, telling Daphne that he would face the wall so she would have a better view, but her eyelids had tightened by a razor's edge and her lips had puckered to the side. She didn't buy his line, but she sat down anyway. He spent an excessive amount of time placing his napkin in his lap. Deus ex machina arrived in the form of a waitress bearing coffee.

"Can I get an old-fashioned donut, please?" Daphne asked.

"I'll do a glazed with sprinkles. Thanks," Oliver said. The waitress left, and Oliver creamed and sugared his coffee. "Old-fashioned. Does that say something your personality?"

"Maybe we could do the list," Daphne blurted out. The

waitress returned and placed their donuts in front of them. She refilled Oliver's mug. It was the slowest pour of coffee in the history of mankind and the cup had only been half empty. Daphne waited until the waitress was back behind the counter. "Or, we could keep talking about donuts."

Oliver reclined against the backrest, interest piqued.

"They had all of these dreams and they never did them. They never even tried. It just seems like a waste."

"It was a waste."

"Yeah. But maybe if we did all these things, it could finally mean something." She was on the brink of tears, swallowing furiously to hold them in. Oliver had never seen eyes as beautiful as hers, simmering with seven years of a grief he understood all too well.

"Maybe." The idea of completing his brother's wish list melded two broken pieces in his mind back together. "But I don't have the money to fly to China or space. Maybe you have money for both of us."

Daphne's laugh cut the air and she shook her head. "There might be another way. An adventure in the abstract."

She aimed her gaze at Oliver with such cold confidence that all of his doubts froze over. He would follow her on any adventure, no matter the shape or form.

THE GREAT WALL
OF CHINA

The salt and pepper shakers on the kitchen table weighted down a green bill. This was the alliance between the three remaining Bowmans. Her mom pretended that her dad didn't drink most of a bottle of whiskey over the course of a day. In exchange, her dad pretended that her mom still loved him. And for Daphne's silence on all the pretending, her mom left her money for takeout every morning.

Sometimes it was five dollars, sometimes ten, sometimes twenty. Somewhere between the bedroom and the front door, her mother must have gotten confused about the fluctuation of food prices and did her best job at guessing. Today, her guessing had taken the form of the genocidal face of a twenty. Jackpot.

"Going to Janine's!"

Daphne didn't know why she hollered as she ran out

the front door. The lie shone bright in the morning sun. It wasn't like anyone had asked where she was going.

She speed-walked until she reached Sacred Heart. The plan was to meet Oliver in the school parking lot instead of at her house, in case one of her parents surfaced at the wrong moment and asked questions. Daphne knew the best way to not get caught in a lie was to not tell one. She cursed herself for being such a good girl, someone who had barely done anything that would earn her disapproval. Amateur.

Despite the general lack of rules in the Bowman household, one decree was made clear: Daphne was forbidden to date. When Daphne was fourteen, her mom had marched into her bedroom. Her forehead and temples were stained black from the box dye-job-in-progress that she'd applied to cover up her gray roots. Her hair was an oil spill on the top of her head, shiny and confused. Amidst this natural disaster, Daphne was handed her first box of tampons, and her mom declared that she couldn't be alone with boys. Daphne found this new rule strange because a month earlier she'd spent many hours alone with Janine's fifteen-year-old cousin, Brandon, who was visiting from Florida. Their lips had practically been suctioned together during his two-week stay. Janine had groaned and eye-rolled and sighed with her full body, but eventually allowed them to use her room as a make-out den for a full week. They'd gone to second base, and as he tried to round third, fiddling with her fly button, she'd pushed his hands away.

"Leave my fly alone." She kissed him.

His hands went right back where they left off.

"No." She said it lightly, still kissing him.

He pushed the fly button out of its hole and pulled down the zipper. Daphne jumped back, zipped up, and buttoned.

"What's wrong?" Legitimate confusion paraded across Brandon's face.

Daphne didn't need to explain the meaning of the word *no* to someone who spoke English. Or any Romance language, for that matter.

"Let's get something to eat." She marched out of the room to find Janine.

The rest of the day, they hung out as a threesome, and Brandon was in a foul mood. He didn't want to eat anything or watch any movies or go to the beach. He wanted to be in Janine's room with Daphne. When she said *no* to this request, he finally understood, as if a moment from a muddled dream flashed in his mind with sudden clarity. He answered her *no* with more sulking, a clenched fist when she reached to hold his hand, and a turned cheek when she tried to kiss him. Daphne found this behavior unacceptable. She wasn't a prude and refused to be treated like one.

Without asking for a goodnight kiss, Daphne greeted the night air and trotted home. For the next week, Daphne didn't answer or return any calls from Janine in case Brandon was using her phone.

After giving a few days of buffer to ensure Brandon's departure, she called Janine. Daphne never spoke Brandon's name again and never berated Janine for giving him her number. He called a few times, but after no response, he finally realized that *no* meant the opposite of *yes* and gave up.

Janine never mentioned Brandon. Daphne was so grateful for this that her affection for Janine grew to new depths, somewhere near the bottom of the ocean. Their friendship became closer than ever, and Janine never knew why.

After the Brandon incident, Daphne didn't pay much attention to the restriction on boys. Not that Brandon had turned her off to the opposite sex, but nor was anyone knocking on her fly button. The likelihood of being alone with a boy was minuscule. If it did occur, it would be a happy accident.

She was reluctant to ask her mother about the current standing on this restriction, as questions would be sure to follow. These questions would have no concrete answers because there was no boy, but her parents wouldn't believe her. After Emily, they doubted everything. So Daphne chose to let it lie. Therefore, she assumed the ban hadn't been lifted. However, if she was caught with a boy, she could still plead statute of limitations. She'd grown old enough since the restriction was implemented that any irrational teenager would believe it to now be null and void.

At the alley before the Sacred Heart parking lot, Daphne slowed. She massaged her scalp to volumize her hair, straightened her shirt, and brushed the lint off the front of her jeans, all in five seconds. She took a breath and rounded the corner into the school's line of sight.

A quick scan over the parking lot found two half-rows of cars, their owners a collection of overachievers not taking a weekend break. The angle of the light on the dashboards made it difficult for Daphne to tell if anyone sat inside, and she regretted not asking Oliver what kind of car he drove. After approaching close enough to cut the glare, she found the cars all empty.

He had stood her up. Anger rolled around in her stomach and traveled upwards, tightening around her lungs until she heard the crunch of asphalt under car wheels. The tension left her body just as quickly as it had risen. She let out a long, steady breath. An old sedan rolled down its window. The havoc that was Oliver's hair indicated that he had stumbled out of bed only minutes ago.

"Sorry. I'm always late." He lobbed out this excuse as though he was powerless against a clock.

Daphne attempted a grin, the result of which was a grimace. She climbed in the car and hoped the movement blurred her expression.

"Thanks for the ride." Her tongue was made of sandpaper, but with the current state of her gut, she was thankful to have articulated a coherent sentence. As they pulled out of the parking lot and turned toward the freeway, words returned to her at a faster clip.

"I read somewhere that running late is an expression of self-doubt. Like you don't respect yourself enough to show up on time because you don't think you deserve to. Or something."

"Do I look like a guy who's full of self-doubt?" His smile appeared unnaturally large, but it wasn't enough to prove her theory.

"Maybe you just hide it really well."

"Nah, I'm not that good of an actor. And it's too much effort. I'm pretty lazy, not big on the effort thing."

"You're doing this."

"For now."

A wave of dread pushed against Daphne's skull. She closed her eyes, leaned into the seat, and told herself over and over: *For now is Now. For now is Now. For now is Now. Until it isn't.*

Thirty minutes later, they moseyed up the streets of Chinatown, crossing under the two bronze dragons guarding Broadway. Even though the downtown skyscrapers were right behind them, with her back turned she may have been on an altogether different coast. The warm, sweet, fishy-sour scent that wafted from every grocery store was as foreign to her as Asia itself.

The next block housed a giant market. They wandered through stall after stall, each vendor mashed into a maze-like space that wound in seemingly never-ending rows. Every inch of floor and wall was being utilized to sell cheap clothing, sunglasses, and knockoff handbags.

"I never knew shopping could be claustrophobic," Daphne said.

Sensory overload etched lines in Oliver's forehead. "Want to get out of here?"

"Yeah, but I don't know how," she laughed.

"Me, neither."

Oliver pointed his arms out, aiming for a straight line in front of them. They weaved together through the chaos, trying their best to adhere to the invisible line. They broke into a playful run and bumped into a stack of fake Louis Vuitton luggage, leaving wheels spinning in their wake.

Daphne spotted a beige door between two stalls. "I don't care where it goes, we're taking it."

They burst through the door and emerged into sunshine and the sidewalk's distinct confines.

"Close call. Didn't know if we were gonna make it out

alive. Nice save with the door." Oliver wiped a trickle of sweat from his temple.

"Anytime."

After rounding a few corners, they ended up in a plaza draped in red lanterns swinging against the blue sky. At the center of the plaza, an unexpected wishing well beckoned them. The well was a six-foot-tall waterfall that looked like it was made out of papier-mâché. Along the water flow, little bowls were perched next to placards for each particular wish: Health, Wealth, Long Life, Love, Peace, Prosperity, Happiness, and Good Luck. Small, cheerful Buddhas were nestled amongst the bowls, assuring all wishes come true.

Oliver dug into all of his pockets. "I have a quarter, that's it."

Without much thought or aim, he tossed it at the Wealth bowl. He missed.

Daphne searched her purse. She came up with three pennies, two nickels, and four dimes. "Jackpot."

She handed him half the coins. He alternated his tosses between Wealth and Prosperity, never hitting the rim of the bowl.

"This is why I don't play basketball." He gave a bitter laugh.

Daphne aimed for Good Luck and missed.

"Good luck? People make their own luck," Oliver said.

"So say the lucky. Better than just wanting to be rich."

"Or prosperous."

"Is there a difference?" she asked.

"I'm sure there's some philosophical difference…but no, not really."

She tossed a coin at Serenity and missed. "I didn't want to be serene anyway."

The half of Oliver's face she could see was bored. He turned away, heading toward the road. Daphne tossed her last coin at the Love bowl. The coin bounced off the bowl's rim, rolled down the waterfall, and plunked into the pool at her feet.

Oliver was hungry, so they ducked into the first restaurant that looked like it wouldn't smell like fish. He slid into the booth facing the door, bouncing on the worn springs in his seat. He cracked open the menu and gave micro reviews of random items. "Beef with broccoli—too healthy. Velvet chicken—sounds too much like a sofa cushion. Bean curd—just…no. Nothing good could come from that."

Resentment rippled through her. He wasn't embarrassed to be seen with her here because the probability that any of his friends were in Chinatown was nonexistent. She had to travel across half the city, practically to another continent, to see him exhibit natural behavior.

The server brought tea, and Daphne poured them each a cup.

"Should we share something?" she asked. "I'm not picky."

"Do you like spicy food?"

"Definitely."

"Shrimp?"

"Sure."

He ordered the slippery shrimp with two orders of white rice. Daphne preferred brown rice but didn't say anything. She'd just declared herself not picky and held herself to those words.

Oliver cleared his throat. "So what do you do in school?"

Getting to know you, getting to know all about you. Those *The King and I* lyrics always comforted and amused her when someone asked a vague question that didn't want an answer. Did Oliver even care? She responded in an equally vague manner to test him.

"Uh, I think I read and write like everyone else."

"Are you in AP classes? You seem smart."

This was where things got tricky. She wanted to come off as smart. She knew she was smart, and she enjoyed being smart. But she didn't want the *smart girl* label from Oliver. She figured that *smart girl* also meant *boring girl* to him. And she wasn't boring. Was she? And why did he automatically assume she was smart? Probably because she wasn't pretty enough to be average. But, attractive or not, Daphne didn't want to be average. She hated taunting herself with this rabbit hole internal questioning.

"I'm in some AP classes. Are you?"

She knew it was a stretch. He was intelligent, but too loose in his shoulders and swagger to be in AP classes. He didn't appear worn down and hardened by the competition and unrealistic expectations and vast amounts of homework in the race for valedictorian. She had already judged him the same as he'd judged her, but her question made it seem like she hadn't.

"This…" He gestured up and down his torso. "Is not AP material. Sorry to disappoint."

"Can't judge an AP book by its cover."

"Eh, I think most of the time you can."

Too much AP talk. She needed to change the subject fast, before she had time to be offended. "I'm auditioning for the school play tomorrow." She nearly imploded after she said it. Now she was not only the *smart girl*, she was the *drama freak*.

"Oh, yeah? What play?"

Could he possibly be interested in theatre? "*Our Town*."

"Mmm, I don't know that one."

"It's pretty famous. It has one of those crazy statistics about being performed somewhere in the world every day or something. I mean, it's no *Romeo and Juliet*, but it left its mark. I don't really know why. It's kind of boring."

"Well, if you're in it, I'll go see it."

Her face flooded with warmth. Thankfully, the platter of golden fried shrimp bathing in a syrupy sauce was placed in the middle of the table at that moment and absorbed the hungry boy's attention. Daphne flattened her napkin onto her lap and tinkered with her silverware.

Oliver piled a mound of shrimp onto a double serving of rice. Daphne thought for sure he wouldn't be able to finish it. She wasn't even hungry, but she took four shrimp for herself, putting forth a solid effort.

"I bet they eat it just like this in China." She licked a drop of the sweet-spicy-sticky-tang from her forefinger.

He juggled speaking while chewing like a professional. "What? You're questioning the authenticity of a Chinese dish in Chinatown? Blasphemy."

"Deep-fried batter, the cornerstone of world cuisine since the Dark Ages." She peered straight at him, chewing. "It's good."

"I can't tell if you're joking or not."

"Does that make you uncomfortable?" She picked at her rice with her fork.

"Probably not as much as it should."

"You'll figure it out, eventually. And then you'll feel special." She winked at him. The same wink Emily had cast at her about the floorboard. Daphne's grandfather used to wink at her and Emily. It always made Daphne feel like she'd been given a gift, and it must have had the same effect on Emily for her to adopt the trademark. Daphne wondered why no one did it anymore. She became determined to bring back the wink.

Oliver shifted in his seat, taken aback by the wink, reluctantly accepting it. "I don't know, I'm already pretty special."

"Short bus special."

He choked a little on his shrimp when he laughed. "Clearly. I can't even chew and swallow."

"I don't know the Heimlich, so you're screwed."

"Americanized Chinese shrimp isn't the worst way to go," he said.

She laughed for half a second before thinking, *A better form of asphyxiation?* Her eyes flashed up at Oliver and saw the same mood-killing question on his regretful face. He opened his mouth and tried to come up with something improving on apology. He took a drink of water instead.

They spent the rest of the meal trying to leave—flagging down the server, waiting for the check. Oliver polished off his plate of shrimp effortlessly, proving Daphne wrong. He threw down a wad of bills from his wallet while she reached for her purse. He shook her off.

"I got this one. You get the next."

"Okay." There would be a next time. Containing her excitement made her ribcage buzz.

After lunch, they returned to wandering the streets. They passed more red lanterns hanging on wires strewn from rooftop to rooftop. Daphne wished they'd come at night to see them illuminated, glowing hearts swaying in the black breeze. Staring at the lanterns, she wished for a message that wasn't coming. Oblivious to the lanterns, Oliver checked out the cute Asian girls as they pranced by, leaving Daphne alone and frustrated in her contemplative state. She quickened her pace, and he followed her.

Daphne wanted to avoid Oliver's bored expression. A gurgling despair was folding into the slippery shrimp in her stomach. She wasn't going to find what she was searching for in Chinatown. Not that she had a clue what she was hoping to stumble upon. The passing pet shop provided an opportunity to stall and regroup.

"I'm going in. I'll be out in a minute."

She expected some sad animals and the scent of cedar. Instead, she was bombarded with the sound of screeching birds and the piercing assault of ammonia. Hopping from perch to perch, a hundred parrots, parakeets, finches, and cockatiels sang their songs simultaneously, all musicality lost in the melding of their voices. In great numbers, the birds' innocent chirping warped into a nightmarish cacophony.

The unrelenting sound surrounded Daphne and quickly closed in on her. She shut her eyes, unable to fight against it, until all she could see was gray. Powerless to move her feet in the screaming storm, almost to the point of panic, all Daphne had left was her mind. Is this what Emily felt like? Trapped in the gray noise, her thoughts lost in the flap of feathers. Daphne needed to get out of there, fast. She pushed against the thickness in the air, her heart pounding against the wall of sound, and willed herself through the door.

When she stumbled outside into the blinding sunshine, her head felt as though it was floating above her body. She needing to be centered by the sense of gravity that only came with time. Grateful that Oliver was distracted, his eyes feasting on all the people intersecting in front of him, Daphne leaned against the brick wall to recover. After her knees stopped shaking, she trudged over and passed him without speaking. Again, he followed.

Another block and hopelessness settled in.

"Uh, Daph?"

Great, now he was going to voice his boredom. And Daphne didn't like being called Daph. Only her dad had that privilege, and that was only because her dad had given her the name in the first place. But the abbreviation didn't sound so bad coming from Oliver's lips, and this exacerbated her annoyance. He already knew how to break her rules.

"I don't know why I brought us here. I don't know what I expected to find."

"I think you found it." He was gloating up at the store sign: THE GREAT WALL COMPANY.

Daphne's face hurt from the effort of holding back her joy. "What do you think they sell?"

"I don't know, but we're gonna find out."

Oliver's smile was complete, not trying to impress, only full and open. It was his real smile, and this was the first time she'd seen it. Daphne caught herself at that moment, recognizing what was happening as though she was standing on the sidewalk outside of herself, watching her and Oliver smiling at each other. It was the moment her heart involuntarily opened for Oliver Pagano, and he walked in without knowing.

The shop's window display of ceramic plates, serving dishes, pots, pans, and tea kettles served a stark contrast to the collection of decorative knives hanging on the wall in the back. The blades grew in size the further up they went, culminating with five machetes. Daphne and Oliver's wide eyes scaled the weapons to the ceiling. Most intimidating was the handwritten sign: *Must be 18 to touch anything.*

"Well, I'm always in the market for a new machete," he said.

"I like this one." Daphne wanted to prove that she was more than an AP, chapel-studying, drama nerd. She picked up a small knife with a creamy, white handle and gold details. It felt good in her hand, the curves hitting all the right places. Wielding a weapon gave her an unexpected sense of power. "Maybe I'll have a career fighting crime in dark alleys, vigilante style."

"You need a name for this alter ego."

"Any suggestions?"

"The Chinatown Slasher."

She crinkled her nose. "That's a serial killer name."

"Well, in the eyes of the law, vigilante-murder and murder-murder are the same thing."

"Not if I put on a mask and a pair of tights."

Oliver inhaled, preparing to refute. Daphne narrowed her eyes and tilted the blade toward his throat, three feet away.

He jumped back and threw up his hands in surrender. "I would enjoy seeing you in a mask and tights."

"That's right. Think about the big picture before you kill my dreams."

Oliver laughed. She was becoming addicted to his laughter, the sound where truth met fact.

"How about Gothique?"

She pondered a second too long. "That's stupid."

She loved the name and hadn't gotten any better at lying in the last three hours. Worse yet, she could tell by the way Oliver sneered that he knew she loved it.

The shopkeeper stepped out from the back room with a warning glance. Daphne's stomach jumped, and her cheeks went bright red. So much for playing cool while breaking the rules. She returned the knife to its slot on the wall.

Oliver grinned. "Busted, Gothique."

"Guess the alter ego will have to wait another year."

Eighteen. The year when her life could begin.

• • •

Daphne's feet landed on her driveway and the glory of the afternoon evaporated. She was still seventeen. Emily's birds flapped against her skull, and the warm wind blew the same as it had on that infamous Tuesday seven years ago. Today had been all about Emily and Jason. She stood still on the driveway, staring down the garage, and didn't fight the memory.

The thick haze escapes as the garage door opens. Her mom throws open her car door, tries to jump out with her seatbelt still on. Her seatbelt reaches the end of its give and yanks her backward.

"Oh, God." Her dad unsnaps his seatbelt and turns to Daphne in the backseat. "Stay in the car. Don't move."

Seconds after the garage door fully opens, the vapor thins to transparence.

Emily and Jason's names echo in the garage. Her mom repeats Emily's name over and over with increasing volume, as though Emily has gone deaf. On the passenger's side of the car, her dad's voice quivers as he shakes a body hidden behind the seat. Jason.

She closed her eyes, and the tears made warm trails down her face. But her running mascara was not going to give her away and become a topic of conversation with her dad. She pulled up the bottom of her shirt and dabbed under her eyes. She'd developed such a skill for this that she no longer needed a mirror. She knew her makeup well, had examined all of its boundaries. Judging the duration and intensity of her spilled tears, she knew exactly how hard and long she needed to wipe so she appeared normal. Whatever that was.

Daphne crept inside. The light from the TV bounced off the walls and the whiskey bottle on the coffee table, but the La-Z-Boy was empty. She bounded out of the foyer, through the living room, and reached the safe border of the hallway. Three more strides and she was inside her room. Despite her naysaying, one of the coins from the fountain must have brought her some luck, after all.

Thinking about coins, she noticed *The Catcher in the Rye*'s bare spine. She pushed her chair out of the way, searching the floor, calm at first. She lifted her laptop and books with increasing speed and disregard for gravity. By the time she reached the hairbrush and cosmetics, she was treating her dresser like an air hockey table, pushing items left and right to clear the space in front of her.

"Dad!" She ran out into the living room.

The clatter and thunk of the closing refrigerator door startled her. "In here." Her dad's small voice barely travelled past the kitchen.

She charged into the dark room, where he peeled the plastic off a slice of cheese and centered it between two slices of mustard-coated white bread.

"Did you take a nickel off my desk?"

He tilted his head, giving the question an inordinate amount of thought, as if a proverb had landed on his sandwich.

"I think so."

"Why would you do that? What were you doing in my room?" she growled.

He took a bite of his sandwich, not bothering to cut it in half. "I found some change in the couch cushions. I thought I'd do a sweep through the house and cash everything in at the bank. Every penny counts, right?"

"You deposited it?" Daphne clenched her jaw and recognized the hateful shriek in her voice.

"Come on, we're going to Pepe's. Taco Tuesday." The cheerfulness in her mother's voice is tentative.

"I'm not going." Emily clenches her jaw, not budging, Jason beside her.

Her mom blocks the living room doorway, the only route to Emily's bedroom.

"Listen to your mother." Her dad stands behind Emily and Jason. They're surrounded.

Daphne sits on the couch. Ties her shoes. Ready for tacos. Knows she'll have to wait another half hour.

Her mother attempts to appease Emily. "Please, come. You can bring Jason."

It's too late. The first shot has been fired and both women blame the other side. Emily's voice reaches inhuman octaves, a hybrid of angel and demon speaking in a language Daphne doesn't understand. Or doesn't want to. Daphne picks out her own name among the jumble, spat out like venom.

"I'm sorry I'm not your perfect daughter like her. You only want me to go tonight so you can grill me! What school am I going to? What's the plan for the REST OF MY LIFE?"

"You're graduating in eight months," her dad says.

"We're not trying to pressure you," her mom says. "These are normal questions."

"I'm not normal! I'll never be normal. And why do you even care what I do after high school? It's not like YOU did anything. You got knocked up and dropped out of college."

"Hey!" Her dad closes in on Emily. Daphne's never seen him this angry. Will he hit Emily? Her mom abandons her stronghold in the doorway to jump between the two of them.

Emily sees the hallway opening and takes it, like this was her plan all along. "Your life's work. Here it is. And I'll never be good enough for you."

"Stop saying that," her mom pleads.

"All your dreams are heaped on my shoulders, and I want none of them." Emily flees down the hallway. Jason slinks behind her. The slam of her bedroom door is the last they'll hear from her until breakfast the next morning.

Her dad had heard Emily in her voice, too. Terror played across his blue eyes. "I haven't deposited it yet," he croaked.

Daphne blinked hard, resetting. She wasn't going to sound like Emily. Her life depended on it. "Where is it?" Her voice wavered in its normal range.

He dug through his full pockets, change rustling on both hips. He opened his palms, full of silver and copper. She picked out the nickels and read their dates, dropping them in his right hand when they weren't a match. 2006. She held onto it and checked the remaining three: 2011, 2013, and 2008.

She buried the 2006 nickel in her palm. Her body relaxed but her voice still pinched. "Please, don't touch this. Do you understand?"

Her dad raised his hands with his sandwich. "No more nickels. Got it." He swallowed. Daphne found it aggravating that someone who drank so much could have a dry throat.

He wasn't a mean drunk, and Daphne was grateful for this. But no matter how upset she was, she shouldn't be disrespecting her dad like this. She wanted him to lose his temper and yell at her, summoning the power he once held over her and Emily. Daphne longed to hear the strength of his voice, the security in the tempestuous father-teen relationship. Instead, his tall, sturdy body was now frail and sloped. The weight of his eyebrows and slagging skin at his jawline made him look more like a grandfather than a father. She hated that she had his eyes, thankful for inheriting her mom's round nose and thin lips.

"Good." Daphne held her target, unblinking, waiting to be put in her place.

He forfeited, drifting away, no apology demanded. His

focus crawled past her, into the darkness. He'd lost the will to fight, lost the will to do anything.

"I'm sorry I yelled." She offered the olive branch anyway.

"You've got some pipes."

"Yeah…" She shrugged.

"Mmm-hmm."

The conversation was over. Like most of the conversations with her parents, the punctuation could never translate to another language. It made no sense outside of her family's dysfunction.

She trudged down the hallway. The weight of her dad's detachment seemed to press her into the floor. Every step compounded her frustration. When she crossed the threshold to her bedroom, her eardrums were on the verge of exploding. Her fingers shook while she set the nickel on the edge of her desk and rotated Jefferson's three-quarter profile upside down.

It had been many months since she'd been this angry at her parents. The last time was what would've been Emily's twenty-first birthday—alcoholic liberty, an event to celebrate. Daphne had set her alarm for 5:00 a.m. to see her mom off to work, expecting a hug or an acknowledgement of the sad date. Her mom had groggily handed her a ten-dollar bill instead of leaving it on the table. She used the money to split an order of Pad Thai with her dad for dinner. They'd even sat at the kitchen table and used chopsticks instead of forks. Neither parent had spoken a word about Emily. It had been any old miserable day at Casa Bowman. Daphne was no more or less alone on Emily's birthday, yesterday, today, or tomorrow. The lack of change had pushed her voice to the edge tonight. She hoped her dad had really heard the Emily come out of her, hoped she had made him feel even smaller.

• • •

After the final bell, Daphne stepped on stage for her audition. For the past three years she had painted sets and smeared stage makeup on the actors because the thought of being in front of an audience made her body go hollow. This year, fear was not going to be the protagonist in her life story. Confronting Oliver with the list had been the scariest question she'd ever asked and getting his answer had led to greatness. She wanted more. She deserved it.

Mrs. Baker, head of the drama department, gave Daphne an encouraging nod and prepared to write on her notepad. "Daphne, what part are you trying out for?"

"Emily."

Mrs. Baker's head shot up. Daphne wondered if the abrupt head lift was due to the coincidence of the name *Emily* or because Daphne had never auditioned for any school production and was now trying out for the lead.

"Okay, whenever you're ready." Mrs. Baker said.

Daphne projected and enunciated, imagining her half-deaf grandfather sitting in the last row of the theater. The adrenaline of being on stage accelerated the pace at which she spoke her memorized lines. She could hear the words gushing out too quickly and tried to slow them down, but they only poured out faster. Unable to control the clip of her speech, she let go and went with it.

"Goodbye, Grover's Corners. Mama and Papa. Goodbye to clocks ticking…and my butternut tree! And Mama's sunflowers…and new-ironed dresses and hot baths." Sorrow and hope trembled within her voice.

"And sleeping and waking up! Oh, Earth, you're too wonderful for anyone to realize you! Do any human beings ever realize life while they live it—every, every minute?" Everything she'd been through with her sister Emily was coming out through *Our Town* Emily. It was a therapeutic breakthrough combined with a feeling of free-falling into jagged rocks.

"I'm ready to go back now." The monologue came to an end. A murmur passed over the students waiting in the auditorium. A boy in the front row clapped three times before regaining his bearings and sinking down in his seat. Mrs. Baker's mouth hung open, exposing her astonishment. The irony of Mrs. Baker being a former Off Broadway extraordinaire, yet having such a terrible poker face, only increased Daphne's pride.

"Thank you, Daphne. I'll be posting the cast list tomorrow at 3:00 p.m."

A day. Enough time to get her hopes up. Luckily, she had a distraction for the rest of the night.

Trying to be home as little as possible, Daphne had applied for a job at Sweetie's Ice Cream Shop the day after her sixteenth birthday. She worked two nights during the week and one weekend shift scooping out artisanal ice cream from the deep vats in the display freezer. Besides walking to and from school and work, scooping was the only form of physical activity she undertook.

Daphne didn't recall getting to Sweetie's that day. A hypnotic trance carried her down the blocks, her body numb and warm and unaware of its movement, fueled on pure satisfaction. The minutes of her shift ticked away like seconds.

The exhilaration settled throughout the evening. Daphne had no illusions. Seniority and cumulative body of work would outweigh her solid audition. She would not get the lead on her first try. She probably wouldn't even get a part. The victory was the audition, joining the ranks of the unafraid. The person she most wanted to tell was Oliver. She didn't know why, and she was done trying to figure it out.

After her shift, she pulled out her phone to text him and found his text waiting for her: "*How did the audition go?*"

Her glee was as subtle as Mrs. Baker's drooping jaw.

"*Really well,*" she typed. "*I'll find out tomorrow.*"

• • •

At 3:00 p.m. the next day, she approached the auditorium door with a heaviness in her creepers. A small group of students gathered around a piece of paper crudely stuck to the wall with masking tape.

"Yes!" Holly, the lead in last year's fall play, clapped and pumped her fist.

There's your Emily, Daphne predicted. Another girl dashed by Daphne crying tears of rejection. The doubt crept in. *That's going to be me.* Daphne wanted a part more than she'd allowed herself to believe. She rushed up to the cast list, forcing the misery to begin.

She scrolled down and found her name. Her name! She had a part! She scanned across the dotted line to the character's name: Mrs. Soames.

Daphne smiled in that dopey, mouth-breathing way she only did while watching movies alone or in the dark, when no one could see her. Now, she was surrounded by people and didn't care. She grabbed her phone and texted Oliver: "*I got a part! Nov. 4th. Save the date.*"

She stared at her phone, willing it to respond. And it did. "*SUPER JUICE!!!*"

JIM MORRISON'S GRAVE

"I'M NOT TELLING." KATRINA RECLINED AGAINST OLIVER'S locker. She stretched a lock of hair to cover her lips.

Oliver did his best to fend off annoyance. He loved homecoming, but he could've done without the dance. The formality was fine. Oliver liked getting dressed up in a suit. He liked seeing his date in a slinky dress, teetering in high heels, wearing twice as much makeup and hairspray as usual. He enjoyed showing off with the guys in the middle of the floor as much as slow dancing with his date, pressed up against her, breathing in the perfume on her neck, carving a private cave around them amongst the other couples. All that was good. It was the dinner beforehand that had to be somewhere *nice,* which really meant *expensive,* that he dreaded. Making conversation while out came course after course—that was a lot of talking that could lead to places he didn't want to go. He also hated those damn flowers.

He'd never met a boutonnière whose pin hadn't stabbed him in the chest.

"I need to know what color your dress is so I can buy a matching corsage," he said.

"I want it to be a surprise."

Oliver noticed the blind optimism in Katrina's eyes. Nothing had ever gone truly wrong in her life. There was that one time freshman year when she didn't make the cheer squad and was named an alternate, but Caitlyn Mendelson broke her ankle a week later and Katrina was added to the permanent roster. This year, she was the team's beloved captain and Caitlyn a mere shadow in the bleachers.

Silly girl. Katrina thought a surprise could only be something good.

"I just don't want to show up with the wrong flowers and ruin the night," he said.

"You couldn't ruin it if you tried. I can't wait. It's going to be a night to remember."

Oliver slung his backpack over his shoulder. He leaned in like he was going to kiss her and at the last second pulled up and kissed her forehead, leaving Katrina hanging, lips puckered against the wind. She whimpered and punched his arm as he took off down the hall.

"That's what you get for not telling me," he called over his shoulder.

When Oliver arrived at the chapel for the second time in two weeks, he realized how infrequent his visits there had been, except to shortcut through from the football field to the parking lot. He had no idea how Daphne could concentrate in the five o'clock shadow of Christ. But there she was, furiously punching the keys on her graphing calculator and scribbling in her notebook.

"For a minute I thought you were gaming. I was going to light a candle in your honor."

"Aw, and I was one candle away from sainthood." A corner of her mouth dimpled her cheek.

Daphne continued calculating, jotting down equations, circling the final answer and resting her pencil before giving him her full attention. Her dedication astounded him. No commitment in his life equaled her attentiveness to a single math problem.

"Are you coming to homecoming?" he asked. "It's this Friday."

"Do you need a date to the dance?"

Trepidation intersected with flattery and the combination took Oliver off guard. Was she asking to be his date? She had the ability to disarm him with simple questions. This fight was unfair, yet something deep inside him enjoyed the challenge.

She rolled her eyes at his hesitation. "I'm kidding."

"Yeah, I know." The hoarseness in his voice forced him to clear his throat, making it all the more obvious that he had not been in on the joke.

"I didn't even go to my own school's homecoming. Why would I come to yours?"

A tinge of hurt pinched at the small of his back. He ignored it. "The chicken suit, of course. I got some new moves."

"Are they going to shoot you out of a cannon? Because that I would go see."

"So you'll only come if my life is in jeopardy?"

"Pretty much."

"You're a tough audience, Daph."

She crossed her legs, signaling a refocus to the heart of the matter. That was why he was standing amongst the chapel pews after all, for *hearts* and *matter*.

Defeat weighed down her voice. "I've been racking my brain on Jim Morrison's grave."

"Don't worry, I got this one." He gave a reassuring nod.

Daphne's nod fell into sync with his. "Okay, you're on. This weekend?"

"It's homecoming."

She tensed again and picked up her graphing calculator. "Oh, right. I thought, Sunday, maybe."

He hated letting her down, but his parents were conveniently out of town this weekend. He hoped the carnal midnight after the dance would stretch into daybreak—especially given Katrina's current state of forgiveness and overall enthusiasm. The thought of jumping out of his twisted sheets and spending the day with Daphne felt dirty. He didn't know why. It probably had something to do with him not telling Katrina about the Top Ten list, and how he wouldn't ever be divulging that information to her.

"Next Sunday. Bring a Sharpie. And red lipstick," he said.

Daphne bent an incredulous eyebrow and returned to her homework. "You better wear the chicken suit to the dance, or I'll be very disappointed."

For half a second, he considered it. Katrina would kill him.

• • •

Homecoming was a typical game with a higher box office. As the Sacred Heart Hawk, Oliver ran back and forth and back and forth, energizing the rambunctious crowd. Sacred Heart was winning so handily and exuding such school spirit that no extra encouragement was needed, but Oliver kept running, jumping, and cheering, as he had for the past season.

Oliver had spent all of middle school trying to bulk up for football and praying to grow five more inches for basketball while throwing ten thousand footballs and shooting a million free throws. He'd earned the friendship and respect of all his teammates, but after sitting on the bench in both sports for his entire freshman year, he'd grown tired of the pity in his coaches' eyes.

During sophomore year, while he prepared to sit on the bench before the homecoming game, he read an article that profiled a college mascot. The young man bore the broiling heat and relentless cold all for the sake of the fans. How selfless. The accompanying photo depicted this small man being hoisted on the muscular shoulders of the football team, their faces focused upward in admiration. It didn't hurt that this scrawny, not-conventionally-attractive fellow alluded to having zero trouble in the lady department.

Oliver knew he needed a powerful ally in the mascot game, and Coach Anderson was the mark. Anderson was the merciless football maverick that the high school revolved around. A new trophy case was always under construction for his end-of-season accolades. The Math Team trophies had been stuffed into the teachers' lounge to clear shelf space. If Oliver could win Anderson's approval, the school board would blindly follow.

On the first day of practice junior year, Oliver marched into Coach Anderson's office with straight shoulders and made his announcement. "Coach, wouldn't it be great to have a mascot who pumped up the crowd at every home game?"

Anderson mulled it over for a moment. "No, that's what the cheerleaders are for."

"But the Hawk would be the living embodiment of the team, and fans love mascots. He could interact with the cheerleaders. We could play off each other."

"We?"

"Yes, I would be the Hawk." Oliver debated whether he should have led with this information while Anderson scratched his forehead.

"You're a football player and you want to be a bird?" Anderson curled his upper lip.

"Coach, I want to contribute to the team. All I do is sit on the bench. And I'm not blaming you for that. I suck, I know. And I'm not getting any better. If I could be the mascot, at least I'd be doing something." Anderson inhaled his irritation. Oliver kept going. "I just don't want you to waste your time on me, Coach. You've already spent more than enough."

Anderson perked up. "You used to play baseball, didn't you? Heard you were good. Made the All-Star Team, right?"

Oliver hung his head, the shame of unwelcome accomplishment. "I did. But I don't play anymore. Baseball's not for me."

Anderson didn't bite. Oliver knew he needed to go even further, bring his argument back around, but he couldn't do it on his own. He needed to play the dead brother card.

"Things have been kind of rough at home, Coach. I really miss Jason…"

After two years of devoting every fall afternoon to the gospel of Anderson, Oliver had learned the only sure way to terrify the football coach was to mention feelings. Oliver averted his eyes so Anderson could openly shudder.

Jason had been an elite wrestler, making it to the State Finals his freshman year, finishing as runner-up his sophomore year, avenging for a win as a junior, and defending his title senior year. Though Anderson hadn't known Jason, his athletic prowess had grown into a tall tale after his death. The legend had scaled the school walls and spread throughout the San Fernando Valley. Anderson had remarked on more than one occasion, usually when Oliver was struggling to block anything with two legs, how Jason's talent was rare and how it was a damn shame that it had been wasted.

Anderson cleared his throat to cut off Oliver. "I think it's a good idea. I'll see what I can do."

On his way out of the office, Oliver tried to shake off the guilt he felt. Wasn't this the least Jason could do for all the anger, confusion, and every other negative emotion in the English language that he'd unearthed in his absence?

By the home opener, Oliver was the embodiment of the most expensive mascot costume in the San Fernando Valley. He ran back and forth along the stands, hyping up the crowd. He danced with the cheerleaders, even joining in some of their choreography. Like the scrawny *Sports Illustrated* mascot had prophesized, the ladies loved the the Hawk. More than once during a steamy make-out session he'd been asked to leave on the bulky body of the furry bird until the last possible moment.

Through the eye slits in the headpiece, Oliver enjoyed the view: the roaring crowd, the men on the field, the bouncing cheerleaders, Katrina. She never took her eyes off Oliver, even when she was at the top of the pyramid. For a split second, her ankles faltered, and his heart dropped, but she steadied herself and beamed down at him from the top of the world. He knew that even if she did fall he would catch her. Or, at least, soften the impact.

On Katrina's front doorstep, Oliver slipped the pale pink corsage around her wrist. "You look gorgeous."

Katrina sauntered to his car without responding. She didn't have to. Her long, bare legs spoke for her, stretching out underneath a short dress of royal blue sequins. He charged ahead of her and opened the door, right on time for her to slide in.

The tiny, reflective discs on her dress scratched Oliver's hands, but he figured he deserved a little pain to go along with his pleasure. He had convinced Katrina to forgo a romantic solo dinner and hitch onto the Mitch and Joe supper wagon. Oliver concocted this scene as a sure way to avoid any boyfriend drama. Or, in their case, lack-of-boyfriend drama. Mitch and Joe would mess around and barely avoid a food fight, and Oliver could make eyes at Katrina while they played footsie under the table. Katrina had balked at the suggestion, not because she didn't like Mitch or Joe, or even because she had wanted Oliver to herself, but because Mitch and Joe's dates, Jamie and Mandie, were dumb as hell. Hanging out with them was a chore, but without the sense of accomplishment at the end of the agony.

Katrina and Oliver were the last to arrive, mainly because

they had pulled over to have an impromptu make-out session in Oliver's car, during which Katrina forfeited half the sequins on her dress to the back seat. The geometry of her updo had been pushed a few degrees off-kilter. Neither she nor Oliver cared. A glorious precedent had been set for the evening and neither Jamie nor Mandie (formerly Mandy, she changed to an "ie" to match Jamie) could hinder them.

The dinner played out like a bad sitcom. Mitch and Joe and Oliver ribbed each other, Jamie and Mandie (Oliver nicknamed them the "Ies") shared a single order of french fries. Katrina managed to respond to all of the Ies' frivolous observations on the following topics with one-word answers: Their proudly overpriced dresses, their gaudy corsages, the blotches in their fake tans, their unbroken-in shoes that had the nerve to give them blisters, and even the paint on the restaurant walls, which was deemed "perfection." It helped that the Ies took five trips to the bathroom together over the course of the meal. Five. Even Oliver noticed.

"Maybe one of them will come back pregnant," Oliver whispered to Katrina as he stole one of the Ies' french fries.

Katrina snorted a little too loudly, and Oliver had to backpedal to explain the outburst to Mitch and Joe.

"I told a lawyer joke." He shrugged.

By this time, Katrina was in tears. She could barely get out the words. "My dad's a lawyer."

"Tell it, man." Mitch and Joe gaped at Oliver like he was a traitor for not sharing the best joke ever.

Retreat was the only option. Oliver stood up. "I can't. I have to go the bathroom."

Katrina drowned in a new pool of laughter, and Oliver

marched to the bathroom. Mitch and Joe turned to Katrina for the joke, but she shook her head, leaned back, and hung her napkin over her face until Oliver returned, which was well before Jamie and Mandie did.

Oliver and Katrina spun every which way on the dance floor. By the end of the night, the skin on Oliver's hands had become numb to the sequins. He couldn't tell the difference between the scaled dress and the soft skin on Katrina's arms, the same arms she wrapped around his neck during all of the slow songs. Swaying in the center of the gymnasium, surrounded yet isolated, she whispered in his ear how they were like the old song that was playing by the band she didn't know. *Two worlds collided and they can never tear us apart.* Oliver liked the romanticism, but he was pretty sure that her arms would let go of him with little resistance. One pin prick into that tender skin and she would jump twenty feet away. He tightened his grip on her waist knowing she would let go before he would.

In the darkness of his bedroom, it had all gone according to plan. Well, not that Oliver had an actual plan. He wasn't an evil sex genius by any means. It had all gone according to hope. To dream.

He plucked stray sequins from Katrina's bare body and kissed each spot after removal. Their breath and soft laughter took on a musical quality, the roll of a timpani.

"Oly. Will you be my boyfriend?"

And the cymbal clanged.

Every expletive in the book ran back and forth between Oliver's ears. He kissed her, praying the moment would pass, but she pulled back, demanding a response.

"Oly?"

A sequin stuck on her cheek, which made it difficult to take her seriously.

"Katrina, you know I don't do the boyfriend thing."

He reached up to pluck off the sequin and she slapped his hand away, surprising both of them. Undeterred, she looked directly into his eyes.

"We spend so much time together. Why do I feel like I'm your dirty secret?"

Dammit, there were going to be tears. Oliver hated tears. Even more, he hated being the cause of them. He went out of his way not to cause them, and still, it rained.

"We went to the dance together. I didn't dance with anyone else." He bowed his head and rested his forehead on her shoulder.

"Did you want to?" She rolled her shoulder out from under him.

Frustration coiled inside of Oliver. Why had she waited until neither of them had any clothes on to have this conversation?

"No."

"Why not?"

The room smelled of coercion. He gritted his teeth. "Because I like you, and only you. And we're having fun."

"This is fun for you?" She sat back and crossed her arms.

Every response was a question. There was no winning this game.

"It *was* fun. But this isn't fun. I guess it needs to stop. If you want it to."

"Oh. You won't be my boyfriend, but I still have to do the breaking up part?"

Katrina grew smarter with each question. Oliver ached

with sadness. Good things always looked better when they were putting their clothes back on and disappearing from his life.

"That's not what I want, but it sounds like what you want," he said, crossing his arms.

"Are you putting words in my mouth?" She threw her arms down to her sides. Her disdain for Oliver was so great that she couldn't even wear her arms the same way as his.

The argument ran a few laps, always ending in the same place, with Oliver thinking he was crossing the finish line and Katrina feeling stuck in the starting blocks. Ultimately, the race came to a close with Katrina cursing Oliver down the hallway, out the front door, and into the fall night air while she searched not-so-silently for her car. Neighbors came to their windows to see the shimmering blue wreck in the streetlights.

Oliver was deleting her contact info from his phone when it rang. A familiar number glowed in the darkness.

"Hello?"

A shivering voice growled out of the phone. "You picked me up. I need a ride home."

"Oh, yeah. Sorry. I mean, about the car. I totally forgot—"

"Just take me home!"

He hung up, pulled on his pants in two hops, zipped his hoodie, and followed the trail of blue sequins out to his car.

• • •

The trauma from the night carried over into the next day. Oliver's mind overflowed and emptied at the same time.

Little aftershocks rolled through every surface he sat upon—his bed, the sofa in front of the TV, even at the dining room table. When his parents arrived home in the early evening, the ground stabilized. Oliver basked in the normalcy of his dad's pestering about *college applications* and *his future*.

Oliver's parents owned a furniture store, Pagano and Sons, three generations strong. The name was a dark cloud hanging over the fourth generation. At times, Oliver wished they would change the name to Pagano and Son, if only to acknowledge the burden of being the only son in a family business with "Sons" in the name.

The Pagano furniture business was a successful endeavor. Oliver's grandfather and father had expanded the stand-alone store to several chains. Every time his parents entered a restaurant, they buzzed about how great the chairs were and brainstormed about how they could mass-produce a cheaper knockoff, all before the hostess had taken their name. This shared interest bound them together, through everything. The furniture business was the reason Oliver's family remained intact, kept their sanity after losing Jason. Oliver wanted to express his gratitude by dedicating his life's work to Pagano and Sons, but he had zero passion for furniture. More problematic, he didn't have a better alternative. Oliver had no idea what he was passionate about, couldn't picture himself doing anything day in and day out for decades. Thinking about it made his head throb, and he blamed the dangling "s" on the end of "Sons."

Fortunately, his parents had agreed to pay his college tuition no matter where he went and what he studied, as long as his grades were strong and he graduated in five years. The plan was to go somewhere out of state where no one knew him as the only heir to a small furniture empire and figure out his life.

That night, Oliver filled out a college application at the dining room table. Jason's empty chair was a distraction.

"Full ride!" His mom reads a piece of paper and rips open another envelope.

Jason sits back in his chair, his parents tower over him.

"We are pleased to inform you…" His dad laughs and drops his piece of paper on a growing pile.

"Another full ride!" His mother claps.

"Jason, you got in everywhere!"

The energy in the room is palpable. Jason smiles at his parents' excitement, but his smile is purely cosmetic. Even eleven-year-old Oliver sees the pry in his upper lip.

"College is your oyster. Where are you going to make your pearl?" His dad beamed.

Jason shrugs. "Wherever Emily's going."

His parents exchange a worried glance.

His mom laughs it off. "Well, Emily should strongly consider somewhere you have a scholarship. There are a lot of great schools to choose from."

Tonight, the focus wasn't on college. Again, Opposite Possum. His dad flipped through interior design magazines and yammered to his mom about upholstery while she stirred spaghetti sauce at the stove. Coupled with his exhausted daze from the sleepless night, the room didn't provide the best environment for concentration, but the noise made the essay questions less painful.

If you could only bring one thing to the University of

Montana, what would it be? He debated the ways he could answer.

1. A photograph of my parents because of all they've given me.

True, but it tasted too saccharine.

2. My glowing attitude and bright outlook to the future.

He groaned—too generic.

3. Nothing. If I wanted anything from my past to follow me, why the hell would I be going to Montana?

He had a feeling that rebellious essays, like fervidly misguided speeches to parole boards, only worked in movies. Splitting the difference, he peppered the essay with all three inclinations and sealed the envelope without proofreading.

• • •

One week and vow of short-term chastity later, Oliver cruised down Sunset Boulevard with Daphne at his side. This wasn't the Sunset Boulevard in West Hollywood, with its outward appearance of musical history and infamy. On a Sunday afternoon on this eastern stretch of Sunset, many of the shops were gated, giving the neighborhood a slightly dangerous flavor.

After a brief internet search, Oliver had discovered that Jim Morrison was buried at Père Lachaise Cemetery in Paris. Obviously, they couldn't fly to Paris, so he had had to dig deeper inward. Who was *his* Jim Morrison? A singer with the talent and charisma to influence generations, with the small caveat that the musician needed to have died young and tragically. The scan through the bass lines of his memory had been quick. Melancholy guitar had taken over, strumming the answer. Oliver knew exactly where to bring Daphne and finished explaining all this as they arrived in front of a wine bar. Its façade was a painted piece of red, black, and white street art.

"The Elliott Smith Wall." He made a grand gesture with his arms to downplay the humble nature of the wall.

"Elliott Smith? I've never heard of him."

"You have now."

Oliver pulled out an iPod and ear buds. A tinny sound vaguely resembling music dissolved into her as he tucked the buds into her ears. She squirmed and readjusted them.

"Jason got me hooked on him, so I guess it's even more appropriate. This wall was one of Elliott's album covers."

He'd cued his favorite song, a ballad whose acoustic guitar fell like raindrops. He couldn't hear the bitter lyrics in Daphne's ear buds, but Elliott's sarcasm sang along in his head.

Someone's always coming around here, trailing some new kill. Says, "I seen your picture on a hundred dollar bill." What's a game of chance to you, to him is one of real skill. So glad to meet you, Angeles.

Daphne blinked three times, processing. "This song's about L.A. and how much it sucks."

"Uh-huh." Had she gotten all that from the first verse? It had taken Oliver five listens before he'd figured out that Angeles wasn't a person.

Picking up the ticket shows there's money to be made. Go on, lose the gamble, that's the history of the trade. Did you add up all the cards left to play to zero, and sign up for evil, Angeles?

"You listened to this when you were ten? Pretty hardcore in the sad department."

"Not exactly when I was ten. I inherited Jason's music library, and Elliott Smith was one of his most listened to. I wouldn't have discovered him otherwise."

"I like it. It's so different from what Emily listened to. The Ramones, The Clash, The Sex Pistols, The Doors, Bowie. All the music my parents rebelled with in their youth. Oh, the irony in those chord progressions."

He laughed. The chord progressions in Daphne's humor played in the right key.

Daphne stepped closer to the wall and Oliver followed her lead. They examined the four thick black lines curving up, down, and around again before merging together into a thin point, something of a warped racetrack. Threads extended from the convergence point, forming infinity signs that connected to a pair of pliers. It didn't make a lot of sense to Oliver, but that was the point of art, wasn't it? To imitate life when words had given up.

Gratitude, condolences, dedications, proclamations of love, and senseless obscenities graced the wall's white background. People from all over the country had left their mark.

"Have you been here before?" Daphne asked.

"Nah. Didn't seem right to be here without Jason."

Oliver noticed the vast amount of gum residue splotched all over the sidewalk. Something once so pastel and sticky now blackened and smooth. The sight unnerved him. He returned his focus to the wall while Daphne pulled a Sharpie from her pocket.

"You remembered." His chest puffed up. So few people cared enough to remember the things that came out of Oliver's mouth, he'd started to forget himself.

"I take basic instruction like a pro. If it was a sport, full-ride scholarship right here." She pointed her thumbs at the meat of her shoulders.

Foreboding lit within Oliver and sent his heart into overdrive. If she handed him the Sharpie, he had no idea what to write on the wall. He loved and admired Elliott's music and couldn't bear the shame of writing something meaningless just to write something. An inkling of perspiration spotted his hairline until Daphne saved him by plucking off the cap, kneeling down, and writing without hesitation. She'd known what to write since the moment they'd arrived. She inscribed the sterile cursive of a perfectionist, the letters exactly as taught in elementary school: *Emily & Jason.*

She stepped back. They stared down the words together as though the letters might leap from the wall and run away.

"That's about it." Oliver said.

Daphne shrugged, "For better or for worse."

"I hope they found their better."

"Part of me hopes they've had to watch our worse." She twisted the closed Sharpie cap around the marker, and the revolution squeaked in her palms.

Oliver's body swayed, the reality of her wish moving

him. His thoughts had often taken similar positions, but he'd never said them out loud, and certainly not to another human being. Not even his therapist. Although, maybe now he would. Daphne couldn't face him. Her upper lip twitched, and he sensed regret. He wasn't going to allow it.

"I hope they've had to watch our best and be sad about what they missed."

His words didn't turn her toward him. Her eyes remained connected to the wall, reading something he couldn't see. His first instinct was to grab her hand, squeeze it, remind her they were both still alive. But lately he'd found that his first instincts were often wrong when it came to girls, so he stood motionless, putting it back on Daphne. Plus, he was pretty sure she knew she was alive.

He started despising himself for his nothingness, his pulse beating in his forehead. A soft set of fingers brushed through his. Oliver dipped his head in scant shame. She was braver than he, and always would be. He was getting used to being a step or two behind her, beginning to find reassurance in the warm cloud of her perception. She gave his hand a little squeeze and he responded with a flexing and tightening of his fingers against hers. She dipped her chin a few times, first at the wall, and then to Oliver. He detected a tiny movement at the corners of her lips. Was it a smile or nerves? She headed toward the car before he could decide. He looked down and discovered his hand empty.

"We're not done." He called after her.

Oliver couldn't see her face to tell if she was happy or exhausted. She was already too far ahead of him.

• • •

A few neighborhoods west, near the postcard version of Los Angeles, the buildings were taller, the streets wider, and the towering palm trees more pronounced. Oliver led Daphne down a narrow driveway tucked between two parking structures.

"I think this is it."

"I always thought if I was murdered in a dark alley, it would be in a less gentrified neighborhood," she said.

"Did you also think you would go so willingly?" He snickered and ducked under a small archway.

"Little known fact, I'm actually very stupid."

She ambled through the gateway into a small, secluded cemetery. There were no other visitors, no one else between them and the dead. Daphne came to a halt. Oliver realized the flaw in his plan, so wide and apparent his legally blind great-aunt could've seen it. Cemeteries haunted as often as they consoled.

"Oh no. I wasn't thinking. Are you okay? We can go back."

"No, I'm fine." She swallowed and took a breath. "I wasn't expecting a cemetery. It's beautiful. Peaceful."

She stepped forward and they looped along the driveway past the simple gravestones of varying shades of gray and bronze and rose.

He masked his relief by pointing around. "There are a lot of famous people buried here."

"Figures they would get the good cemetery. Where did you bury him?"

"The guy I killed last night? That secret stays with me."

"No, the other guy."

Serious Daphne was back. Something about the tone in Serious Daphne's voice lured the truth nestled deep inside him with unsettling ease. When he heard this tenor shift in her voice, the hairs at the base of his neck prickled.

"He was cremated."

"Please don't say he's sitting on your mantel."

"No! My family is dysfunctional, but they're not anywhere near your level of morbid, sicko. We spread his ashes in the Pacific."

"Jason loved the ocean?"

Oliver cackled. "He hated the ocean. Hated the sand. Hated to swim. Hated the seagulls. Supposedly, and conveniently out of my range of memory, he loved to swim and surf and build sandcastles and barely even cried when he got stung by a jellyfish. I don't buy it."

"They reimagined him as Jacques Cousteau. Emily gets reimagined as Sally Ride because she asked for a telescope for Christmas when she was eight. And you know who actually used that telescope?"

"I have a strong feeling she's walking right next to me."

"I moved it to my room the summer after she got it, and it had so much dust on the lens, I thought I'd discovered a new galaxy."

"Now every time I say I'm going to the beach my parents get all sentimental, like I'm going there to grieve or something, when I'm just hanging out with my friends. With my parents, every aspect of my life is a reflection of Jason. Sometimes it's really hard not to remind them about how much he hated the damn ocean."

Daphne let out a little laugh. He realized he didn't need to apologize for venting. The blood in his veins was replaced with air and lightness inflated him.

"Where is Emily buried?"

"Up north, near San Fran, in my mom's hometown where my grandparents are buried. It's this huge cemetery with zero personality. They threw in a couple weeping willows here and there, but it's not helping."

"You go up there a lot?"

"We went up on her first two birthdays after to plant flowers. Then nothing. Having her grave so far away made it even easier to not talk about her."

"We could go."

"Nah. But thanks. I don't feel any closer to her there." She swallowed. "There's nowhere I can go where I feel close to her."

"Well, this is the Père Lachaise of Los Angeles. Emily and Jason wanted to see Jim Morrison's grave. Maybe you could come here."

"I guess that's all up to you and why we're here. This better be good, Pagano."

He responded to the challenge by lengthening his stride. They passed two sanctuaries filled with stacks of crypts and rounded a corner.

"Oscar Wilde eternally rests in Père Lachaise. People come from around the world to kiss his grave and leave giant lipstick marks. So who is Westwood Memorial's Oscar Wilde?"

Daphne scanned the sanctuary as they passed. One crypt, second row from the bottom, second row from the left, stood out from the rest of the gray-white slabs. Its deeper, blushing-beige face wore a coating of red-lipsticked kisses.

Daphne smirked. "Marilyn Monroe."

"Did you bring the lipstick?" Oliver knew, certain as the graves before him, she had brought it.

Daphne pulled a small tube from her pocket. Oliver scrunched his face.

"What is this?" He snatched the red-tinted lip balm from her fingers.

"In case you haven't noticed, I'm a neutral lip gal. I don't own a red lipstick. This is the closest thing I had. I even looked through my mom's makeup."

"Oscar would disapprove."

"Well, maybe he'll write a tragic character based on me for his next play running in the afterlife."

"Oh, yeah. This is Greek chorus worthy."

"A girl is told by a ridiculous boy to bring red lipstick to an unknown place for an unknown purpose. She gets hung up on the red detail and brings lip balm because it's red, when any lipstick would have worked for the occasion, which is to kiss a grave."

"The ridiculous boy is definitely the hero of this story."

"Yeah, you're right up there with Oedipus."

"So, kiss it."

"Ew. No."

"Are you a germaphobe?"

"Are you going to peer pressure me into defacing a grave?"

"Fine. I'll do it."

He popped off the cap and pressed the balm hard against his lips, rounding over them again and again until a thick ring of bright red circled his mouth. Daphne fought back laughter.

Oliver noticed her struggle. "All the cool kids aren't doing it," he joked at himself.

He closed his eyes and leaned into the wall of crypt, pressing his lips firmly against the pink marble until his nose touched. He rested there for a few long seconds, praying the color would adhere to the stone. He pulled away feeling like he had blown out birthday candles and opened his eyes to see how many were still aflame. To his pleasant surprise, a faint but distinct pair of pink lips kissed back.

"It could be better," he said with an air of pride.

Oliver turned to Daphne, doubting she'd be impressed, but encouraged by her glimmering eyes. Still, he braced for impact against merciless teasing when those eyes shifted to his mouth.

"Well, it couldn't be worse." That was all she was going to say.

Oliver's laugh carried them toward the entrance. Daphne refused to hasten her slow pace, forcing him to walk backwards to talk to her.

He pointed at her, square between the eyes. "You like when I look stupid."

"I guess that's why I like you, because you look pretty stupid all the time." A half-smile unzipped the corner of her mouth and revealed a quadrant of teeth.

He clasped his hands, leaving his index fingers straight, and tapped their tips against his chin. "Daphne, has anyone ever told you what a pleasant, flattering young woman you are?"

"You look like you painted your face with a lollipop. It's giving off a psychotic clown vibe."

"Hey, I bet I look pretty good compared to all the other psychotic clowns out there."

"I can't believe I just watched you make out with a grave." Daphne buried her laughing face in her hands.

"And she was great." He threw his arms out, full wing-span. "Thank you, Marilyn!"

On the drive home, the stillness between them evolved into a hum of contentment. Daphne closed her eyes and rested her head against the seat, listening to Elliott Smith on Oliver's iPod. Occasionally, she opened her eyes to see Oliver pumping his fists in celebration or pounding the steering wheel in agony while he listened to the Rams game. His lips were still eight shades pinker than skin.

When they reached the empty school parking lot, Daphne removed the ear buds and handed him the iPod.

"Keep it," he said. "I have three of them. Dead-older-sibling-slash-bad-parenting-guilt-money buys a lot of MP3 players."

"I'm financing college with my guilt money."

"Well, you're always gonna be three steps ahead of me, aren't you, Daph?"

She climbed out of the car and closed the door. "Learn to walk faster."

She thought about what she wanted to say for a notice-able length of time. The car window framed her, the setting sun haloing her head, her eyes gazing off into the distance. She was so close, yet all puzzle. A smile pulled at the corners of her lips but didn't materialize.

"Thanks."

A single word after all that thought. The smile finally came when she turned away toward her house. Oliver caught only one curve of the dimple on her left cheek. He was disappointed not to see the whole thing.

Oliver went home and had the strangest urge. He dug out a stylus from the bottom of a desk drawer, plopped down with his tablet, and started doodling the moments of the day. The abstract racetrack of the Elliott Smith wall. The lipstick on Marilyn Monroe's crypt. A boy walking backwards in front of a girl through the cemetery. Stick figures, nothing serious. His brain needed a few more minutes to remind his hand how to draw.

He had no formal training. The only art classes he'd ever taken were walking to the comic store with Jason on Wednesdays, buying all their favorite titles. Then they would come home and draw for hours, half-tracing, half-creating. Oliver had given up comics, filed them under Opposite Possum, buried them in a box in Jason's closet to collect dust.

This isn't cheating, he kept telling himself. There were no superheroes or villains, not a stitch of spandex or latex or leather. It wasn't the same.

Oliver opened a clean page. He drew a face with huge eyes that he framed with heavy, uneven streaks of hair. He drew lips, not too small, not too big, pinched but not puckered. He filled them in, how red lipstick would appear in black and white. But she didn't wear red lipstick. He was making her a superhero, giving her an alter ego she probably didn't want. He smiled, knowing how pissed off she'd be by a dumb boy drawing her so inaccurately. She might even drop phrases like *hypersexualize* and *testosterone eyes* and *misogynistic fantasies*. The glare and snarl might be worth it to hear the deservedly feminist rant this false representation would inspire. He erased the lips and redrew them without filling them in.

He drew more hair, procrastinating. It was weird having a picture of Daphne sitting in front of him, inaccurate as it was. Unsatisfied, he drew a line over her face, and another one, a few wavy curves and sharp edges. Making the drawing something more, because despite barely knowing Daphne, it was clear that she was more. More than her eyes. More than her Goldilocks lips. More than the sister of his dead brother's dead girlfriend. He connected the last line, and puzzle pieces covered her face.

And then it hit him. He already knew Daphne's alter ego, one that wouldn't make her cringe. One that would make her smile so big she wouldn't be able to bite her lip to hide it. He started over, but this time added a black mask across her forehead and temples, leaving her eyes unobstructed. He squiggled a nose, but it was too small for her perfectly proportionate face. He erased, tried again. It was better, but still wrong.

He sat back and absorbed the full picture. The face looked nothing like Daphne. The nose and mouth weren't quite right, but he didn't know how to fix them. The eyes weren't expressive enough. But he could practice and improve. The next time he saw her, he'd pay better attention to the mechanics of her face.

• • •

Oliver and Daphne hadn't spoken directly about her play since texting when she got the part. She'd dropped a few hints reminding him about the show dates that he pretended not to pick up on, but he'd never verbally committed to attending. Besides, she hadn't gone to any of his football games. Which had stung. Well, not stung so much as left him doubting the Hawk's allure. Not that he wanted to allure her. The point was, he owed her nothing. But he was practicing being the bigger person. He wanted to see the surprise on her face when he showed up.

He watched *Our Town* sitting in the back row of the surprisingly full auditorium, a bouquet of the freshest supermarket daisies in tow. Daphne was right—it was kind of boring. Life and death and whatever comes after. Blah, blah, blah. The mystique was gone for Oliver. He felt he'd lived longer than any of the characters, even the grandparents. Despite all this, his throat constricted to uncomfortable levels during Emily's farewell speech, when Jason and his Emily slipped into Oliver's mind. Oliver pushed them out and focused on Daphne, who was pretending to be a dead, old woman on the stage. Harsh lines had been painted on her face to mimic wrinkles. She wore a wig with a matronly bun and pantomimed knitting, because for some inexplicable reason there were no props in this play. The set consisted only of tables and chairs.

The strange workings of his mind began to morph the tragic scene in front of him into comedy. Seeing Daphne, this young, vibrant person made up to be old, wrapping invisible yarn around invisible needles—the whole thing was absurd. He knew this was his brain's way of fighting the lump in his throat from Jason and Emily, but he didn't know how to counter it. The tickle started in his knees and inched up through his hips and abdomen. He could feel a set of the giggles coming on, crawling up his esophagus, a thousand cactus pricks in his throat. The only way to prevent laughter was to cause pain. He bit down on the fleshy part of his hand between his thumb and forefinger didn't let go.

He closed his eyes. For a few eternal minutes, the hot pulse in his hand throbbed against his teeth. Applause rang out, and he unclamped his jaw, revealing a hand with broken skin and flecks of blood in the deepest impressions. Oliver cradled his hand while the actors took their bows, and the curtain closed. He filed out with the rest of the audience and waited patiently in the hallway with daisies and damaged nerve endings.

Daphne was one of the last cast members to emerge from backstage. For a moment, he thought he caught her eyes searching the hallway, but he couldn't confirm it. She maneuvered through the crowd, granting hellos and accepting congratulations. Four girls and a guy breezed by her.

"See you at Gizzarelli's?" one of the girls asked.

"Yeah, I'll see you there!" Daphne waved.

She landed in front of Oliver as though he was the target she'd been aiming for the whole time. If she was surprised by his presence, his senses weren't acute enough to identify it.

"You came."

"I don't make idle promises when it comes to extracurricular activities."

He handed her the flowers. "Congratulations, on your theatrical debut. *The Oliver Times* declares your performance mesmerizing, transcendent, and…"

"Geriatric."

"Really geriatric," he grinned.

"Did you like the knitting? I came up with that myself." She rolled on her feet, heel to toe, inching closer to him before tilting back.

Oliver was surprised at missing those few inches of closeness when they went away. "That was my favorite part."

"Who the hell is this?" A lanky girl with long, black hair barged in on the conversation.

Oliver examined her from head to toe and diagnosed that she might be decent looking if she didn't have a permanent case of pissy face.

"Janine, this is Oliver. Oliver, this is Janine."

Janine performed the same once-over of Oliver that he'd given her. She announced her verdict in the rolling of her eyes. Her expression didn't say, *Oh, this is the Oliver that I've heard all about in relentless repetition.* It was more, *This dude is a jackass. I can smell it.*

"You're still going to Gizzarelli's, right?" Janine crossed her arms.

"Of course. Give me a couple minutes."

Janine threw one last warning glance at Oliver before turning on her heels and leaving.

"The Drama Crew is celebrating its success. Mostly that the curtain didn't fall on anyone, and the lights stayed on the whole show. Tiny victories."

"Janine's protective of you," Oliver said.

"Yeah, you don't need birth control if you have a Janine."

Oliver snorted. "Super juice."

This Daphne girl was something. He liked not knowing what.

CLIMB MOUNT EVEREST

GIZZARELLI'S WAS THE BEST: CHEAP, DELICIOUS, AND HUGE portions. Daphne twirled a mound of linguine around her fork and opened wide. Her senior year pact with bravery had included unforeseen benefits: friends. Holly, Macy, Anna, Kyle, and Danielle had all been in the play, and Daphne dubbed them The Drama Crew. Holly had played Emily and Kyle had played the male lead, but neither was a diva. Daphne wondered if the negative actor stereotypes were all inaccurate. The only thing actor-y that Holly did was talk and laugh louder than anyone else. That wasn't such a bad thing. Holly sounded like a trumpet, her laugh was jazz.

The Drama Crew liked going to movies and discussing them for hours over coffee at Frank's Diner afterwards. Janine, normally a moth in the swarm of social butterflies, fluttered around the light of The Drama Crew and landed. At Gizzarelli's, she sat next to Kyle and chatted for hours about his boyfriend, who was a year older and went to college on the East Coast. They'd left things open, and Daphne's heart hurt for him, but Kyle didn't mind the arrangement. He reminded everyone how cold the East Coast winters were and how warm his bed would be over break.

The people sitting around the table weren't Daphne and Janine's new best friends that they made plans with every day. The Drama Crew were every-third-weekend friends that ensured a good time. Their caffeinated all-nighters filled an unspoken emptiness between Daphne and Janine that had been vacant for three years.

Daphne had vaguely known Janine Grajian when Emily was alive. Janine was that girl in class who always got caught passing notes to Penny Layton. Right after Emily died, most of the other kids hadn't known how to say they were sorry for Daphne's loss and kept their distance, preserving the grief bubble. But Janine and Penny weren't like the other kids. They'd skipped straight up to Daphne during recess, said they were sorry about her sister, and asked her to join them on the monkey bars. After swinging those bars together, the threesome was inseparable. Sleepovers every weekend. Long trips to the mall where no purchases were intended. Seeing every non-R-rated movie playing at the theater.

Everything was fine in Daphne-Janine-Penny Land until freshman year, when Penny decided to try out for the dance squad. Apparently, Penny's mom had told her that she had cheerleading legs, and Penny started seeing herself in a new light. A light with backlit short skirts and pom-poms and a boyfriend.

Janine thought this was the worst idea in the history of the world. "A cheerleader? But you're not stupid. How will you understand what they're saying?"

"That's so, like, racist against cheerleaders. And I'm not trying out for cheerleading, it's dance. We don't even wear skirts." Penny admired her reflection in her locker mirror and smoothed the deep brown flyaways on the crown of her head.

Okay, maybe Penny wasn't as smart as Janine thought.

"Truth." Janine pumped her fist.

Daphne made a stone of her face so her opinion on all matters would go unquestioned.

"It's a completely different sport," Penny said. "That's like confusing soccer and football."

"Well, most of the world refers to soccer as football, so there you go," Janine said.

"I want to make some new friends. What's wrong with that? Plus, I have nice legs. My mom says I should use them before I lose them." Penny repeated the phrase in Thai, transforming into her mother instantly.

"Since when do you listen to your mom?" Janine scoffed.

Penny ignored her and applied a fresh coat of lip gloss.

"I guess we're not good enough for Penny Layton." Janine said it casually, but Daphne detected the agitation in her voice. They both knew Penny was slipping from their friendship circle. Unlike Daphne, Janine was unaccustomed to loss.

Daphne had her own philosophy about Penny. With a name like Penny Layton, her mother had destined her to cheerleader-dom. It had only been a matter of time. Daphne was supportive of Penny's decision to try out for the dance team, which drove a small rift between Daphne and Janine. In the end, Janine was vindicated because even after all of Penny's promises of *best friends* and *trying something new* and *nothing will change*, Penny's appearances at sleepovers and the mall and movies dwindled. Within two months of making the team, Penny ceased to socialize with them entirely. The ultimate betrayal came sophomore year in the form of the dance team snickering in the school cafeteria. Five pairs of eyes from Penny's table scoured Daphne and Janine, three tables away.

"They're inseparable. It's weird." Penny said it too loudly, saw that Daphne and Janine had heard. Penny's face lost all its color, a Technicolor movie in reverse. "So what are we doing Saturday night?" Penny tried to cover, but the damage was done.

Daphne and Janine had skulked away, gripping their lunch trays with white fingertips. Daphne wished to forgive this isolated incident, but Janine wouldn't let her.

• • •

"What's super juice?" Daphne climbed up the paved, winding trail and glanced at the Verdugo Mountains behind her. She tried her best to fake being in better shape, pretending the uphill climb wasn't pushing her angry lungs beyond their limits.

"It's like *awesome sauce*, but *awesome sauce* was already taken."

"Originally derivative." She huffed out the words.

"I prefer *uniquely* derivative, thank you."

She changed the subject without attempting a transition. "Does your family eat dinner together?"

"Yeah. Does yours?"

Daphne shook her head. "Right after Emily died, people kept bringing us food. You probably went through that, too."

"Our fridge was full for weeks."

"Right? And the things people define as casseroles. They clean out their fridge and pantry, mix it all together and bake it. Because if you're grieving, you forget what good food tastes like."

Oliver laughed. "I don't remember it being that bad. Maybe the grief food is meant to remind you that you can set the cooking bar really low and still feed yourself. Life will go on, it just might taste shitty for awhile."

"My mom didn't get that memo. After the condolence casseroles ended we got takeout every night. But we still ate together. It seemed like the only thing we could do. Must. Eat. Survive." She punched her fist up through the air, conquering the wind. "But then my parents decided that dinner is a concept only for families of four. My mom filled her plate with school and work and my dad started drinking, so no more dinners."

She let the words dangle. My dad's a *drinker*. This new information had leapt forth from her before she'd had a chance to weigh the consequences.

"My mom makes dinner every night," Oliver responded. "But she hates cooking. You know how if food is made with love you can taste it? Well, my mom's food tastes like outdated gender roles."

Daphne cracked, and her distinct, true laugh poured out in a full, rough burst. Oliver laughed in surprise at the sound.

"I'm trying to imagine what outdated gender role chicken tastes like," she said.

Oliver grimaced. "It's a little dry. And other parts are salmonella pink."

"Mmmm, tasty."

"So, what are your plans for Thanksgiving?" he asked.

"My mom will be working."

"She works on Thanksgiving? Where?"

"It's a holiday tradition. After…"

Oliver nodded. He knew what she meant, wanted to hear it out loud even less than she wanted to say it.

"…My mom decided to do some good for the world and all the other Emilys and Jasons in it. She enrolled in nursing school, got her degree, and works at a mental health clinic. I get it, they're understaffed and in demand on holidays. So, for Thanksgiving, she usually leaves my dad and me a turkey TV dinner in the freezer."

"That's funny."

He thought she was joking. Daphne didn't know whether to be amused or disheartened that the level of her family's dysfunction was inconceivable to a person belonging to the second most dysfunctional family she knew.

"Wait, she really leaves you a TV dinner for Thanksgiving?"

"Sometimes it's a pot pie."

He shook his head, a little disgusted. "You want to have Thanksgiving at my place?"

"Uh, the way you've built up your mom's cooking, I don't think my stomach could handle that culinary amazingness."

"No, it won't be that bad. They always buy a pumpkin pie from somewhere good and we have the spray whipped cream. That stuff's awesome."

"Is that you or the whippets talking?"

"Hey, I am an upstanding young man. If I need to huff something, there are plenty of toilet cleaning products to get the job done. The whipped cream is for pie and pie alone."

"I do like pie."

"Well, think about it. The offer stands."

He sounded genuine, like someone who wouldn't openly invite her into catastrophe. Luckily, her answer could be delayed, saved by the end of the trail arriving under their feet.

"This is it," she said.

At the top, they stared down. On the other side of a chain-link fence, the back of the Hollywood sign jutted out from the hill. The white vinyl appeared less substantial up close. It resembled the cheap siding of the shed in her backyard that stored the forgotten gardening equipment. Somehow it was appropriate for the symbol of Hollywood to be as much a façade as the film sets on its studio lots.

"They should put lights all over it for the holidays," she chirped.

"Another missed opportunity for gaudiness," he snarked back.

"It would be fun, the Hollywood sign floating in the night sky in twinkle lights." Under her steely exterior, Daphne had a soft spot for holiday decor.

Oliver immediately exploited this vulnerability. "You're so festive. How many reindeer sweaters do you have?"

"None. But I have a headband with antlers."

Oliver was so repulsed by a reindeer antler headband that he moaned and clutched his stomach. Daphne could respect this. It was the way she felt about homecoming, but she didn't want to hurt his feelings.

He turned a slow 360. "Nice view from up here."

Daphne gazed out to the west, where the ocean would be if it weren't hidden behind a layer of smog on the warm fall day. "Well, it's not the Himalayas."

"The way you were puffing up the hill, I thought it might be."

"Yeah, I should put more effort into P.E." She tried to laugh, but her face went bright, and she turned away from him.

Daphne did her best to skirt the embarrassment, but her cheeks were a sure tell. Here she stood, pink and mute, unable to come up with a witty or self-deprecating comeback. At this point, Oliver apologizing would paint a pointing neon arrow above her head. He didn't make that mistake.

"When you summit Everest, how long do you stay up there?" he asked.

"As long as your oxygen-deprived brain and all the other oxygen deprived brains waiting in line behind you will allow. Not very long."

"So you travel around the globe, put yourself through hell, risk your life, for a couple minutes at the top of the world?"

"People die for less every day." It was the noble thing to

say. The words felt smooth against her tongue as they slid out of her mouth, but she didn't know if she believed them.

"Would it have been easier if Emily and Jason had died scaling Mount Everest?" he asked.

"Than in my dad's car in our garage? Yes, probably." Her voice was one decibel short of an exclamation.

Oliver shook his head.

Curiosity overtook the warmth in her cheeks and she faced him. "You don't think so?"

"I think we'd still have questions, just different ones."

She sighed in half-agreement. This argument was unable to be won, all speculation and conjecture and trying to think for people she didn't understand. "The great thing about Mount Lee is that there isn't an oxygen shortage, and we can stay for however long we choose."

"Do you want to sit down for a little bit?" He glanced around for an open space to settle.

"Sure."

He took off his jacket and spread it on the ground beneath them. Daphne folded her legs under her and they sat speechless for a few minutes, a half an hour, she couldn't say. Time became a theory floating in the hazy atmosphere. Hollywood spread out before them on a sloping platter, a vast expanse of desert metropolis. The beginning and end of dreams and dreamers.

In seventeen years, Daphne had seen so little of Los Angeles, only recognizing a few small enclaves among the miles upon miles of concrete and palm trees. Her entire world stretched out before her. For once, she enjoyed feeling so small.

• • •

After the visit to Marilyn Monroe's grave, Daphne became fascinated with the icon. Bat your bedroom eyes, smile bright enough and no one will see the pain. It's even harder to see if your lips are painted red. Had Emily owned red lipstick? Daphne had no recollection of seeing Emily in makeup of any kind.

"Move over!"

"Stop it!"

Emily and Daphne elbow each other in front of the bathroom mirror, battling for sink high ground. The elbowing escalates into a duel with hairbrushes. The bristles pierce Daphne's knuckles.

"Ow!" Daphne cedes her ground. The end of the mirror cuts off half her face.

"Crybaby," Emily says. She brushes her hair. "You're so lucky you got Mom's nose."

"But, it's big."

"You'll grow into it, though. Dad's boxy nose, no hope. It's like a sculptor got chisel happy."

"Jason likes it."

Emily blushes. "Yeah, he does."

The nose was their most dissimilar facial feature. Perhaps that's why Daphne took much time and care with her own makeup—the similar facial features needed to distinguish themselves.

Finding her perfect red involved luring Janine to the mall three times in one week with the promise of cinnamon pretzels. Daphne subjected herself to an onslaught of salespeople, each with a different opinion about which undertone would best suit her. The process had expended an entire box of tissues, copious amounts of lip balm, and five downward turned thumbs from Janine before a nod of approval. The truth was found.

Standing on the Paganos' welcome mat, Daphne wore the oxblood lipstick out in public for the first time. It made her ivory skin lean even closer to the shade of snow and darkened her hair. One swipe of the deep maroon distanced her further from the California girl image, the antithesis of blonde and bronzed. This filled her with immense delight.

She ran her tongue over the front of her teeth one last, precautionary time before ringing the doorbell. The two chords hit the notes of optimism and dread. Daphne reminded herself that this was any other family, any other dinner. It might as well be Janine answering the door. But it wasn't Janine, it was Oliver, who may have stepped out of a parallel dimension, wearing a chunky sweater clearly gifted to him by a relative who hadn't laid eyes on him in a decade.

"Hello, Marilyn." He whistled at the lipstick.

Her cheeks went hot, and an insult was the only defense. "You wish, Grandpa."

Oliver tugged at the sweater. The pattern looked better when stretched against his chest. "Christmas present from last year. It makes my mom happy."

"Which great-aunt?"

He nodded, impressed. "Second cousin, actually. But, close."

"Six degrees of bad-sweater separation." She crossed the threshold, easing into the warmth of the house, much warmer than her own.

Oliver grinned in agreement and returned to the topic of the lipstick. "And, no, I don't wish you were Marilyn Monroe. You're way too smart to stand over a subway grate in a skirt."

Daphne sighed. "That was a character she played, not her. That's like me judging you for the bird suit."

"You *do* judge me for the bird suit."

Daphne rolled her eyes for show, but she didn't mind being caught in her contradiction. "Well, no one's perfect. Plus, this isn't even Marilyn's shade of red."

"Well, I like it."

He led her down the hallway and couldn't see her fail at holding back a grin.

"You look ready to kiss a grave," he added.

Not the compliment she'd hoped for. The grin fell from her face.

He pointed at the wall covered with framed photographs, giant tiles connecting and filling all of its blank space. "This also makes my mom happy."

The photographs were old and new, every possible combination of the four Paganos. Oliver's hair was blond as a kid and he smiled with his top and bottom teeth. Jason looked happy in all the photos. Perhaps more pensive in the final candid ones, but Daphne figured she was reading too much into a stolen moment.

Daphne wondered what Emily looked like in her last photo. In the months following her death, all family photographs containing the four original Bowmans mysteriously vanished. Only photos with Daphne and her parents remained. Since these photos were somewhat recent, there wasn't a lot of smiling going on. It was *American Gothic* with the pitchfork swapped out for a dark-haired teenager wearing smoky eyes. In photographs, the family became a band that lost the original singer but still played all the old songs, no big deal. Except that it wasn't the same.

One day, out of boredom, she was rooting around in the china cabinet and found a framed photograph buried under a stack of plates. In front of Sleeping Beauty's Castle at Disneyland, Daphne's smile was full of missing teeth, Emily's full of braces. The four Bowmans in the photo were now strangers, people exuding an aura of happiness so unfamiliar that she could scarcely believe it was her own face grinning back at her.

"I was such a cute kid," Oliver said, trying to prove that he wasn't embarrassed by the photo display.

"Yeah. What happened?"

Oliver laughed and escorted Daphne into the kitchen.

If Stella and Blake harbored any ill feelings toward the sister of the girlfriend of their dead son, they smothered them with their hugs. Two big squeezes and Daphne took a seat at the table across from Oliver.

Stella and Blake appeared much more alive than her own parents. The way they weaved around each other in the kitchen like a blundering dance, the frazzled search for extra hot pads when the timer went off. They also came dangerously close to finishing each other's sentences. Oliver's family horror film was her rom com. It all depended whether you were on the screen or in the stadium seats.

A half-carved turkey, three shades lighter than the crisp brown of a well-cooked bird, sat in the center of the table, the ideal mascot for the meal before them.

"Everything is delicious, Mrs. Pagano."

Stella sat a little taller. She had Oliver's smile. "Thank you, Daphne. I hope the stuffing isn't too dry."

"No, it's perfect."

Daphne took a sip of water, drowning her white lie. Oliver coated his stuffing in cranberry sauce, making it edible.

"Oliver, you didn't get any sweet potatoes. Here." Stella picked up the casserole dish to pass.

Oliver waved her off. "I don't like sweet potatoes, Mom."

"But they're your favorite." Stella's voice pinched.

"No."

His cold, flat tone made it an easy riddle; Daphne deduced that sweet potatoes were Jason's favorite. Age and time swirled her own mother's memories, she and Emily's traits blurring together like clouds joining in the sky. Daphne always tried to not let these confusions upset her. Nevertheless, it was insulting for her own personality to be forgotten and replaced with one who'd abandoned them so long ago. Oliver didn't expand on his mother's error, and Daphne bargained with higher powers for Stella to move on. But, as holidays proved again and again, higher powers took the day off, too.

After brief contemplation, Stella came to a conclusion. "Oh, you're right. Sweet potatoes were *Jason's* favorite."

Oliver said nothing, impaling his stuffing with his fork.

Daphne perked up. "I'll have some. I like anything with marshmallows on it."

She could feel Oliver shifting in his seat, annoyed that she was running damage control. His disdain had more seasoning than any of the food on the table.

"Glad you're not a picky eater like this one." Taste wasn't Stella's only sense that was dead.

Daphne had often turned to her own father with the same pleading expression Oliver now offered his. The last hope.

Oliver's dad was as oblivious as hers. "Jason loved every food. I remember him particularly loving the green bean casserole."

The pressure from Oliver's elbows sent a small tremor through the table. Only Daphne noticed the tingle of silverware and wavering liquid in their drinking glasses. She watched hopelessness settle into his face. Oliver had brought a guest to the table and, still, the dinner cycle could not be broken. If anything, she was accelerating its course.

Oliver spoke with quiet rage. "Except for the fried onions. He used to pick those off and hide them in his napkin."

"Did he? I don't remember that." Blake turned to Stella. "Do you remember that?"

"No, not at all."

Oliver gritted his teeth. "Because he hid it from you."

Oliver was about to lose it. Daphne knew what he felt, what he was seeing. The black splotches that clouded his vision, the room closing in around him. The chords in his throat tightening, on the brink, unable to restrain the swell of his voice, so desperate to be heard. But now, a mile away from her own dining room, she could see everything clearly. And she had an idea of how to free him. Free all of them.

"I heard Jason loved the ocean." Daphne shoved a heaping forkful of mashed potatoes in her mouth and rolled the mush around.

She winked at Oliver and verified herself as an ally

instead of an audience. The violence in his eyes dissolved, the blackness surrounding him disintegrated, and the room opened.

Uncontrollable laughter rose inside him, his strength too depleted to squelch it. His fork tumbled onto his plate and he keeled over, laughing with such force he had to push back his chair to avoid knocking his head on the table. Daphne choked down her mashed potatoes and joined him in free-flowing giggles.

"Oh, yes. He did." Though skeptical of Oliver's laughter, Stella's face warmed with pride. "You told her."

Oliver nodded, still unable to speak.

Blake studied Oliver's odd laughter. Finally, his dad's timing caught up with the situation. "He loved the ocean. But not as much as you do."

"That's true," Stella said.

Their admission was a welcome antidote to Oliver's laughter. It steadied his breathing.

"Can you please pass the cranberry sauce?" Daphne asked Oliver.

He passed her the dish and touched her fingers in the exchange. It was an accident, a coincidence, until he cleared his throat. His eyes thanked her. She replied by spooning an ample dollop of gelatinous fruit onto her stuffing and taking a big bite.

"Mmm."

With mouths full of subpar food, Daphne and Oliver gazed across the table at each other. Common sense told Daphne that better Thanksgivings had taken place in her past, but they weren't in her memory.

• • •

Daphne handed two ice cream cones with bright green scoops to a man and his six-year-old daughter. Janine sat at the counter, scowling at the scene. Heavy breathing and muffled screeches emitted from the little girl, in a tizzy over sugar.

The kids that came into Sweetie's were Daphne's favorite part of the job. She loved the excitement on their faces, the wonder of cold-smooth-sweet ice cream and a crunchy cone. The children never bored of ice cream, and she never bored of their innocence.

The bell over the door rang with the father-daughter exit, signaling privacy and the opportunity for Janine to opine.

"Who the hell orders lime sherbet? There's twenty-five flavors and he picked lime sherbet and passed that horror onto his kid." Janine shuddered.

"Maybe he likes the color."

Janine pushed herself off of the counter. "Then get mint chip or pistachio! Poor kid. She's going to hate him forever when she tastes real ice cream."

"She'll go ice cream crazy to make up for lost time, and she'll never take it for granted. In the end, she'll love ice cream more than both of us."

Janine squirmed in her seat. "What's this Happy Heather bullshit? It's that Oliver guy, isn't it? You like him."

It was Daphne's turn to squirm. There was no point in lying to Janine. It was more difficult to pull off than lying to herself. "Maybe."

"After you graduate college and law school and get a

unicorn job at a high-paying nonprofit, you want to have 2.5 of his babies."

Daphne couldn't deny that this was exactly how she pictured her future, minus the babies and Oliver as a life partner. "What do 2.5 babies look like?"

"I could say a lot of politically incorrect things right now."

"I've thought of at least five. Want some lime sherbet?"

"Give me two scoops of mint chip before I describe in vivid detail what half a baby looks like."

Daphne heaved herself into the freezer and furiously scooped.

• • •

In the chapel, Daphne typed numbers into her graphing calculator with authority and scribbled down her conclusions.

"It's holiday break. You have two weeks to do homework."

She softened at the emergence of his voice but didn't take her eyes from her notebook. "If I get it all done tonight, I have two weeks of utter freedom."

"You and I are very different people."

"Yes, and I'm coming out on the better end of the school stick."

"True."

He dropped his bookbag from his shoulder and searched inside. "Well, since you're here, I'll give you your present."

Jason clasps a silver heart locket around Emily's neck. She spins around and kisses him.

"Merry Christmas, Em."

"Merry Christmas, Jason."

Oliver sat down, putting his bookbag between them and leaving space for an additional body. He pulled out a 5x7 cardstock. Similar to a comic book, it was bagged with a cardboard back to keep it flat. "I had an idea, so I ran with it."

Daphne knew even before accepting it that it was the best gift she'd ever received. But when she saw it she found that it was even better than she'd expected—a drawing of herself, dressed in a black catsuit, wielding the white knife from The Great Wall Company. Her figure stood in a dark alley under a full, cratered moon.

"Did you draw this?"

Oliver shrugged. "It won't get me a job at Pixar, but I think it turned out okay."

It was so much of everything that she couldn't speak for three seconds. She covered by studying the details of her alter ego portrait. The black mask. The shine in the blue eyes. The concentrated purse of the lips. The red lanterns in the background. "I love it. You were even respectful to female anatomy." In the drawing, the proportion of Daphne's breasts was depressingly accurate.

"I hate how comic books do that with the boobs."

"Oh, you're a feminist?"

"Yes, I believe in a full range of arm motion for everyone." Oliver swung and crisscrossed his arms in front and behind him. The blur of his fingertips almost touched her shoulder.

"Seems fair. Thank you, Oliver. This is awesome."

She had a present for him, too, which was now humiliatingly inferior. She'd debated giving it to him for weeks, treating it like a school project and making a pro/con list.

In the end, she'd decided to gift it only if he gave her something. She never believed the something would happen, much less be a custom work of art. But, here she was, digging in her bag, presenting him with a crudely wrapped, slightly torn rectangular object. It was better than nothing. She hoped.

He accepted the package, pleased. "You even wrapped it. Impressive."

Oliver tore off the reindeer wrapping paper and held up the half-filled cologne bottle. "Are you trying to tell me that I smell bad?"

"I found it under the floorboard with the list. It was Jason's."

"Oh." Oliver scrutinized the bottle, trying to concoct words.

"I thought you should have it. I'm sorry, it's kind of a lame gift."

"No, it's not. I'm glad to have this." The clunkiness of his words highlighted their truth. "Thank you."

"You're welcome." The sick feeling in Daphne's gut battled the jubilation rising in her chest.

Oliver tucked the bottle in his bookbag. "So, New Year's plans?"

"Hanging out with Janine. Maybe The Drama Crew."

"Sounds fun."

It sounded weak, but New Year's with Janine was always fun, filled with board games and dumb romantic movies that they both made fun of, yet secretly swooned over. Since July, as she had the past two years, Janine had been siphoning small amounts of booze from the bottles in her parents' liquor cabinet. Five water bottles nearly half-filled with various alcohols lined the wall of Janine's closet, concealed behind her shoes, waiting for the year to tick up. Explaining this to Oliver would make their grand evening sound even less cool. "What about you?"

He expelled a bored sigh. "A party. I think it's a girl that goes to your school who's throwing it. Penny Layton?"

The breath in Daphne's lungs turned cold and icicles crackled along her windpipe. Words started tumbling out in an attempt to warm herself. "Oh, yeah. That's the party I was going to. I mean, Janine and I are going to."

"You're friends with Penny?" He lifted his forehead in surprise.

"Yes." She contemplated explaining that she and Penny weren't as close as they once were, deciding against it because her lying skills needed work. Suddenly, she threw everything into her bookbag. Oliver jumped at the unexpected movement.

"Maybe I'll see you there. Happy holidays! Thanks for the drawing." She slung her bookbag over her shoulder, raced out of the chapel, and only turned around when she was through her front door.

• • •

Daphne stood at the end of the Laytons' driveway. A labyrinth of candy canes, glowing reindeer, and a Santa Claus decorated the lawn. Every tree and bush in the yard was bound tightly with twinkle lights, as if to keep the trunks from escaping the holiday spirit.

She strolled past Penny's bright red Mini Cooper parked in front of the garage. The car's ownership wasn't a mystery due to the license plate: CH33RZ with a heart. Those stupid hearts on license plates, who decided that could be a thing, anyway? It was bad enough that you could cheat words with numbers. Penny's license plate made Daphne want to take a shower.

She shook it off and rang the doorbell. She hoped the approaching footsteps belonged to Penny, but luck was never on her side.

Mrs. Layton opened the door. Her black hair was flat ironed into submission and lay stiffly against her scalp. Some of the wavy kinks at the roots weren't going down quietly. The smooth skin on her bronze face startled with minimal resistance, and Daphne deemed the Botox job above average. Mrs. Layton's jaw relaxed, and her eyes twinkled with nostalgia. Daphne was a beloved childhood toy that had stuck its head out of a storage box.

"Daphne! It's been a long time. You look…Cute haircut! Come on in." Mrs. Layton had been born and raised in Bangkok, and she took great pride in her American accent. It was especially flawless when delivering backhanded compliments.

"Thanks."

Daphne had always appreciated Mrs. Layton's half-honesty. The woman spoke lies, but her intentions could always be read on her face. Not even cosmetic injections could change that. When Penny went to college and the contact with her mother turned into a phone relationship, Daphne worried that Penny wouldn't have the mental strength to blindly play that mind game. But that was Penny's problem. Daphne was here for her own problems.

"Penny!" Mrs. Layton called down the hallway.

Penny stepped out of her room, creating her own wind just like she did in the school hallways. Beachy waves of hair framed a full face of makeup. She didn't take the weekends off.

"Daphne's here. Do you guys want some lemonade? Freshly made. It has mint."

Reminded by the suspicion on Penny's face, Daphne remembered her plan to make this visit as short as possible. "No, thanks. I have to go soon."

"Okay. Well, good to see you again, Daphne."

"You, too."

Mrs. Layton disappeared into the kitchen.

"Um, hello?" In the past few years, Penny had mastered the uppity tone that demanded an explanation without asking.

"Hi, Penny." Daphne nodded toward the door and Penny followed her outside. In front of a jury of candy canes, Daphne pled her case. "I heard you're having a New Year's Eve party and I want to come."

Penny laughed. Not a *You've got to be joking* laugh, but a *You are so clueless and I pity the ground you walk on* laugh, which was a slight upgrade. "It's a party, and I won't have a bouncer, so you do what you have to do."

"I didn't want it to be weird for me to show up."

"Well, it won't be weird for me, but it will probably be weird for you being in a place where you have no friends." Penny swept her hair over one shoulder.

Daphne wanted to ask Penny if people who sounded bitchy all the time were oblivious to it, or if they could hear it in their own voice and chose to ignore it. Since their conversation, a gymnastics tournament of subtlety, was going better than she'd anticipated, she stuck to the New Year's party. "So, I'm invited?"

"Oh my god, it's not like I sent out invitations. Yes, you're invited."

"I want to bring Janine."

Penny huffed and rolled her eyes. "Attached at the hip, as always."

"I thought there wasn't a bouncer. Why do you care if she comes?"

Something twitched on Penny's face. It happened so fast, Daphne couldn't tell if it was her eye or forehead, but some nerve had failed her.

"Janine is…" Penny pondered way too long to come up empty. "She hates me, and I hate her. It's traumatic to be in the same room with her. I'm sure she feels the same way."

"Actually, I'm pretty sure she's over it."

Penny's face twitched again. This time it was definitely her eye. "Why do you guys want to come to my party?"

Daphne debated confessing the truth: a boy. But there would be the who, what, when, where, and why follow-ups. She stuck with flattery. "Everyone is talking about it at school."

The compliment worked, and Penny grew another inch. "Who's everyone?"

"I didn't take down names, but I've been hearing murmurs in the hallway and locker room."

Penny bounced with glee. Daphne worried she might burst into a choreographed dance.

"This is going to be epic!" Penny squealed.

"Yeah, I'm not doing that with you."

Daphne's unwillingness couldn't keep Penny's feet planted on the ground.

• • •

Her nose an inch away from her bedroom mirror, Daphne patted glitter eyeshadow on her inner eyelids. Janine sat on the floor, leaning against the bed, peering up at the ceiling with winged eyeliner and a touch of metallic sheen at the corners of her eyes. Although Janine was beautiful barefaced or made-up, Daphne hoped that she was secretly enjoying her brief transformation.

Janine sipped from a water bottle and screwed on the cap, a "V" scrawled in black permanent marker on the top. She handed the bottle to Daphne. "We don't even need fireworks, you have them on your face."

"Compliment or criticism?" Daphne asked.

"Please. You know you look like a rock star."

Daphne winked and drowned her humble-brag with a sip from the bottle. Janine stood and hovered over Daphne's dresser.

"Still no movement?" Janine asked.

From the mirror, Daphne saw the nickel in Janine's fingers. "Nope." Daphne continued dusting her cheeks and temples with bronzer. The brush kicked up that Tuesday in March seven years ago along with the pigment.

The snap of the seatbelt. The screaming of names. Daphne's forced to remain in the car, a helpless spectator to her parents' frantic despair in the garage. A glint catches the lower corner of her eye and proves a useful distraction. She digs out the nickel jammed between the seat and backrest. Her fingers trace around the smooth rim and across the slight waves of Jefferson's forehead, hair, and jowl. 2006. She would've been six. Or five. Kindergarten or first grade. Back when her favorite color was purple. She closes her eyes and wills the sounds of the garage away, drifting off to a place that's warm and dark and quiet. She falls asleep before the ambulance shows up.

After Emily's death, Daphne held onto the 2006 nickel. She carefully monitored its placement in her bedroom. She waited, hoping Emily would visit and move it an inch to the left or right. A ghost was better than nothing, and she wanted something to believe in. The nickel never moved.

"Way to be a happy drunk, Janine." Daphne patted highlighter on the tops of her cheekbones.

"Sorry. New Year's fail." Janine placed the nickel where she found it, Monticello at the same angle. "Probably going to be a lot of those tonight."

"Again with the happy drunk. I think we have your New Year's resolution."

Janine groaned. "Are you sure you want to go to this thing to stalk some guy? We could just stay here. I have all the water bottles labeled this year, so there's no mystery mix."

"But mystery mix gives the best hangovers." She applied another layer of red lipstick. "I think it'll be good to try something new. Plus, you look hot. Someone other than me should enjoy that."

"I'm your ugly duckling turned swan. You know, my eyes kind of look like a swan's, don't they? Maybe I should speak to you in quacks all night or whatever noise swans make."

Janine made a series of guttural squawking noises trying to sound like a swan. It mostly sounded like terminal pain and led to Daphne collapsing against the wall in laughter, barely able to eke out her words. "How can something so beautiful sound so ugly?"

"Don't judge a swan by its honk!" More honking ensued.

Daphne and Janine collected themselves, coaching each other on how to pass the sobriety test if they ran into Daphne's dad on the way out. Focus, focus, focus, eye contact, breathe through your nose, always through the nose.

"Okay." Daphne raised her arm.

Janine high-wristed her. "We got this."

Nine times out of ten, no matter where her dad lurked within the house, Daphne could breeze past without question or remark. Sometimes he would call out a goodbye that she could ignore, and she was hoping for that option. But New Year's wasn't a holiday to be ignored, especially by the drunks.

Daphne and Janine filed quietly down the hall. In the living room, her dad filled a garbage bag with empty cans and bottles. Some of the bottles were half full, though Daphne saw them as half empty.

"Hi, Dad. Winter cleaning?"

"I'm quitting. I'm done, Daph. Done."

He'd made half-hearted attempts at going cold turkey before. One time it had lasted for almost two months. Daphne had marked the days on her calendar, all fifty-four of them, each one crossed off in strokes of pride and hope. After that relapse, all faith in her father had been shaken and crumbled at her feet. But she had never heard these words before. He'd never had the courage to say it out loud, admit there was a problem. That had to mean something, didn't it?

"Well…good." After years of strife, she'd been rendered

defenseless. She felt guilty that *good* was all she could come up with, which led to her being pissed that she felt guilty. The clank of glass and aluminum rustling against the plastic bag heightened her confliction. "I'm staying at Janine's tonight."

"Okay, be safe out there." He'd put on his Dad cap.

In an attempt to prove her sobriety, Janine said a little too loudly, "We will, Mr. Bowman."

Daphne nudged Janine out the front door. "Bye, Dad."

Daphne closed the door behind them. She paused for a moment, pushed it back open, and stuck her head inside. "I'm proud of you."

His eye contact contained the clarity that she so often longed for. "I'm doing this for you."

"Happy New Year."

"Happy New Year, honey."

She closed the door and joined Janine walking down the sidewalk.

"Do you believe him?" Janine asked.

"I want to. Maybe he'll break his record."

"I hope so. He owes you that."

Daphne agreed with Janine, but she also knew that the people who owed her the most had no idea how much they'd borrowed.

• • •

Janine tossed the empty water bottle into a recycling bin as they approached Penny's driveway. Even from the outside, a party was evident. A low bass thumped into the windows. Shadows danced against the closed curtains.

"Ready?" Daphne's voice shook.

"We could still go back to my place and make a mystery mix. I'll let you do the shaking."

Daphne looped her arm through Janine's and led her up the driveway. "Nope. Come on."

No one questioned their entrance. No one noticed at all except for a couple nervous glances from two people on the swim team who were insecure about their own presence at such a party.

"He's here." Daphne nodded across the room to the kitchen doorway before conducting a full evaluation of the scene. Once she did, her stomach fell to her knees. Oliver was surrounded by five dancers showing considerably more skin than Daphne. His laugh rolled across the room.

"Seriously, Daphne? You fell for a lady killer," Janine said.

Between laughs, he leaned against the counter, sketching something on a paper napkin. Probably a late Christmas present customized for every girl in the room.

Daphne felt stupid. She'd seen Oliver with Katrina, but they'd broken up. She had envisioned him standing by himself at this party, alone and open. That's the only way she knew him, when she had him all to herself. The captive audience made complete sense. He was a charmer. And funny. And gorgeous. Of course he didn't need Daphne Bowman to be entertained. She wasn't even supposed to be here. "Maybe we should do the mystery mix."

"Oh no. We've crossed the threshold. Now you can see his true colors," Janine said.

"I know his true colors."

"Then go talk to him. Or wait and see if he'll talk to you."

"Why do you hate him? He's a good guy."

"I've barely met him. You're projecting your fear onto me."

A seismic shift occurred in Daphne's core. If Oliver ignored her tonight, could she ever push the resentment far enough away? Could she resume the Daphne-Oliver-alone bubble and be fulfilled? Why couldn't she muster the courage to walk up to him? The whole thing was disgusting and there was a simple solution.

"Let's find the liquor," Daphne said. It was a demand more than a suggestion.

Three Jell-O shots and one beer later, Daphne graced the dance floor with alcohol-fueled confidence. Janine swayed near her, but Daphne danced with whoever was closest to her. Some cute guys even brushed up against her, moving to her over all the other girls on the floor. She exuded power, magnetism.

Suddenly, the music switched off and a booming voice yelled.

Ten.

Nine.

Everyone joined in. Daphne thought of the Top Ten list. How they had only completed numbers one, two, and three. She tried to push Oliver out of her mind, forget that they were in the same room ignoring each other. Or, at least, she was ignoring him.

Two.

One.

Some random guy kissed Daphne on the mouth. Before she could object, he moved on, kissing the next person over, male or female. His lack of discrimination meant she could neither be offended nor flattered.

Janine crashed into Daphne with a hug. They said their Happy-New-Years, dancing as the music faded up. Janine leaned near Daphne's ear.

"I'm going to go…" Janine was confused about how to end the sentence. "I'll be back."

"Okay, Mysteriosa."

Janine stuck out her tongue and headed toward the kitchen.

"He got you."

His voice. Daphne was so happy to hear it, she forgot to feel relief. Now that he was watching, she swirled her hips in a greater circumference and turned around to face him. "Yeah, the kissing bandit got me."

Oliver bobbed and swayed, moving with her. "I didn't know what crime to charge him with. You're going with theft?"

"Petty theft. Stealing closed-mouthed kisses is a victim-less crime. Unless he gives me the flu. Then I'm suing."

"You can't mess around with people's mucus."

"I love New Year's. New year, new possibilities, new lips." She stepped closer, cutting the distance between their own lips to six inches.

His neck tightened, but his feet didn't shift. "You're a pretty good dancer."

"Pretty good?" She spun around, careful not to touch him. "I'm fairly awesome."

"Ugh!"

Out of nowhere, Oliver was shoved from behind and flew forward, crashing into Daphne. Drunk laughter erupted behind him, and she recognized the face from the football game when she'd met Oliver. It was the meathead.

"Just helping you out, man." He grinned at Oliver.

Oliver played it cool. "Thanks, Mitch."

All of a sudden, recognition sparked in Mitch's eyes. "Hey, that's Emily Bowman's little sister." Mitch lumbered off the dance floor, no response necessary.

"Good friend?" Daphne asked, attempting to mute her sarcasm.

Oliver shrugged. "I guess."

She phrased her question as a statement. "He said that on the football field, the night I met you. 'Emily Bowman's little sister.'"

"Sometimes I think Mitch is a robot and he's only been programmed with a certain number of phrases and he says them over and over again."

Daphne laughed. "How does he know who I am, though?"

"Facebook."

She held her face steady, kept it from falling, but he heard her silence.

"I haven't told anyone about the list." He swallowed. "It's ours."

The pressure pulling her face down now lifted her cheeks. *Ours.* It was the best word he could say.

The fast dance music dissolved into a slow song. The moment of truth. He would put his hands on her waist. Or he would go get a drink or run to the bathroom or some other form of translucent rejection. Daphne decided to complicate the situation. She clasped her fingers behind his neck and pulled herself six inches closer to him.

He didn't cringe, for that she was grateful. His eyes searched in unease, but his hands came to rest on her hips.

"What do you think Emily and Jason's New Year's together was like?" she asked.

He glanced upwards, as if words were illuminated on the white ceiling and he was carefully choosing which ones to use. "Probably romantic. Alone. Intimate. The exact opposite of this."

"I bet we're having more fun."

He shrugged, doubtful.

"What? You're not having a good time?"

"I am. It's just…"

The seriousness in his eyes worried her, but she kept dancing, hoping it would dissipate after a few more blinks.

"Daphne…don't." He stopped moving and she stopped with him. The darkness in his eyes thickened. He took another breath. "Don't fall for me."

"Someone took their cocky pills today."

"It just happens, and it never ends well. So don't do it. You're too good of a friend."

The alcohol swirled around her head and disoriented her emotions, rendering her unable to shield against their sabotage. Crying was unavoidable. The compression built on all sides of her eyeballs and tingled her jaw. She did what she did best and sucked it all in. She had about ten seconds before the bomb of tears would explode.

"I think you're afraid," she said.

The darkness drained from his gaze and exhaustion filled in its place. She didn't have time to decipher the meaning behind his crooked squint. She stepped close and put her lips to his ear.

"You're afraid of falling in love with me. Happy New Year, Oliver."

He wouldn't be able to tell if she was serious or joking. To further confuse him, she put her hands around his neck and planted a fat kiss on his cheek. It left no mark, her lipstick gone hours ago. Daphne swaggered away and prayed with her entire body that he wouldn't follow her. He didn't.

Time expired down to zero. The tears detonated and combined with her eye makeup to make a Jackson Pollock of her face. Wiping the moisture would only make it worse and spur the production of more tears. Luckily, everyone else's level of drunkenness exceeded her own and she was able to waltz from room to room unnoticed. The search for Janine took her through the kitchen, the hallway, poking her head into bedrooms, seeing things she desperately wished to file off her retinas. Teetering back and forth between alarm over Janine's potential kidnapping and fury from Janine's (more likely) bailing on her, Daphne was ready to make a bed in the bushes against Penny's house and call it a night.

She was trudging toward the front door when Janine tumbled out of a closet in front of her, falling back against the door so it slammed closed behind her. Janine's ponytail was a gathering of static-charged, matted lumps, and her cheeks bore a flush from guilt or exertion.

Unaware of her own dishevelment, Janine beheld Daphne. The whites of Janine's eyes blazed with sympathy. "Whoa, what happened?"

"Holidays are a bitch. Why were you in a closet? Are you high?"

"No." Janine cleared her throat. "Maybe, a little. Just a pinch." She squeezed together her forefinger and thumb.

"I need to leave."

"It looks like you needed to leave fifteen minutes ago."

"Well, I'll always know where you land in the nature versus nurture debate."

"Look up."

Daphne obeyed. Janine smoothed her thumbs over the puffy bags of Daphne's eyes, erasing the raccoon smut. "Do I need to kick his ass?"

"No, you need to kick *my* ass for crying over a boy."

Janine bent her knee and kicked her foot up and to the side, lightly tapping Daphne's backside.

"Thanks," said Daphne, her grief dissipating.

"Come on. Let's bail. We can still go to The Drama Crew's party."

It was Janine's turn to loop her arm through Daphne's and weave among the mass of sweaty, buoyant bodies reverberating music and alcohol. Daphne pretended not to see Oliver dancing with Penny as Janine pulled her out the front door.

• • •

The next morning, Daphne crept into her house with an arch in her shoulders. She made sure the lock slid with little sound, the knob turned completely before its release, even though both her parents knew she was spending the night as Janine's, giving her no reason to sneak in. She was ready to cross the hall with feline silence when she saw something glinting from the living room. She proceeded to the glowing triangle, the sun reflecting on the round corner of the half-empty whiskey bottle, the light shooting off in all directions. Her father slept next to it on the La-Z-Boy, his mouth open, softly snoring in last night's clothes. *Slept.* That was the Happy New Year's way of saying it.

Daphne towered over him, judging him with the ferocity only known to the helpless. Stomping down the hall, she made as much noise as possible, hitting every creaky floorboard with echoing force. Regret guided her steps. She wished she'd thrown the bottle into the wall or done something equally dramatic that scared him into sobriety, even for a day. It wouldn't make any real difference, but she might have somehow been absolved, bathed in the holy spirit of whiskey on the wall.

Daphne slammed her bedroom door with all the strength of her frustration. Even she jumped at the sound of the door meeting the frame. Surely, she had woken him up. But as she lay down on her bed, the weight of the previous night and the now heavy morning piling on her chest, she wasn't sure of anything.

SKYDIVE

Oliver sat on the bleachers watching the purple-orange of the setting winter sun. He hadn't seen Daphne in two weeks. He'd sent her some vague texts, lame greetings that made him cringe while he hit "Send":

"How's it going?"

"How was the first day of your last semester?"

"Happy One-Week Post New Year's! Why isn't that a holiday?"

Each text had elicited equally vague and lame responses:

"Fab."

"Meh."

"You should lobby Hallmark."

Whatever had transpired between them at Penny Layton's New Year's party, he was sure he'd messed up, but he wasn't sure how. He wondered if even Daphne knew. If he asked her, would she tell him?

He replayed the dance floor scene every time he saw a girl

with short, choppy hair or a girl wearing black. He'd never noticed how many of these girls existed. His mind was hitting rewind in all of his classes and in the hallway between.

He and Daphne had been dancing, no big thing. Before New Year's Eve, he'd imagined dancing with Daphne would be like dancing with one of his ex-girlfriends, a relationship so far removed from his present that the memory felt like fiction. Tricia Grasso, to be exact.

Oliver and Tricia had dated in seventh grade for a month. They'd held hands and kissed a few times. One day he'd opened his locker and a note dropped down to his feet.

> *Dear Oliver,*
>   *I don't think we should date anymore. I hope you understand.*
>
>   *Sincerely,*
>   *Tricia*

Oliver still felt a pang in his abdomen whenever he remembered that note. In seventh grade, he was finally adjusting to athletic rejection in every sport he participated in besides unwanted baseball. With fifteen words and a carelessly folded piece of notebook paper, romantic rejection had fallen upon him as well.

He'd held it together at school that day, but he'd cried as soon as he hit the safe confines of his bedroom. It was the ironic *Sincerely* that tore him up, a heart dotting the *i*, all the other *i*'s dotted with the same paradox. What was sincere about breaking up with someone through a note? *Sincerely* would have been dumping him in person, or even the dignity of a phone call. Tricia would've been forced to accept his response, even if it was only dumbfounded speechlessness. A note held no consequence for her. There was no justice between those blue lines. And it didn't help that she was dating someone else on the basketball team the next day. Someone who didn't sit on the bench the whole game.

The years had passed. Other than a tinge of bitterness every so often, Oliver held little more than indifference for Tricia. From a distance, he half-admired the way she chose her boyfriends. The boys wrapped themselves around her little finger, silk ribbon eager to be twirled in whichever direction she desired. She gracefully discarded them when their edges frayed or showed resistance, same as she'd done with him. His interest in Tricia ended there. While undeniably pretty, he never checked her out as she swept down the hall, turning the heads in her path. The thought of kissing her, even touching her, repulsed him. It would be like kissing his sister, if he had one.

That was the sensation he'd expected to feel when dancing with Daphne Bowman. After resting his hands on her hips, he'd waited for her to become the imaginary sister. Instead, her body kept moving under his hands, warm and free, magnetizing his torso into sync with hers.

He'd tried willing her to feel like Tricia Grasso, but his body had kept moving, unobstructed, his heart pumping hot blood to the beat of the music. The odd feeling in his stomach wasn't curdled milk. It was something more complicated, a mixture of complete joy, utter dread, and borderline hysteria. Daphne especially hadn't felt like Tricia when she leaned over and purred in his left ear. Two weeks later and he still recalled her breath flowing into him.

When school had returned to session, Oliver had avoided the chapel. He could predict that future. He'd see her sitting there, not know what to say, and sneak away before she spotted him. Also, he was afraid to find her absent. He didn't know what to do with an empty pew.

Two weeks had been a long time, the amount of time he needed to confront his cowardice. As far as he could tell, Daphne wouldn't let a little intoxication and well-meaning warnings at a party cause her to abandon her homework haven. She was probably halfway done with her calculus assignment, and all the time he devoted to imagining the bare chapel was wasted seconds/minutes/hours of his life. He slung his backpack over his shoulder and bounded toward the cross, eye level with his seat in the bleachers.

Oliver stepped inside, confident she would be there, but the room was empty. His footsteps echoed against the stained glass windows. Jesus, Mary, the angels, and all the sheep mocked him. Oliver inspected the pew Daphne usually occupied. No grand prophesies or holy wisdoms trickled down with the dust through the beams of sunlight.

Oliver sat down in Daphne's place, putting himself in her pew. He pulled the book *Of Mice and Men* from his bag and flipped to the dog-eared page. Concentration eluded him. He read the same paragraph over and over again, unable to absorb a single word. His vibrating cell rescued him, a text from Penny: "*What r u up 2?*"

The letdown that the text wasn't from Daphne was quickly soothed by Penny's adoration. A hot girl liked him. Nothing bad about that. Nothing bad at all. Before he could respond, she'd already sent another text: "*Want 2 hang 2nite?*"

He did. His whole body was in full smirk as he typed. Then it hit him. It was Thursday. He threw *Of Mice and Men* into his backpack and broke into a run. His steps echoed off the walls and the holy figures seemed to scowl at him.

He was halfway to Sweetie's before worry slowed his steps. What if she hated him? What if it was going to be weird forever? What if she didn't want to do the list anymore?

The last question brought him to a full stop. The last few months, the list had become shiny texture poking through the surface of dull days. Was he about to lose that? Had he already lost it? Would she complete the list without him? Had she already? He prepared for the worst: she never wanted to see him again. Oliver didn't want to do the list alone. It would only make him sad. Depressed. Like Jason. And the last thing in the world Daphne Bowman was going to do was make him be like Jason.

He neared Sweetie's doorstep, his feet leaden with doubt. Oliver was out of options, so he did something he never did with Daphne. He faked it.

Oliver pushed through the door, a deep grin on his face. She washed a set of ice cream scoops in the sink, glanced over at him without moving her head, and refocused her attention to her hands under the faucet. She still wore red lipstick. That had to be good sign, right? Or maybe she didn't associate the lipstick with him, never had. His mind went blank, what he imagined a blizzard to feel like, never having been in one—cold, white, nothing. All the clever things he'd envisioned coming out of his mouth as he'd pushed open the door washed down the drain with the ice cream drippings.

Daphne turned off the water. "Of all the ice cream parlors, in all the towns, in all the world…"

At least she was speaking to him. His vocal chords unclenched, making conversation possible.

"I like yours the best." He stepped up to the counter.

She tilted her head down and peered at him incredulously. "You've been in here before?"

He liked the way she forced honesty out of him. Instead of a smooth injection, Daphne shoved truth serum down his throat.

"No, but I like yours the best out of all the ones I haven't been in. Because you're here." It was the right sentiment tacked onto the wrong sentence. He broadened his smile to balance his inner cringing.

Daphne remained unmoved. "Lucky me."

She wrung out a sponge and wiped down the counter, eager to do something other than tolerate him. The humming squeak of wet friction against stainless steel became the only sound between them. Oliver browsed the ice cream case.

Daphne acknowledged his perusal. "Cup or cone?"

"Cone."

She rinsed her hands. "What flavor?"

"What's your favorite?"

"Vanilla."

Oliver gasped, "Vanilla? No one's favorite flavor is vanilla. It's so boring."

"It's timeless. And you never get a bad vanilla. My palate doesn't like disappointment."

"Well, my palate likes actual flavor, so I'll have cookies and cream."

"One scoop or two?"

"One, please."

She dug the scooper in the black and white frost, "That will be three fifty."

"Friends don't get free ice cream?"

She stopped mid-scoop, leaving the scooper wedged in the cookies and cream. "Oh, we're friends?"

And there it was, the dreaded rhetorical question. At some point in grade school, was there a secret session where the administration pulled all the girls aside on their way in from recess and gave them this valuable life advice? *When a romantic interest offends you, but you sense that he or she doesn't know how or why, instead of stating the offense, merely raise or lower the pitch of your voice and repeat some benign phrase that the offender has spoken. This will signify that you are offended, and the offender needs to scramble to fix it. If an amicable solution is not reached, repeat until desired outcome occurs. Or someone leaves the room.*

Oliver found it best to use few words in these situations. "Yes."

Daphne rolled her eyes. She expected more from him, like everyone else. "See, that's what I thought. But on New Year's we were acting like friends and having a perfectly civil conversation surrounded by our inebriated peers, and you started laying out guidelines for this so-called friendship. Friends don't do that. Friends just be and then they stage an intervention when you need one."

The argument slid from her mouth without calculation. Her eyes weren't buried so deep in emotion that she couldn't see him, like other similarly frustrated females in his life. She wanted to be friends. Nothing more. Now he was embarrassed that he'd warned her off. All along he'd been the one imagining a romance between them. On New Year's, those delusions had tunneled out from his subconscious and broke free at the front of his mind.

"You're right. I staged an intervention when you didn't need one. I'm sorry."

She nodded and packed the cone with an extra shaving of ice cream.

Oliver noticed the gesture. "That must mean a truce."

"Enemies truce."

"Then let's agree not to truce."

She held out the cone. As he reached for it, she pulled it back. "You still need to pay."

Oliver put on a show of reluctance and pulled out his wallet, gladly paying pennies for dollars.

Later that night, he responded to Penny Layton's invite with an apology, saying he'd been busy. She suggested another meetup. The texts lit up his cell phone without pause. He considered cluing her in that she would read more desirable if she played harder to get. Ultimately, he decided against it, realizing that a transparent Penny was easier than the murky waters he navigated with Daphne. These girls were two vastly different lakes. After the ice cream make-up, Lake Daphne was the only place he wanted to swim where he couldn't see his kicking feet.

He told Penny he'd text her after the weekend. He expected her to respond with a chipper "*Gr8!*" and five emojis, or at the very least "*ok*," but a response never came. He instantly liked Penny Layton a lot more.

• • •

The weekend rolled around. Oliver waited anxiously for Daphne's shift to end at Sweetie's. He picked up his room, rearranged the mess on his dresser. He pulled out the bottle of Jason's cologne, stored under his workout clothes, hidden from the world by a barrier of mesh and elastic. He sniffed. It smelled like intimidation—the notes held power and strength. This was the scent of a man. Against his nose, the richness made him feel like a boy, unworthy. He had the sudden urge to spray himself, but he remembered his parents were downstairs. He'd need to say goodbye to them on his way out and feared recognition. Oliver didn't want any questions. He didn't have any answers.

He contemplated arriving at Sweetie's early but didn't want to come off too eager. Playing video games in his bedroom was the best remedy to pass the time, but his thoughts refused to hold still. The only place he could find silence was the point where his stylus met his tablet. He didn't have any good ideas, so he recreated the Sweetie's logo with a modern font and a waffle cone with an ice cream scoop for the "i." While it wasn't a work of art, the finished product was an improvement over the current design. He might even show it to Daphne. He glanced at his phone to check the time and did a double take. The half hour had passed like a finger snap. He grabbed his keys, wedged his feet in his shoes, and ran to his car.

An hour later, he and Daphne stood on Venice boardwalk. Beautiful people played beach volleyball as an excuse to show off their toned figures. A yoga class namasted on the grass. Muscular bodies that defied human anatomy hoisted massive barbells and grunted with every press.

Daphne set her eyes on the empty beach in front of them. "There used to be a zipline here. Janine and I came down a couple summers ago and the place was flooded with gross teenagers everywhere."

"You're a gross teenager," Oliver pointed out.

"I'm a sophisticated, gross teenager."

"Yeah, that sounds much more appetizing. Did you go on the zipline?"

She threw him a look of absolute disgust, as though he'd suggested going to Hollywood and Highland, the biggest tourist trap in the city.

"No." Her defense softened. "We walked up to Santa Monica, ate a funnel cake, and rode the Ferris wheel like respectable Angelenos."

Oliver watched all the curves and lines in her face, searching for clues to whether she was serious.

"It was fun," she conceded.

"Did you want to go on the zipline?"

"No."

Oliver threw up his hands. "Then why are we here?"

"It was the closest thing to skydiving that I could think of."

"We could try parasailing?"

"It's too expensive, I already checked."

"Daphne, do we have the smallest inkling of desire to do anything resembling skydiving?"

"I think we've already established that *I* don't."

"Then we agree."

Daphne sighed, "I feel like we failed."

"Well, there's always that one thing on the bucket list that doesn't get done."

"Or ten." She rolled her eyes, more frustrated at herself for making a bad joke than annoyed by his reassurance.

Oliver plodded on with his postmodern optimism. "So maybe this is the one thing that doesn't get done. And we're extra diligent about the rest of the list."

"Fine. Skydiving was a poor choice, anyways."

"But it brought us here, to this place, to this moment."

"Oliver the Philosopher." She drew in a long breath. "You know, there is something I've always wanted to do."

A half hour later they pedaled mountain bikes up the Venice boardwalk, racing the fading sun.

Oliver challenged her. "Bet I can beat you to the pier."

He pedaled faster, harder. She equaled his speed and force, squealing in delight with the exertion. Oliver caught as many glimpses of her face as he could while weaving around slower cyclists and rollerbladers. This was the first time he identified her as truly happy, all the mystery wiped away, only the sunset bouncing off her cheeks. Seeing this new beauty in her pleased and pained him at the same time.

"Never!" She leaned forward and surged ahead of him.

The night sky oiled over the remaining purples of the sunset. Bikes returned, they strolled along the pier past the cacophony of the arcades, the click and swallow of inserted quarters rising above the black noise.

Daphne scoured the beach. Oliver turned in the same direction, meeting her focal point. A ball of orange glowed in the darkness.

"What's that?" he asked.

She whipped her head around to face him. Her eyelids were weighed down without appearing tired, and her eyes shined extra bright with a new idea.

"Let's go check it out." She was ten feet down the pier before he could answer.

As they approached, the orange glow dimmed, shielded by the crowd of one hundred gathered around it, blocking the light from spilling onto the beach. A hailstorm of drumming poured from the center of the circle: kettle drums, snares, buckets, anything in the vicinity with a flat surface that would produce sound. The rattle of a tambourine slithered in and out of the beat.

"Sounds like a good time," Oliver said.

He would've been happy standing on the outskirts, catching glimpses of the fire inside when enough people shifted a couple inches to the left or right at the same time, revealing keyholes of orange between the seams of their bodies. By now Oliver knew the bold quiet of Daphne swam straight to the mosh pit at concerts. He wasn't surprised when she stuck her toe into the bonfire crowd and began wading to the front of it, pushing against and floating with the current. He drifted into her path before it could close behind her.

The intense heat of the giant bonfire held the circle at bay. The nine drummers were all men, teenager to gray with wrinkles. The blaze illuminated parts of their faces and covered other parts in shadow. A flurry of callused hands pounded without fatigue. Closest to the fire, dancers shuffled their feet in the sand, offering their rhythm up to the night with the rising smoke and embers. Of course,

Daphne wanted to dance. She gyrated into the dancing donut hole and thirty seconds elapsed before she flung her head back toward Oliver. He stood motionless on the donut's edge.

"Come on!" she shouted.

"I don't dance without alcohol."

"Oil to your machine," she laughed. "You're human. You can dance whenever you want to. It's the benefit of having a soul. And not living in a dystopia."

"Okay, then. I choose not to dance."

"That I can respect." She turned her back to him and kept dancing.

The beating of the drums hammered through Oliver. He'd expected Daphne to beg him to dance with her like many of his previous dates, bestowing him with gratitude when he finally surrendered. But this wasn't a date, he reminded himself. Daphne didn't play by the same rules. She didn't have any rules, which was unsettling. He didn't know her game, so he didn't know how to play her, or how she was playing him.

All of a sudden, he longed to be sitting in Joe's garage drinking a sixer, listening to Mitch and Joe talk about all the somewhat-real-but-mostly-fake sex they were having. He wanted someone else's problems to be larger than his own. He wanted to be in the backseat of Penny's Mini Cooper, hushed and unbuttoned.

A crackling snapped him out of fantasy. One of the logs had disintegrated, failing like crushed bone beneath the burning matter. The fire's foundation shifted down and to the left, spewing embers in a sigh of smoke. Something in his own foundation was shifting. Daphne was the first person he'd encountered who had the ability to make him feel excluded. She'd challenged him to dance without directly challenging him. Now he wanted to meet that challenge.

Oliver stepped into the donut hole, swaying over to her. He braced himself for Daphne's teasing. *So, you changed your mind*, or some other quipping. *I was right, and you were wrong.* But the *I told you so* never came. She simply danced with him, satisfied for him as much as herself.

He never touched her. He didn't want a repeat of New Year's, but this dancing was different from that night. As they slowly circled around the fire, she never moved into him, never asked anything of his hands. Oliver surveyed the faces surrounding him. Everyone was a stranger. Seeing Daphne's face full of orange and sweat, even she felt like a stranger. He threw his hands up and out and danced freely in the closed circle of anonymity.

Hours later, on a deserted patch of beach with the drum circle as a lamp in the background, Oliver and Daphne collapsed on their backs into the sand, an arm's length between them. Oliver liked this distance. It was close enough that he could reach out and touch her. Not that he wanted to, just that he could.

The sun had been under the horizon long enough that the sand beneath their bodies had cooled to the point of feeling wet. Oliver burrowed as deep as his limbs would pull him down. He glanced over and saw Daphne doing the same, her shoulders shifting back and forth, heels pressing up and down, making a well for her legs. The sensation of cold cement crept up his arms and around the sides of neck.

He stared up at the sky. "Nice night. Wish there were

more stars." At times, he spotted pin pricks of light poking through the black expanse above him. Eventually, he came to the conclusion that he had only seen stars because of how badly he'd wanted to believe they were there, like Santa Claus or the Easter Bunny.

"What would you wish for?" Daphne asked.

"I don't know. What would you wish for?"

She'd been to this rodeo before and tossed his question back at him like a bucking bronco. "I'm not the one wishing for stars."

"I would wish for world peace." He kept a straight face.

"There are two kinds of wishes in this world, the attainable and the implausible. I prefer mine attainable."

"A wish is a wish because it's unattainable."

"You wish for things that you know you'll never have. A wish for you is a fantasy. I wish for things I can actually accomplish."

"That's a goal, not a wish."

"It's all semantics." She shrugged her shoulders into the sand.

"So, what's your wish?" he asked, again.

Her words were automatic, no thought required. "To get into Berkeley, and then Stanford law."

Though new, these wishes were unsurprising. Jealousy prodded him between the ribs, how she could envision her future with such conviction. "Well, your semantics expertise will do well there. Plus, you'll be closer to Emily. The symbolic Emily buried in San Fran."

Daphne pressed her neck deeper into the sand. "Hmm. I never thought of that. I will be much closer to the symbolic Emily."

Oliver worried that he'd pointed out the single flaw in her master plan. He'd reminded her that she couldn't escape the past, no matter how many counties she removed herself. He'd also reminded himself.

Daphne laughed softly into the night. "I could celebrate her birthday again. And the Day of the Dead. Might be soothing."

Sand tickled the base of Oliver's neck as he nodded. He carried out the hypnotic motion again and again, long past being a mere response. He was lost in the uncertainty of his own future, so he turned to the uncertainty of someone else's past.

"Why didn't they leave a note?" he asked.

"Isn't that the point of suicide? You have nothing left to say."

"I mean, do you think they planned it? Or was it spur of the moment?"

"I've thought about it. A lot. I don't know what I want to believe. The evil premeditation or the hopeless spontaneity."

"You think they wrote the list near the end? Maybe they were trying to talk themselves out of it."

"I like that. I'm gonna keep it." The exertion of the fire had stripped Daphne down to nothing but her truth. "Do you ever get scared that you'll get it? Mental illness, depression, go bipolar. I mean, I know you don't catch it like a cold. But it's genetic. I feel like it's inside me and someday it's going to take over. One day, the darkness could settle, and I won't be able to escape."

"I think about it sometimes. But there's help. You know the history. Our families know."

"But help wasn't enough for them." Worry strained her voice.

He wanted to comfort her, but he couldn't comfort himself.

Oliver wipes the midnight sleep from his eyes and stumbles into the bathroom. Jason stands over the toilet, sprinkling pills from a white bottle. He and Oliver both jump, startled by each other. Jason drops the bottle into the bowl and fishes it out.

Oliver says nothing. What could he say?

A great number of things, turns out.

"Don't tell Mom and Dad, okay?"

Oliver says nothing.

"Oliver, okay?" Jason demands.

"Yeah, okay."

He'd kept his word. And now they were here. Oliver turned to her, his ear against the sand. For a moment, he considered confessing the middle-of-the-night pill run-in with Jason, but she might not forgive his silence as easily as his parents had. Plus, there was another truth to tell. "You know they went off their meds, right?"

The parting of her lips turned his question into a revelation. Her voice was weak. "No."

"They stopped taking their medication months before. There was no trace in their toxicology, and my parents found full bottles of Jason's pills. I always assumed they quit together."

"Why would they do that?"

"They were in their love euphoria, I guess. They thought they didn't need the meds, so they stopped without telling anyone. And they came crashing down."

"Why didn't my parents ever tell me?"

"Because you're fine."

"Yeah, I'm fine." Daphne cackled at the sky. "You're fine. There's some more semantics for you."

Oliver laughed with her until calmness set over them.

"It's getting late," Daphne said to the absent stars.

Oliver didn't want the night to end, and he wasn't tired. "Yeah."

Neither of them moved, staring up into the dark abyss, now lightening to blue at the corners.

"What are you doing for Valentine's Day?" What was he asking? How had that question escaped his lips?

"Are you asking me to spend Valentine's Day with you?"

He didn't know. Did he want to date her? He deciphered nothing from her question. No delight, no distrust, no anger. She would be completely blameless in any misinterpretation. It all rested squarely on his shoulders.

"No." But he'd expelled his *no* in a guilty laugh. It had been a *yes*. What was happening? He'd asked Daphne Bowman to hang out with him on Valentine's Day. Nothing good could come from that. It would only make everything more confusing than it already was. The imaginary stars above him spun around the sky.

"I have plans. Watching a rom com with Janine that we both pretend to hate but secretly love. Probably *The Notebook*." She'd saved him. And she knew she'd saved him.

"Gosling is hot." It was his best attempt to smooth the situation.

"So is McAdams."

After that, Daphne went quiet. They still spoke, but there was no more discussion of semantics or philosophy. She was inside her own head, and Oliver was annoyed at himself for sending her there. The birds had begun their song when she opened her mouth to speak. He knew she was going to say something that made everything okay.

"Thanks for dancing with me, Oliver." Sleepiness weighed on her vowels.

"Any time."

One thing he knew for certain: he liked dancing with Daphne Bowman.

THE SAHARA DESERT

OLIVER PAGANO HAD KINDA/SORTA ASKED HER OUT ON Valentine's Day, and she had said *no*. As she lay in bed staring at the ceiling, that fact grated her like scratches on a turntable. She tried to convince herself she'd done the right thing by shutting him down. He hadn't exactly asked her out, anyway. His *no* had sounded like a *yes* to her, but a *no* was still a *no*. Either way, she felt manipulated. If she'd accepted, he probably would've recanted and given her another speech about how she shouldn't fall for him.

Be a good little girl. It made her entire body clench.

Valentine's Day arrived as another unassuming Wednesday. Flowers and balloons begot squealing girls at school. Other than a few more eye-rolls than usual, it was just another day for Daphne. She'd successfully buried Oliver Pagano somewhere in the back of her brain.

Had she known of any further Valentine's drama, she would've bypassed the western wing hallway, going outside and around the campus before reentering through the door nearest to her physics classroom to avoid Penny Layton's locker. But she hadn't taken the long route because as far as she was concerned, it was just another day. Penny Layton was just another squealing girl. Daphne had almost made it out of hearing range when the name "Oliver Pagano" banged against her eardrums. The sound brought a stop to her feet. As she gaped down in disgust at her motionless combat boots, another tiny piece of her heart hardened.

She wanted to unhear his name. She couldn't rewind, and she couldn't move forward, the soles of her shoes stuck in the wet cement of St. Valentine. It took all her strength to scoot to the side of the hallway to avoid becoming high school road kill. While she tried to will her legs to work, she was tortured by the fading in and out of Penny's gushing to a group of dancers: *He's so sweet...red roses...no, we can't...chicken pox.*

Sympathetic moaning and groaning from the peppiest of the pep squad wafted over to Daphne. For the first time in her scholastic career, she contemplated cutting class. She decided against it as the normal sensations of her lower limbs returned. Right now, she needed physics, needed the blend of math and theory to reaffirm her existence, that it all meant something. In the alternate universe of mathematics, everything made sense.

By the end of the day, Daphne made her Valentine's peace. Despite her best intentions, she liked Oliver. Despite her best intentions, he didn't like her. It was that simple. She was never going to be Penny Layton. Nor did she want to be. But the Oliver Paganos of the world never fell for the Daphne Bowmans, and she was not going to watch some stupid romantic comedy with Janine that night that tried to prove fantasy over science. They'd watch a horror movie instead. Preferably one where all the pretty people died.

In the end, Janine ditched her anyway, citing that she had to study for a test the next day. Janine wasn't the studying type, but it was impossible for Daphne to discourage healthy student behavior just so she didn't have to be alone on Valentine's Day. Especially because she didn't *have* to be alone. Oliver *had* kinda/sorta asked her out. Even though she'd deactivated this landmine hours ago, the fuse now burned brighter than ever. Once again, she became lost in the smoky aftermath.

The Drama Crew was hosting a movie night, but Daphne declined. She'd chosen to be alone and, dammit, she was going to be alone. It was time for pity popcorn, a concoction coinvented with Janine that involved melted butter, Parmesan cheese, and a touch of sriracha.

She settled on her bed with a heaping bowl on her lap, Elliott Smith singing through her earbuds. The sound from that Tuesday seven years ago snuck up on her, leaving her unprepared for the attack. Daphne tried to quash it.

The sound.

The sound.

The sound of suffering that emanates from her mother's body as she shakes Emily's dead weight in the car. It's the moan of a wounded animal Daphne saw on a nature show. Was it a bear? Or an elephant? Or a sea lion?

She cranked Elliott Smith all the way up, but it wasn't loud enough. Her heart still beat into her stomach.

Since that Tuesday wasn't a bad dream she could wake up from, it often became the twisted lullaby that coaxed her into sleep. Tonight, all of the nightmares would be scared away. Ready to surrender to the Day of St. Valentine, she would've missed her ringing phone if it hadn't vibrated against her leg. She answered without reading the caller name, assuming it was Janine.

"I made pity popcorn," she said with a mouth full of kernels.

"Can I have some?"

Daphne sprayed popcorn spittle, almost knocking over the bowl at the sound of Oliver's voice. She tried to swallow and choked, hacking into the phone.

"I better not. It sounds lethal." He chuckled. "So, why the pity?"

She swallowed, regaining control of her voice. "Not a great day, that's all."

"Details?"

"Not worth mentioning."

"Oh, come on."

"Because I'm not spending Valentine's Day with *you*." She said it coyly, with a little bite. She didn't even know what she meant, so she knew it would confuse the hell out of him. It had the dual effect of shutting him up, and she took immense pleasure in listening to him suffer through the silence.

"Just kidding," she chirped. A relieved exhalation travelled from his end of the phone. "Don't you have a date?" She regretted asking before the sentence was out of her mouth.

"I do."

Was he really so clueless to call and brag about a date? Daphne shoved a wad of greasy cheese popcorn in her mouth to keep from saying something mean and bitter but true.

"Her name is chicken pox."

Ah, Penny's blurbs started to make sense. The mouthful of popcorn had been a gross miscalculation. She started chewing furiously.

He talked over the chomping, "She's quite the catch. Get it? Because I caught it."

How did he have the power to make her smile when she was feeling seven kinds of awful? The half-chewed popcorn scraped against her throat when she swallowed. "Fever dreams, crazy itching, inability to keep food down. You should really break up with her."

"I think I'll give her another seven to ten days."

"You didn't get vaccinated?"

"I did, but the CDC can't handle my awesomeness. Maybe I'm a mutant."

"Hmm. We have to figure out what your superpower-slash-curse is, now that we know one of the side effects is catching eradicated diseases."

"So you can exploit it?"

"Hell, yeah. No use having a friend who's a mutant if I don't get anything out of it."

"Don't worry. I would mutate for you anytime."

She grimaced. "Sounds messy. Lots of nasty sound effects."

He laughed into her ear and the line went quiet.

"Oliver, why are you calling me?"

"I'm sick and bored."

"No, I mean, why are you calling *me*?" *Because I have it*

*on good authority that you sent a dozen roses to someone who
is not me.*

The question hung in the air somewhere between the mile that separated their bedrooms. He responded slowly, carefully. "Because you're the only person I wanted to talk to. You're the only person I wanted to make me feel better."

"And did I?"

"Haven't you learned yet? I'm never wrong."

Molten laughter bubbled deep inside her and erupted into the phone.

"It's not that funny," he said.

Trying to stop laughing only made her amusement thicken.

"I'm so glad I could entertain you," he grumbled.

"I'm sorry." The laughter subsided, and she regained her words. "Sorry. I'm back."

"I think you're sicker than I am."

"I probably am."

Oliver cleared his throat. His voice strengthened and signaled his true intention for calling in the first place. "So, I should be virus-free by spring break. I have an idea."

• • •

A month later, the day in March arrived as it did every year. The marine layer hung over the afternoon for an extra hour, graying out the sun. Daphne studied for exams, books sprawled across her bed. Between subjects, she counted down the days to spring break: two weeks. Oliver hadn't called or texted today. The date was a pop quiz she didn't want to hand out, but she was grading him, nonetheless.

Daphne's phone buzzed with a text. *"It's our day, not theirs."*

He'd passed.

• • •

Daphne stuck a Post-it on the counter saying she was spending the night at Janine's. She waited until snores accompanied her dad's dozing before leaving the house with her overnight bag.

She hustled to the school parking lot, scared that a divine intervention would emerge from her home or fall from the clear sky and stop her road trip with Oliver. Daphne wasn't much of a believer in the stories of the Bible, arks and whales, walking on water, water into wine and the like. At least, not literally. But when she saw Oliver's car pull up, met his beautiful smile with a meek one of her own, and witnessed the city vanish into sand, she knew she was part of her own tiny miracle.

After a couple hours in the rising temperature of the car, a faint smell circled under Daphne's nose. The warm aroma held notes of familiarity, but her base memory slipped away like a morning dream, on the brink of recognition and vanishing in the same instant. She glanced from rearview mirror to door, searching for an air freshener, finding nothing. Daphne closed her eyes and breathed deeply, settling into her seat. It came to her with a tickle of smoke. Jason's cologne, now Oliver's. She breathed it in a few more times, marveling at how much more nuanced it smelled coming off of him than it had in her bedroom air or on Jason. Oliver made everything better.

The desert welcomed them with windmill farms. The slow, unchanging pace of the rotating propellers haunted Daphne. A small ache expanded in her gut, the feeling of being left behind at the top of a roller coaster. Instead of quickening and slowing with the fickle wind, the propellers turned in methodical rhythm, unrelenting. These windmills were named of nature but trapped in machine.

The road weaved over rocky hills and when it flattened again, the desert sprang to life with Joshua trees. The eerie trees distanced themselves from each other like children unwilling to share. The ones nearest to the road bore striking silhouettes; the difference from tree to tree the difference between human fingerprints. Their figures loomed as the formidable army of the lost land. With knotted branches for armor and spiked leaves brandished as weapons, the trees extended for miles and miles, only stopping when jagged rocks protruding from the earth interrupted their sprawl.

Their first stop in Joshua Tree National Park was Skull Rock. Daphne and Oliver stood in front of its curves and indentations, critiquing how it only resembled a skull when viewed from a distance. Standing next to it, it was just another rock.

Oliver cocked his head. "I see a gorilla, actually. Gorilla Rock doesn't have the same ring to it."

"I see an elephant seal."

"Well, you would."

"You don't approve of water mammals in rock formations?"

"You always see things more complex than I do."

SO GLAD TO MEET YOU

"I wouldn't call an elephant seal more complex than a gorilla. You'd be insulting your lineage."

"And you went evolution on me."

"You know you like it."

Oliver's voice went rigid. "*If you were a rock, what shape would you erode into?* asked the most pretentious person in the history of the world."

She bit her lip, pondering. "*Does the rock know it's a rock? Is it aware that it's eroding? Does it look down one day and realize half of itself is gone?* asked the second most pretentious person in the history of the world."

"Okay, I'm done talking about rocks," he said.

"Good."

They drove further into the park, the late afternoon sun blinding them. They turned off the main road and crawled down a narrow one made of dirt. Gravel fired into the wheel wells.

"Hope your car can handle this." Daphne's voice bounced against the bumps under the wheels.

"Me, too."

An eternal mile later, they reached a small clearing that served as a parking lot. The giant rock formations surrounding them reduced Skull Rock to a pebble on a beach.

As they roamed on foot through Joshua trees from one towering plateau to the next, the desert humbled Daphne. So many of the ground plants had perished. The dead bushes weren't so different from the live ones next to them, except that all the brown had been sucked out, leaving an ashen bouquet of rot. These briers had fought so hard to live, withstood lethal conditions long enough to leave behind a mass of decay. Joshua Tree was full of reminders that even the strong didn't survive.

Oliver struggled to climb up a boulder. He tried to make it look easy, but his jacket and track pants quivered as he searched for the next stronghold. With one last surge of his knees and a muffled grunt, he hoisted himself up to the top.

Daphne regarded his success with a scowl, impressed at his determination and bored by his bravado. "You look like a cat up a tree."

"Do you want me to meow for you?"

"Not really."

"Mrow, mrow, mrow." He yowled long, domesticated calls into the wild.

"Purring would be better."

"This cat doesn't purr."

Unprompted, Oliver wobbled and fell over. Daphne gasped as he disappeared from her line of sight.

"Oliver? Oliver!"

His head didn't pop up.

"Oliver!"

She pulled out her cell. No reception, same as since they'd entered the park. She didn't have the car keys to go get help. Her eyes darted around in panic. The parking lot—empty. The direction of the road—nothing. The wilderness surrounding her on all sides—no one.

"Oliver!"

Silence.

Daphne started up the boulder following Oliver's route. In comparison, he'd made it look easy. Her arms and legs trembled in resistance, her muscles trying to protect her by shaking her off the rock. She'd gotten four feet off the ground when she heard the scrape of sand against rock at the top. Oliver peered down at her, his face pale and his lips pinched.

"Okay, I'm really, really sorry. I saw a way down on the other side, so I thought I'd prank you and then run up behind you and surprise you right when you started climbing up. But it took longer to get down than I anticipated, and I didn't want you to totally freak out, so I had to climb back up, which also took more time than I thought."

Her red face twisted into a snarl and her eyes narrowed to angry slits. "I hate you."

"Let go, you're only a few feet off the ground."

"You don't understand. I have a fear of falling. I have a reoccurring dream where I fall and die."

"Everyone has that dream."

"I'm always rock climbing when I fall."

"Because you're an avid rock climber, no doubt."

"Oliver." Her eyes pleaded up to him with the solemn helplessness of starving children on commercials. "I can't move."

He ran to the faster way down, the crunch of desert cinders under his feet the only sound Daphne could hear. She hoped his descent would be quicker this time after the practice run. Her convulsing limbs threatened to expel her from the rock at any moment. Her fingers slipped with sweat, but she was too terrified to adjust her grip. Her heaviness multiplied by the passing of each second, settling out and away from her center. It was all going to go. Soon. One, two, then ten fingers, too exhausted to claw at a second chance.

Losing consciousness, her mind tumbled down a wormhole to Emily in the car. Her last breaths. The fear, the peace, the finality of all that had come before and would remain after. Daphne had always found it easier to hold on than to let go. Either way, she would end up motionless on the ground. At least Emily's way had been a shorter fall.

Her senses were so numb, she didn't hear his footsteps sprint up behind her. His hands went to her waist. "Okay, let go."

With his touch, she landed back inside her body.

"Daph. Let go."

With pure willpower she pried her fingers from the rock. Her pinky might never fully straighten again. Oliver eased her down. His hands cinched the watercolor roses on her shirt against her ribs even after her feet were firmly on the ground.

He took off his jacket and laid it beside them. "Here, sit."

She folded her legs beneath her with the elegance of a rusty lawn chair.

He sat in the dirt next to her. "Again, I'm so sorry."

Daphne shook her head, half forgiving, half still filled with ire.

"Thanks for trying to rescue me," he said.

Too depleted to be angry, Daphne assessed her surroundings from a new perspective now that she was sitting. Her eyes scaled the giant formation in front of her. It consisted of two rocks. The base rock was much larger, massive enough to cover the horizon. A smaller, rounder boulder sat on top of it at one end. The front of the smaller boulder was covered with texture. Something used to be there. It could've once been a face, erased by wind and time. And the back of it was smooth and sloped. It looked like a helmet—or a headdress. This head was positioned at the front of the longer rock beneath it—a body.

"Do you see it?" she asked.

He mimicked the direction of her chin toward the same two rocks. "No. What?"

"It's a body with a head, and the face is worn off. It looks like the Sphinx."

He smiled. "I see it. Maybe we're not so far from the Sahara, after all."

• • •

In the campground, Oliver unloaded the tent from the car trunk.

"Can I do anything?" Daphne asked.

"Rest easy, Cleopatra. I got this." He grinned.

He pushed the poles through the canvas and attached them quickly and efficiently. Not a single movement was wasted. In less than five minutes, they had a home for the night.

"You are one with the tent," she said. "Are you an Eagle Scout?"

"Nope. I only had a brief stint as a Cub Scout. But three years ago I spent my entire summer in a tent in my backyard."

"Why?"

"I wanted to be alone."

"Amen to that. Your parents let you?"

"I had to eat meals inside so they could make sure I was alive."

Daphne regretted not setting up a tent in her own backyard.

The briefness of Oliver's Cub Scout experience exposed its fatal flaw when they tried to make a fire. The newspaper burned as planned, the gray and white ravaged by orange and blackened into flakes, but the logs would not ignite, no matter how many squirts of lighter fluid Daphne and Oliver doused over them.

"Maybe the wood is damp?" Daphne said.

"We're in the desert. There's no such thing as damp."

"It might be damp from the lighter fluid. The good thing is I'm getting high off the fumes."

Oliver shifted on his haunches. "Okay, Plan B. Mooch off of someone else's fire."

Daphne's stomach went heavy and hollow at the same time. She'd imagined the whole night with Oliver all to herself and now the disappointment traveled through her at a nagging pace. She hit the reset button on her expectations for the evening, kicking herself for setting them above her grasp in the first place. *Silly girl with an unrealistic crush.* Joshua Tree had made her forget that. With all the death surrounding her, she had felt more alive than she actually was.

"Sounds good." She played along.

One of the things Daphne admired most about Oliver was his social grace. She imagined him drifting from clique to clique in the Sacred Heart hallways the same way he wandered from fire to fire with complete ease, natural small talk, and effortless charisma. After they moved on from each fire in search of the liveliest evening, he never made any judgments. He appreciated everyone's fire, even if it wasn't for him. To Daphne, this was the equivalent of a superpower, Mr. Extrovert.

Before they even said hello, Daphne spotted the fire they would be sitting around for the remainder of the evening. Twelve people their age, with a keg, already surrounded it, so the deal was as good as sealed. That seal was stapled when four people in the group turned out to be beautiful girls who hadn't adequately dressed for the desert night. They shivered in their denim shorts, in desperate need of booze and a new friend to warm them. The sight of Oliver transformed them into Pavlov's salivating dogs. Ding. Ding. Ding, ding, ding, ding, ding.

"Hey, how's it going? Mind if we join your fire?" Oliver asked the three guys flanking the keg.

As a response, they handed Oliver a cup of beer.

"Thanks. I'm Oliver. This is Daphne."

Daphne gave a small wave. She stepped up to the fire and everyone made an introduction. The names floated through the space between Daphne's eardrum and brain. She identified the people around the fire by their defining characteristics: Booming Laugh, Eyebrow Scar, Glasses, Dirty Flannel, Freckles, Cheekbones, Dreadlocks, Guitar Boy, and Skanksville One through Four.

Oliver read her snap-judging face and smirked. "Are you drinking?"

After enduring the length of the desert day, the near-death experience, and now being surrounded by unfamiliar faces, the last thing Daphne wanted was a drink. "I'm good. Thanks."

He set down his beer. "I'm good, too."

Before Daphne could enjoy the surprise moment of

chivalry, Skanksville Two and Three closed in on Oliver and sat him down in a lawn chair. Scrutinizing the fire, Daphne could see the night playing out in the flames. Oliver would be preoccupied by whichever body he found the warmest. Daphne would be forced to make awkward conversation with inebriated strangers and pretend that she didn't notice Oliver drift off into one of Skanksville's tents. Judging by their lack of preparation in the clothing department, they probably didn't even have a tent. He'd end up bringing the girl back to his tent. Daphne's tent. Now she was internally stabbing herself for not bringing her own tent. She was more unprepared than Skanksville.

Daphne took a seat next to the most innocuous member of the campfire, Guitar Boy. He strummed a vaguely recognizable tune, and she figured she could gush over his modest talent without having to engage in actual conversation. Besides feeling like a filthy groupie, it was a win-win.

While she set a mental timer to measure how long she could sit without speaking, a body plunked into the seat on the other side of her.

"The fire's warmer over here." The chair creaked when Oliver settled in.

Daphne disguised her joy by digging in her bag and making an announcement to the campfire crew. "Oh, I forgot…" She pulled out five chocolate bars, a box of graham crackers, and a bag of marshmallows. "I brought s'mores."

A chorus of whooping cheers sang around the fire. Fist bumps ensued. Dreadlocks and Glasses snatched the ingredients from her.

"Look at you, camping pro." Oliver nudged her with his elbow.

The warmth of the fire helped redden out her flush. "I do what I can."

The rest of the night, Oliver stayed at her side. Yes, Skanksville was there, too, but Oliver always turned to Daphne when he spoke, made sure she was part of the conversation to the point that Skanksville started to hurl sour looks in her direction. It was magnificent.

The overambitious fire blazed on. One by one, the group retired to the tents, and the Skanksville clan joined whoever would take them in for the night, leaving only Oliver, Daphne, and Guitar Boy, still strumming away beneath the stars. Oliver pierced a marshmallow with his stick and cast it over the fire, where the flames licked its surface.

"You're doing it wrong." Daphne impaled her marshmallow with her stick, held it down near the glowing red-orange coals of the fire, and slowly rotated it. "You have to cook it at the base where the fire is the hottest and keep turning it. That way the marshmallow cooks evenly all the way through and you have a gooey center."

"That looks way too complicated for marshmallow cooking." Oliver promptly stuck his stick into the flames, alighting his marshmallow into a purple blaze of white bubbling to black, a chemical reaction gone wrong. He blew out the fire, plucked the marshmallow from the stick, and popped it into his mouth.

"That was a raw marshmallow with a bunch of carcinogens."

"What if I don't like a gooey center?" His mouth was still full.

"Who doesn't like a gooey center?"

"No one," he admitted.

"My dad taught me how to roast marshmallows. I wanted to stick them into the fire like you." She lifted her stick from the coals and used two graham crackers to slide the fragile, melted blob off the tip. "But he was patient. It was an art form. He really was a good dad, once upon a time." She added two pieces of chocolate and pressed the graham crackers together again. White and brown oozed out. "Plus, it needs to be hot all the way through to melt the chocolate. The most important part." She handed the s'more to Oliver.

"I don't know. You've built up my expectations." Oliver took a bite.

While he chewed, Daphne put another marshmallow on her stick and returned it to the fire.

"Daphne Bowman, you make a damn fine s'more. I think it's your superpower. Especially since you inherited it."

"Ooh, goody. So alcoholism can be my superpower, too."

"Nope. Superpowers have to be advantageous, as well as a curse." He considered this for a moment. "Is that why you aren't drinking?"

"No. Maybe," she mumbled. "I didn't feel like it."

"You're not going to get it. The alcoholism."

"Easy for you to say. Your genetics have less booby traps than mine."

"Well, you're nimble. You'll make it around all of them."

"Nimble? You saw me on that boulder today. I would trip on a booby trap trying to step around it. I'd probably fall into it."

"Okay, but you're smart. And you know yourself. You'll build some contraption to fly over everything so you'll never have to step foot on the ground."

She sighed, lacking both the strength to argue and the confidence to agree. "Do you ever think that we live too much of our lives around Jason and Emily?"

"How do you mean?"

"Sometimes I feel like my whole day revolves around making Emily happy or pissing her off. Like today, when I picked out this shirt, I thought, *Emily would hate this shirt*. She hated florals. One time my mom made Emily take me to the mall with her and Jason. Emily tore through the racks and critiqued each shirt. She couldn't stand anything with flowers because the best thing about flowers is how they smell, and you can't get that from a shirt, so why wear it? But then I put on these boots and I thought, *Emily would like these*. And it made me happy. Stupid."

"I try to be as little like Jason as possible." Uncertainty tainted his voice, the effect of opening a door in his mind after years of keeping it shut.

"You like the same music."

"That's different."

"How?" Her tone was earnest, unchallenging.

Still, her question hit Oliver in a sensitive spot and he flinched. "Liking a few of the same artists and bands isn't being like him. Serial killers probably like Elliott Smith, too. Am I like them?"

He wanted her to retract her line of questioning, to go on eating marshmallows like their siblings hadn't died together in her garage seven years ago. But after those seven long years, Daphne was finally getting answers. She couldn't stop now. "I'm not saying you're like him, I'm asking how you think you're different."

Oliver focused on the fire, took a breath and heeded

the sky. He swallowed. Daphne had only intended to get a simple response and now she braced for some great truth he appeared about to reveal.

"I won't have a girlfriend. Because of Jason."

Her question had been innocent, and so had his response, but Daphne heard blame. Defense crept into her voice. "You think Jason died because of Emily?"

"They were enablers of each other."

"You don't think they were in love?" Her eyes widened at the implausibility.

He stuffed his useless hands under his hamstrings. "I think they couldn't see past the darkness in each other. They felt alone and the other filled the void. It was obsession more than love."

"That's so depressing."

"Well, they were depressed." He wiggled a hand out from under his leg and scratched his jaw, keeping his eyes down.

"Isn't that what love is, though? Except it's the opposite. Instead of the darkness, you don't look past the light in the other person. You don't focus on the bad, the weaknesses, the imperfections. You see what you want to see."

"I want to see everything." His head snapped to her like he'd tossed out an accusation instead of a broad statement. Shadows from the fire cut his face into alternating expressions of anger and hope.

The same shadows danced across her own face. "And that's how you're different from him."

Relief lifted the corners of his mouth.

She knew she'd hit a nerve that sent shockwaves down his backbone, so she struck again. "That's something you'll never get from someone you can't even call your girlfriend."

A sheepish smile flashed across his face as he jabbed his marshmallow straight into the flames.

An hour later, Daphne washed her face in the campground bathroom, scrubbing away the day, inhaling the campfire scent lingering in her hair. She folded her clothes into her bookbag and changed into her pajamas.

As she traipsed around the dark campground to the tent, she cast a glance up at the stars. They weren't as bright or plentiful as she'd imagined. No matter how far into the desert she ventured, she couldn't escape L.A., couldn't escape the past, couldn't escape the present. But tonight, she didn't want to; tonight, she was satisfied with the ground beneath her feet.

Oliver was already tucked in his sleeping bag when she climbed into the tent. He'd laid out her sleeping bag a couple feet away from his.

"Hey, you look…"

He was seeing her barefaced for the first time. She didn't think anything of it. She saw her bare face in the mirror as often as her made-up one. "Pick an adjective, any adjective," she said.

"Good."

She could tell by his awkward swallow that he regretted picking the most generic adjective of all, but she derided him anyway. "Thanks. Next, you're going to tell me how *nice* my disposition is."

"You look different, that's all. Good different."

"There are a lot of girls who write songs about how wonderful and awesome and life-affirming it is when guys tell them they look better without any makeup on."

"Yeah?"

"I'm not one of those girls." She smiled at him.

"I didn't think you were." He smiled back.

"Goodnight, Oliver."

"Goodnight, Daphne."

She turned away with a giddiness swelling through her, thrilled to be sleeping next to him. Tomorrow they would wake up and spend the whole drive back to L.A. together. Life was everything it should be.

• • •

As the new dawn broke, the dreams of yesterday vanished along with the stars in the early morning sky, and the day rose into reality. Daphne woke in a cocoon of pain, the consequence of being spared her life on yesterday's boulder. She awaited teasing for sneaking off to the bathroom and returning with smudgy eyeliner and red lips, but Oliver had no commentary on her morning priorities.

They packed up the camp without saying much. Daphne basked in the comfortable lull while they loaded the truck. It reminded her of how she and Janine could sit in the same room for hours without needing to speak to warm the air between them. Silence had heat of its own. Now a warm breeze blew from Oliver and his able hands as they rolled up the tent.

After the car was loaded, they drove out of the park and into Twenty-nine Palms. Daphne was sure there was a story to the town's name, but she liked not knowing it. Oliver pumped gas and they stocked up on convenience store cappuccinos and junk food for the ride home. The sun shone brightly on their tired faces.

"Ready to hit the road?" he asked.

"Yes, sir."

He turned the key and nothing happened. He turned it again. A buzzing spun from the base of the steering wheel. Oliver peered at the ignition with a mixture of curiosity, agitation, and foreboding. The simple motion he'd acted out hundreds of times before wasn't having the same result. He pounded the steering wheel. Daphne jumped at the sudden motion and sound.

"I'm sorry." Apology was his only available action.

"It's okay. We're not stranded in the desert with buzzards circling. Yet." She tried to remain upbeat. The day was new, and there was still time to reclaim it.

"My parents don't know I'm here." He sounded worried.

"Neither do mine." She shared his concern.

He arrived at a grim conclusion. "I have to call them."

Oliver's car door creaked as it opened and closed. Had it always protested against its purpose, its hinges begging for oil? The minutiae became painfully apparent in the face of impending doom. Daphne stayed in the car while Oliver paced outside of it, his phone to his ear. He was mostly quiet, hanging his head at the ridicule being carried from cell tower to cell tower across the state.

As a distraction, Daphne checked her own phone and saw that she had six voicemails. Dread pressed her legs down into the car seat. Good news never left six messages. She scrolled through her texts: only one message, from Janine: "*YOUR MOM RAN INTO MY MOM AND ME AT TARGET. SHE KNOWS. JUST WARNING YOU. P.S. I'M GROUNDED BY ASSOCIATION. THANKS. PHONE BEING TAKEN AWAY IN 3-2-1*"

Despite the horror in her belly, Daphne delighted in Janine's warning, raging against parental strife until all technology was gone.

The six messages were from her mother, each with its own theme for Daphne to identify. The Six Stages of My Child is Semi-Missing and Lied to Me.

Mild Worry. "*I love you. Please let me know you're safe.*" Aw, she knew Daphne existed and missed her. Sentimentality passed over Daphne, the shadow of a hawk in the desert sky.

Agitation. "*If you don't call me back, I'm going to start worrying.*" Again, the attention was endearing.

Legitimate Worry. "*I'm officially worrying. Call me before I do something drastic like call the police.*" Uh-oh. Now things were getting serious.

Unbridled Anger. "*How dare you lie to me? Who do you think you are?*" Um, she was a normal teenager. Plus, if her mom hadn't run into Janine, she never would have known. It was a revelation of pure coincidence. Daphne's actions harmed no one.

Threats. "*You are going to be grounded until you go to college. Say goodbye to your summer.*" Her mother actually meant, *Say goodbye to Oliver.*

Resignation. "*Just call. Please.*" By this point, Daphne was exhausted, too tired to be amused by her mom's evolution. With a heavy forefinger, Daphne hit "Call Back." The phone rang, and Daphne saw the momentary goodwill between mother and daughter blow by like the tumbleweeds at the edges of the gas station.

"Hi, Mom. I'm sorry, I didn't have any reception…"

Daphne became the mirror of Oliver, still circling outside the car. They shared an empathetic glance and hung their heads at matching angles, absorbing the fierce, tinny voices scolding them.

Sitting in the car, listening to her mother reminded Daphne of the balmy evening in March seven years ago. There had been a good part of the night, before her family discovered the decision Emily and Jason had made.

On the drive home from Taco Tuesday at Pepe's Cantina, her dad gorged within centimeters of his stomach bursting on all-you-can-eat-tacos-for-eight-dollars, he asks from the rear-view mirror, "How was school?"

Daphne reports that karma visited the class bully during dodgeball in gym.

To this day, the scene made her cheeks burn with both giddiness and guilt.

The perfect throw by Andrew Taylor, the runt of the class-room litter: the bully's bloody nose, the keeling over, the nervous laughter and unspoken bonding with her classmates.

Her mom twists around in the front car seat to study Daphne, her face a mix of worry and amusement.

Daphne wished she hadn't avoided her mother's scrutiny. It was the last time her mom would look at her without seeing Emily. Maybe now, Daphne's mom was finally seeing her again while screaming at her from one hundred fifty miles away. Daphne hung up, both defeated and refreshed, as Oliver slouched into the driver's seat.

His voice was more upbeat than his posture. "My parents want to tow the car back to L.A. The bad news is we're both gonna be grounded until we're twenty. Good thing I'm older than you."

"And the good news?"

"I found us a ride."

"Who?"

"Penny Layton."

"I'm still waiting for the good news."

He decided, wisely, not to take the conversation any further. "Let's move this beast."

Daphne switched seats and pulled on the steering wheel with all of her weight, guiding the car into a parking spot as Oliver and two kind recruits pushed. Pinpricks of sweat dotted her forehead when she shifted into park. She climbed out and slammed the door so the draft would blast her face.

"This is the first time I've seen you drive," Oliver observed.

"I hope it's the last."

Oliver chuckled. "Come on. Let's get some coffee. We have a few hours to kill."

He put his arm around Daphne, guiding her toward a small cafe on the next block. Electricity shot into her shoulder from the charge in his hand. She wondered if he felt anything beyond the cloth of her shirt or the curve of her bones.

"Did you tell your mom what happened?" He asked in that genuinely caring fashion that made her resent him even more.

"Yeah, and I don't want to talk about it," she said. His arm against the back of her neck felt so natural, she didn't want it to ever leave. Just the thought of it going away scared her, so she brushed off his hand when they hobbled through the doorway of a small cafe.

"Geez, you're cranky when you don't get enough sleep. It's like poking a bear." He prodded her shoulder. "Poke."

She shouldn't have touched him. But returning his poke

in the shoulder was more cause and effect than calculation. Oliver retaliated by poking her abdomen, to which she poked his bicep and sides. Twice. The game quickly escalated to a poking frenzy accompanied with spastic giggling. Their limbs collided against each other in attack and defense until Oliver, in his haste and laughter, misjudged his finger's trajectory and poked her square in the left boob. She recoiled, cursing her reflexes before she could stop herself from shrinking back.

Oliver's face deflated like a popped balloon. "I'm so sorry."

Daphne's body continued to betray her, cheeks flushing against her will. "It's okay, I think I got your boob a few times in there."

He forced a square smile into the round hole in his face.

"I could give you a titty twister if you think that would even it out." Daphne turned her fist in the air, pantomiming tweaking his nipple.

He laughed, self-consciousness gone, and Daphne laughed with him. She'd redeemed the situation and was grateful, but not as grateful as Oliver. He pulled her close and wrapped his arms around her, hugging her tightly. Her muscles went rigid with surprise before melting into exactly where she wanted to be. Her ear nestled against his neck, his pulse surging through her entire being. In that moment, she would've given up Berkeley to reach up and kiss him. She gritted her teeth, knowing the hug would end momentarily, bracing for the sting.

"Shall we get a coffee?" Oliver loosened his arms.

Daphne studied him. Maybe the moment hadn't ended. Maybe there was still time. She only had to press her mouth into his. It could be so easy.

"Yeah. Sure."

He turned to the counter, and she let him go. She settled her weary bones into a booth. The cushions wheezed under her legs, and something in the sound made her realize that she was always going to want to be more than friends with Oliver Pagano. He would have to wound her in some unfathomable way to change this.

Daphne moved in further to avoid the sun's glare. With the squeak of the vinyl against her hands came an even worse realization. He could only hurt her to that degree from a place deeper than friendship, and that was never going to happen. Daphne was stuck between the Oliver Pagano rock and the hard place of her own heart. She receded into the blind-striped morning shadows and pretended to be tired. Oliver didn't notice anything unusual when he returned to the table with two mugs full of coffee.

Seven cups of caffeine later, Penny arrived. Oliver chivalrously held open the door to the front seat, which Daphne declined. She slid into the backseat, her rightful place as the third wheel, and Penny ordered Oliver to shotgun.

Daphne wanted only music and sleep. She put in her earbuds and discovered, in keeping with the theme of the day, that her iPod was dead as the blackened tree skeletons on the fire-stricken hills surrounding her. She kept the earbuds in so she wouldn't have to be part of Penny's thrilling conversation and could judge invisibly from the backseat: a gruesome basketball injury (nightmare material), the soon-to-be-legendary rager that Oliver had missed last night (greatly exaggerated, certainly, but Daphne could hear uneasiness when Oliver shallowly described last night's campfire), Ava Franklin's pregnancy scare (friends who talk about their friend's pregnancy scare to nonfriends are not friends), and vague allusions to prom (at which point it became difficult to not ask Penny to pull over under the guise of car-sickness). Daphne prayed for sleep that wouldn't come.

Daphne's fingers were already gripping the handle when the car pulled into the Bowman driveway hours later. But the ominous shadow behind the front door of her house kept her from pulling the lever. Instead, Oliver opened his door, much to Penny's surprise.

"Thanks again for the ride, Penny. You're a lifesaver." He climbed out of the car.

"Oly, I can take you home," Penny practically begged.

Oly. If Daphne started calling him *Oly*, would he want to make out with her? It worked for everyone else.

"No, I'm gonna walk. I want to enjoy my last breaths of freedom."

Penny, inexperienced in the department of being rebuffed by boys, did a terrible job of keeping her composure. "Okay. Well, call me. Wait, you'll probably be grounded and won't have a phone."

"We'll figure it out," Oliver said.

Penny opened her mouth to argue, but her voice was stolen by the disturbing scene taking place behind her. Daphne had rolled down her window, drawing all of Oliver's attention. He gave her a little wave. Daphne returned a small salute.

Oliver leaned down to her eye level. "I had a great day yesterday. And night. If I had to go out…"

"You're not going anywhere, Pagano." Daphne rolled her eyes. "And you think I'm dramatic."

He playfully grimaced at her and began the long, solitary march home.

Daphne pulled on the door handle. "Penny, thanks for the—"

Penny cut her off. "Are you and Oliver…together?"

Daphne bristled at the dismay in Penny's voice; at how badly she wanted to prove Penny wrong. "No. We're not."

"Are you hooking up?"

"Penny…" Daphne wanted Penny to cut her off again so she could leave it as ambiguous as possible, but Penny let the question hang until it dropped to the ground at Daphne's feet, forcing her to answer. "No."

"You're taking overnight trips and…nothing?"

Whatever pride Oliver had bestowed upon her with his goodbye, Penny had erased and subtracted extra with the pity in her eyes.

"Thanks for the ride," Daphne muttered. She tripped over the mat on her way out of the car.

"Hope your mom goes easy on you," Penny sympathized, the child of one crazy mom to another.

"Doubtful."

Daphne opened and closed the front door quietly, out of habit. She stepped into the dining room, where her parents waited. They took hesitant steps near the table, unsure of whether to sit or stand. Daphne hadn't seen them in the same room for weeks. Her delinquent behavior was bringing her family closer together. It was almost sweet.

Daphne spoke first. "I'm sorry."

Her parents both jumped a little. The surprise keyed up her mom even more, an unexpected effect. "Daphne. You went to Joshua Tree. With a boy. Without telling anyone?"

"I told Janine."

"This is not the time to be a smart ass," her mother hissed.

Her mom was more embarrassed that her daughter had a life she didn't know about than she was angry at the actual crime. Since Daphne wasn't cowering in apology, her mother's embarrassment frothed into anger. Any controlled plan of attack disintegrated on the spot. Her mom hurled questions at Daphne, who didn't know whether to dodge or absorb the blows.

"Did you have sex?" Her mom skipped straight to the big one.

A combination of laughter and shock coughed from Daphne's throat. She appealed to her father for rescue, but his eyes shifted down to the uneven grains running through the dining room table. Maybe he was thinking of all the dinners the Bowmans had eaten there, happy times when they were a unit of four. When Emily still stuck peas up her nose when their parents weren't watching, goading Daphne into spitting out her milk. Their mom and dad gave half-hearted lectures as they struggled not to laugh themselves.

A thin layer of dust now settled on the chairs. The echoes of laughter reverberated only in Daphne's imagination. Her dad was lost in something beyond memory. Bound by the present, her mom continued pressing for a confession.

"You can tell me, Daphne. I won't be mad. We can still take you to the pharmacy…"

Daphne regained her breath. "No. There is a zero percent chance that I'm pregnant."

Her mother didn't take this reprieve for granted. "Oh,

thank God." She offered herself up to Heaven in gratitude. Daphne noticed the cracks in the ceiling.

Her mom retrained her focus on Daphne. "But you're seeing this boy?"

"No. We're just friends." Daphne's own voice mocked her. How many times today was she going to have to declare that she and Oliver were in no way romantically involved?

The trial appeared to be over. Her sentence would be handed down, and she would be sent to her room for the foreseeable future. It was then that her mom's hand jerked into her scrubs pocket and pulled out a square of paper. Daphne's breath halted at its worn lines and slovenly folds, her and Emily's invisible fingerprints all over it.

"What is this?" Her mother snapped at Daphne like a whip, more accusation than question.

No wonder Emily had hid the list in Daphne's room. Apparently their mom discarded all notion of privacy when attempting to mother. Daphne closed her eyes. Behind her eyelids, she cursed herself with every profanity in her vocabulary for not moving the list to a more secure location than under the floorboard it had rested beneath, solemn and undisturbed, for so many years.

Now, new evidence had come to light. The Exhibit A portion of this trial would be long and arduous. First-degree murder questions would be asked. DNA-level explanations would be given. With Emily involved, the death penalty was always on the table, the chance of parole denied from the get-go.

Maybe it was the utter physical and emotional exhaustion the sunny day had rained down on her. Maybe it was the deep injustice of this woman getting to play her Mom card three turns too late. Maybe it was her dad's inability to speak. Something inside Daphne failed, the way sanity can momentarily lapse in a normally well-behaved person. She needed to act crazy for five minutes, and everything would return to normal.

Her feet started moving. One step backward, two steps, three steps, she didn't stop.

"Mom, I'm sorry…I have to…go!" Daphne zoomed out the front door.

Wordless sounds gurgled from her mom's throat.

Her stuttering dad was forced to call out in her mom's stead. "Daphne!"

"I'm sorry! I'll be back in five minutes, I promise. And then you can ground me adequately!"

Daphne raced down the street, turned the corner, passed the school. She spotted his ambling body three blocks ahead and ran faster, pushing through the stiff pain in her legs, until, finally, her sidewalk met his.

He turned around with his warm Oliver grin. "I could hear you puffing behind me for a block."

Normally, she would return the joke. But this wasn't her usual sidewalk. She wasn't aiming for the familiar road.

"I forgot something."

He opened his mouth, but she didn't give him time to ask. She stepped into him and kissed him with the force of a small, strong girl who'd waited her whole life to tell Oliver Pagano that she forgot something. And then she ran.

Daphne didn't see his reaction, and hope burned in her veins. He had kissed her back. Maybe that was something, maybe it was mere courtesy. But she had felt the soft roughness of his tongue. It had met hers and never receded.

It was the most foolish thing she'd ever done. It was her greatest accomplishment.

OWN A PAIR OF DESIGNER SHOES

No. He shook his head. That did not just happen. The birds stopped singing. Passing traffic carried no roar. The grass and flowers of the neighborhood desaturated to varying shades of gray. The air held no temperature or scent. His mind drained into an infinite funnel, his senses numb to everything except Daphne Bowman.

He spent the rest of the journey home floating in a daze, impending punishment forgotten. His parents greeted him as though he'd come home from school. They sat him down to dinner and gave him a stern sermon about *taking them for granted* and *love* and *second chances*, neither raising their voice. He listened without hearing, nodding once in a while to humor them. The tactic worked—every time he nodded his mother responded with a satisfied, elongated blink.

As soon as he was released to his bedroom, he dug out

his tablet and stylus. He drew the campfire. The stars. The gooey marshmallows. A pair of lips in the sky. And a heart. A heart. Not an anatomical heart—a feminine, lovestruck, accidentally-not-a-circle heart doodle. Erase, erase, erase. He tucked the tablet under his bed and turned on the TV. Eight hours of video games later, his eyeballs dried open, Oliver made up his mind. He was going to pretend like it never happened. Daphne had snuck up on him. He was unprepared and on little sleep, and a simple moment of weakness had led to a large lapse in his judgment. She had poured herself into him and he had drunk her up. He hadn't known he was thirsty until she was a block away, scampering back to her house. A drive-by kissing, the wound of which throbbed inside of him.

It was bad enough that the time they spent at Joshua Tree had conjured magic in its hours. Somewhere between the Hollywood sign and the desert, Daphne Bowman had become a magnetic force. He couldn't stop touching her. Putting his arm around her after the gas station, the poking match in the cafe, the hug that he'd ended even though he'd wanted to keep holding her.

Oliver had played out all the scenarios in his mind, and the only way it ended well was if he became Daphne Bowman's boyfriend. That was not going to happen. She knew it couldn't—he'd been crystal clear through the campfire smoke.

He envisioned Daphne in Katrina's place. Katrina wasn't so dumb once Oliver got to know her, right before he disposed of her, and Daphne had a noticeably higher percentage of brain function than Katrina. Within a week of holding Daphne's hand and making out under the bleachers, she'd probably be able to convince him to paint the "b" word all over his forehead. Even more disturbing was what all of this might say about him.

He didn't want to think about that. He needed to do something drastic, game-changing, to prove—whether to her, or himself, he wasn't sure—that he still had the upper hand in the situation. He picked up his phone. The muscles in his arm tightened, a final warning against dialing the phone. His dialed anyway.

The cheer in her voice filled him with dread. "Hey! You still have your phone."

He took a deep breath. "I have a question for you…"

• • •

School resumed, the home stretch of senior year. When the final bell rang on Monday afternoon, a sixth sense pulled Oliver into the chapel on his way to the parking lot. She wouldn't be there—he knew she was grounded—but he sensed her presence. Sure enough, a hot pink Post-it was attached to her pew: *Any ideas for #6?*

He pulled out a pen from his backpack and wrote on the back of the note: *Yes. When?*

The next day, a yellow Post-it rippled against the pew from the draft of the open door: *Saturday. Meet me at Sweetie's at 4 p.m.*

He wrote back: *I feel like a spy.*

Wednesday: *With a fluorescent paper trail? I can't believe the CIA hasn't recruited us yet.*

Speak for yourself. I'm sworn to secrecy.

On Thursday, the pew was empty, and the room was

cold. He searched the surrounding rows, considering the different possibilities. Maybe Father George or a nun had been in the chapel when she stopped by. Hiding the note would be more Daphne-like than scrapping it altogether. Gritting his teeth, he ran his hand under her pew. Gum, gum, gum, and more gum.

Father George strode into the room and opened the windows. "Hello, Oliver."

How did Father George remember his name? He'd had little interaction with the man during his four years at Sacred Heart, avoiding him whenever possible, which was most of the time. "Hi, Father George."

Oliver expected some unsolicited guidance related to his extended absence from the chapel, all in good humor but patronizing nonetheless. It didn't come.

"How are you doing on this beautiful Thursday afternoon? Almost Friday, right?" Father George flashed a wide grin.

"Yeah. But it's not like you get the weekend off. Sunday's your big day."

"Sunday's the best day of the week." Father George beamed. He meant it. "Come to service, and you'll see why."

"Okay, I will." Oliver wanted to mean it. If he was morally comfortable with fibbing to Father George, his soul was surely condemned. Oliver cleared his throat. The question caught on his teeth and stalled on the way out. "Father George, did you find a Post-it note on one of the pews?" He wanted the question to sound less ridiculous than the possibility that the note didn't exist.

"The second pew from the back? Yes."

"You found it?" Oliver's relief was palpable. Even Father

George chuckled, and Oliver got the impression that Father George had a sizeable understanding of high school woe, despite being celibate. "Can I...I mean, good. Thanks. Do you happen to still have it? I think someone left it for me."

"Sister Candice must have tossed it. I've been letting the notes stay, and reading them, for my own personal enjoyment. I hope you don't mind." Father George strolled behind the pulpit and pulled out a ring of keys.

"Uh, no." Oliver did mind, but he had no desire to argue about it with a priest on holy ground. "If you let us deface your property, you have the right to read it. It's only for this week."

"I'll talk to Sister Candice, see if she can abstain through tomorrow. No promises after that. She's kind of a neat freak, this being the Lord's House and all." Father George unlocked a door to a back room and leaned over a wastebasket.

"Thank you."

The priest emerged from the doorway and extended his hand to Oliver with a yellow Post-it stuck to his finger: *What's your code name?* "Better come up with something clever. Daphne's a smart one."

Oliver gulped. Father George knew Daphne. "Yes, she's a good influence on me." *That's why I got her grounded.*

"Wise men appreciate the positive forces in their lives. Keep it up, Oliver. I hope to see you one of these Sundays." With that, Father George left the chapel as humbly as he'd arrived.

Oliver sat in Daphne's pew and looked up to Stained Glass Mary for inspiration. His best idea wasn't great, but his hungry stomach's growling threatened the quiet of the room. He wrote in small letters so it would all fit: *Frog Murrietta. Because Frog was my first pet hamster's name when I was six and I grew up on Murrietta Ave.*

On Friday, a blue Post-it awaited him, undisturbed: *That's your porn star name, not your spy name. Is this what communication was like when our parents were dating?*

Did she think they were dating? A sharp pain formed behind his eyes. Oliver crumpled the Post-it. Picturing Father George reading the note spread his headache to the base of his skull.

His best distraction was a videogame where he could turn off his brain and focus only on the screen in front of him. But the effect was temporary. The all-nighter left him in a haze, when he was most susceptible to memories of Jason. He noticed that his position on the bed, legs folded underneath him, his back propped against the wall, was no different than it was seven years ago.

Oliver sits on his bed, back against the wall. His eyes are frozen open, staring at the television screen. He pounds on his controller, fighting to keep his characters alive.

"The whole team will be there." Jason's voice carries downstairs to Oliver's room.

"I don't want to go." Emily's voice chases after.

"We could just stop by for a half hour." Jason's voice moves between aggravation and begging.

"Go by yourself. It's fine."

Even with a floor between them, Oliver can tell it isn't fine.

"Just go," she says. "Go." Her irritation sucks the oxygen from the air.

"No. It's okay. I'll stay."

Their footsteps pad down the hall, silenced by the closing door of Jason's bedroom.

Emily had won. Jason had lost. Oliver wasn't going to lose.

He kicked off his covers. Saturday had arrived. The afternoon closed in and Oliver needed to have The Conversation with Daphne. But he couldn't spew familiar words and toss in her name for authenticity. Parts of the conversation could be plagiarized, but with Daphne everything required more.

At 4:00 p.m., he shifted his car into park with a resounding click in front of Sweetie's. He stormed through the door, sending the bell into a frenzy. He had the fullest intentions to make it clear that they were not now, and never would be, together. But at the sight of her, his mouth dried out and his charge weakened to a tiptoe.

She wasn't working, seated next to the counter instead of behind it. "I got three weeks. That's the decree from parents who aren't parents. No phone, no iPod, no closed bedroom door. Straight home from school and work."

He kept staring at her lips. Supple. Neither exaggerated, nor understated. Lips that knew how to kiss. How had he never noticed them before? Outside of the time when they were coated in lipstick and doing their best Marilyn Monroe impression, of course. "Rough," was all he could manage.

"Eh, my friends know where to find me. What was your sentence?"

He lowered his head, both proud and appalled by his admission. "No rental car while my car was in the shop. I already have it back."

"About what I expected. So, I have it all worked out." She winked at Oliver and turned to the freckled boy their age behind the counter. "Okay, Jed. If my mom calls you need to say that I'm cleaning the bathroom and you transfer her to my cell. Got it?"

"Cool." Jed gave her a thumbs up, smitten. A tiny volt of jealousy surged through Oliver and settled in the pit of his gut.

"Thanks." Daphne nodded at Jed in solidarity.

"I thought you didn't have a phone," Oliver said.

"It's for emergencies. My mom checks it every night for calls or texts."

"Intense." Oliver followed her out of the shop. "I feel like I've turned you into a liar."

"You have." Her lips parted into a liar's grin.

They drove over a winding road at the top of a ridge, elevated above the spring dew in the valley. The houses in the hills propped up with stilts appeared ready to teeter over at any moment. A coyote loped through the tall grass and vanished. Had it even been there at all? Oliver focused on the road and tightened his grip on the steering wheel.

Daphne acted like nothing had transpired between them, like he'd made it all up in his head.

"I got into all the U.C.'s except the one I want to go to." She sighed. "I mean, I'm still waiting to find out, not writing it off yet. They have to take me."

"Berkeley?" Oliver asked lightly, trying to lessen her intensity.

Her voice was velvet, pleased that he remembered. "Yep."

"That's a long drive."

"Or a short flight. Depends which transportation glass you want to look at—half empty or half full."

"Except for the train. The train glass is always half empty."

"True," she said.

"So, what U.C.'s have accepted you?"

The twisted road straightened out. Houses lined the street instead of hiding behind hills and fences.

"S.D., S.B., L.A., and Davis. What about you?"

"I didn't apply to any U.C.'s."

"Then, where?"

"U of M."

She evaluated the possibilities and took her best guess. "Michigan?"

"Montana." His enunciation drew out the word, nearly giving it an extra syllable.

"Montana? What's in Montana? Besides buffalo roaming, deer and antelope playing, and seldom heard discouraging words."

"Mountains. Kind of says it in the name, Slow Fry." They hit a red light at one of the few stoplights on the hill, and he tossed her a grin.

"There are mountains all over California."

"You're not the only one who wants to escape. I'm going to business school. Eventually I'll take over Pagano and Sons."

"Is that what you want?"

"At this point in my life, I don't have any better ideas." The relief he thought he would feel after saying this was, in fact, emptiness. The light turned green, and he was glad to have an excuse to focus on the road.

"Does U of M have a football team?"

"Yeah."

"You could be their chicken."

"It's a grizzly bear."

"Everyone will be so drunk they won't know the difference."

Daphne's future burned bright as the Sun. In her solar system, his own future became Pluto, not even good enough to be a planet, just another rock among billions. He changed the subject. "You're not asking where I'm taking you?"

"I trust you."

Every innocent thing she said sounded like a come-on. "You shouldn't."

"Are you a serial killer? Oh my god, I'm trapped in the car. There's no upstairs to run to. I'm going to die…"

The street widened to four lanes and the palm trees grew taller, their pineapple tops meticulously pruned, dead fronds unacceptable.

She continued, "…in *Beverly Hills*. Nope. Beverly Hills wouldn't let me die in it. I'm not posh enough."

They parked off of Rodeo Drive and Daphne followed him up the sidewalk, past the stores of every fashion designer featured prominently in *VOGUE*.

"You need to put a couple extra zeroes in my Sweetie's paycheck for me to shop here."

"So, I'm assuming you remember number six?" he asked.

"Own a pair of designer shoes. Clearly Emily's."

"Look who's sexist. Maybe Jason had a shoe fetish." He opened the door to a tall store that seemed to be made entirely of glass. "I want to get you a graduation present, courtesy of a Mr. James Choo."

She stopped in front of the door. "Now look who's

sexist. You're assuming I'm into designer shoes because I almost have boobs."

"Nah, you have 'em. Can't say I haven't looked. And I poked one." The flirtation tumbled out from Oliver involuntarily and he shifted his eyes to the floor, avoiding her face and chest area. They hadn't kissed, he reminded himself. Never happened. He didn't want to touch her. His hands were rubber to her electricity. *I'm rubber, you're glue.* Grade school defense mechanisms only compounded his shame.

"Well, you're right. About the shoes. But it's sheer coincidence." She sauntered in the store and Oliver followed.

The saleswoman peered down on the teenagers. The arches of her eyebrows came to a severe point over her skeptical eyes.

"Don't worry, he's a trust fund baby," Daphne said to the coifed woman donned in impeccably tailored black.

The saleswoman approached, reserved, still prepared to call their bluff. "Hello, I'm Alana. Is there anything you're looking for in particular?"

Daphne checked with Oliver. If he was planning on folding, now was the time. She cocked her head, giving him one last chance. *You're sure about this?*

He wanted to call off the whole thing. This was all a terrible mistake. They were supposed to have had The Conversation on the ride over the hill. Everything should be as clear as the spotless glass surfaces in the store. The shoes meant nothing except friendship, a relationship forged through tragedy, something pure that had crawled through the ugliness against all odds.

Instead, he nodded in surrender, condemning them both to a harrowing predicament.

All clear, Daphne faced Alana. "Something neutral. Classic. Goes with everything."

Alana believed the intent to purchase, and her attentiveness multiplied by the commission. "We have a few of those. What size?"

"Seven and a half. Or eight. I don't know what size I am in Mr. Choo."

"I'll be right back." Alana glided through the lacquered doors into the back room.

"Thanks, Alana," Oliver called after her, ready to have a good laugh about Alana's dramatic change in attitude. He wore a full smirk on his face, ready to break open with laughter as soon as Daphne cracked. They would make a half-hearted attempt to collect themselves when Alana returned.

"Oliver, go to prom with me."

It was out of nowhere. No lead-in, no warning. He didn't anticipate her having the gumption to ask.

Her voice held its confidence. "I'm not asking you to be my boyfriend. I just want you there with me."

There wasn't a smooth way to say it, so he blurted it out. "I'm already going. With Penny. To her prom. Your prom. It's on the same night as mine." Information he meant to divulge in the car. Revelations he knew would annihilate the admiration in her eyes. The end of times.

He didn't want to see her crestfallen face, but he owed it to her to look.

"She asked you, and you said *yes*?" Thankfully, she was more bewildered than sad.

"Actually, I asked her." The words scratched against his throat.

"You asked her to *her* prom?" Her voice began to crack.

"Yeah." *Because I am a sadistic asshole.*

"The kiss…" She trailed off, unable to compliment or insult herself over it.

"It was a great kiss." He took a step toward her, as if that would prove his sincerity.

"Not that great, apparently." The sarcasm cut with precision.

He spoke slowly, hitting every consonant so she could feel it, know it. "No, it was…the best."

"Oliver, tell me you don't like me."

"I don't want to like you." He said it as flat and robotic as possible, and it still came out sounding desperate.

"Not the same thing."

The conviction in her words fueled him. "I like you, Daphne. But you want more from me than I can give you."

Her voice sliced into him, a clean cut between pity and laughter. "You're predicting what I want so you don't have to find out. Better get your crystal ball checked because you don't know me."

"I know you want what Emily and Jason had. I can't do that." He stared her down, making sure it registered.

Her voice was still sharp. "I want whatever we have. All the good and all the bad."

The line between what Oliver himself wanted, and Oliver not wanting to be Jason, zigzagged on the earthquake-laden ground of Beverly Hills. "I can't do it."

"Taking the coward's way out…" her voice trailed off.

"Like Jason? Little bit of a stretch to compare suicide to saying no to a date, don't you think?"

"I'm noticing the irony. By trying to not be like him, you're being like him."

"And you can't even get dressed without trying to be Emily."

"Wow. Thanks for throwing my honesty in my face."

"Like you're not doing the exact same thing to me."

"So, what is this? You're buying me off with a pair of shoes? Is this what happens? Someone scares you and you head to Rodeo Drive with your parents' credit card? Take me home." She dashed out of the store as Alana reappeared with a stack of boxes.

Oliver had run through all the possible scenarios over the last week. He'd imagined a blowout with Daphne that ended with him feeling guilty, outsmarted, and vacant. He had not, however, imagined that this would take place at the Jimmy Choo store in front of an audience.

He nodded an apology to Alana. She dropped the boxes on the counter a little too hard for how expensive the shoes inside them were, but she got her point across. He hated when people were right about him, especially strangers. And Daphne Bowman.

The car ride home was the longest one of his life. The stoplights taunted him with their measured ability to change.

Daphne took a raspy breath. Thankfully, she wasn't crying. "I'm asking you to be honest with yourself. I don't think anyone's asked you to do that before."

"And I'm responding by saying, 'I can't date you.' You're getting all riled up because I'm saying I don't want you."

She pulled the words from the depths of her throat, "Then say it."

He was even more intimidated by her than usual. "Say what?"

"Say you don't want me."

"I already did." It sounded whiny. He hadn't wanted to sound whiny.

Her pity was back to splicing laughter. "The Oliver *no* is ever ambiguous. And I'm not riled up. If I got upset every time someone in my life didn't want me, I'd be in a constant state of delirium."

"Drama Queen," he said as a dark joke. It cleared some of the frenetic energy in the car but solved nothing.

She took a breath and waited. He knew her next words would be dangerous. They trickled out like the soft rain that rarely fell in L.A. It was always either downpour or a drought. "You're embarrassed to be with me."

He shook his head. "That's not true. I'm with you right now."

"No, I mean, of being *with* me. My boyfriend, or friend with benefits, or whatever your turn of phrase is for what you are with Penny." She parted her hair on the right, using the thousands of extra strands to hide her face.

"I'm not with Penny." He sat up straighter and adjusted his grip on the steering wheel. He was right, and Daphne was wrong, for once.

"Well, you will be, soon enough. You know me? Well, I know you, too." She faced him, waiting.

He glanced over to prove her wrong, but her gloat, bigger and better than his own, returned the curve to his backbone.

They veered onto Mulholland Drive. Oliver used the winding road as an excuse to not face her. "You are an amazing person…"

She almost laughed. "Oliver, if you break up with me one more time I'm going to throw myself out of this car. And as a person with a family history of suicide and depression, I know I shouldn't use that as a threat."

"You forgot alcoholism in there. You want to make a joke about drinking yourself to death?"

"It's too expensive."

"Oh, so this is realistic hypothetical suicide? Should I 5150 you?"

"As long as Jason wouldn't."

The air in the car went so thick and still, it forced Oliver to ask the question he didn't want to ask. "Should we not hang out anymore?"

"I don't know. I think you would miss me a lot less than I would miss you."

"No, Daph. You have it all wrong."

"Give it to me right."

"I tried. I'd just be breaking up with you again."

He glanced at his side mirror to avoid her rolling eyes. But evading her with one sense didn't stop her disgust and exasperation from creeping over to his side of the car.

Defeat swelled in her throat. "You bring out the worst in me."

And you bring out the best in me. He couldn't say it out loud, couldn't tell her how she'd made his senior year the best year of his life. How he knew that even through cancer or Alzheimer's or a horrific car accident, on his deathbed, he would hold onto their conversation at Frank's Diner, when they decided to do the list. He would forever recall the beauty of the desperation and hope in her eyes. The same feeling he'd held inside of him for so long, never having the courage to let it rise to the surface until he met her. She'd opened the cage of something in him that needed to be freed.

He could see black tears streaking down her face. She didn't make a sound. She had mastered the art, a crying ninja.

The silence that was usually so safe between them had grown fangs and snarled at him in the dense air. He snapped back at it. "You want me to change, and I won't."

"You want me to change, and I can't."

Which was worse?

He didn't have to think long before realizing he was the greater of two evils. His adamant refusal to align himself with the best thing that had ever happened to him—it didn't make sense anymore. But change couldn't come in thirty seconds, or even an hour. She had to understand that; she was a reasonable person.

He pulled into the Sacred Heart parking lot where they could continue the conversation without him having one eye on the road. She opened the car door as he pulled into the stall and jumped out before he'd come to a stop.

"Daph!"

All that was left of her was the echo of footsteps on the asphalt.

• • •

At lonely times in his life, Oliver turned to Mitch and Joe.

After a couple hours spent with their simple sentences and bad jokes, life was better. Getting hammered in Joe's garage pushed the future to another day. All that mattered was the night in front of them.

Freshman year, Joe had thrown an epic party one weekend when his parents were out of town. The party had been such a raucous success that three bottles of Resolve and half the JV football team could not get the stains out of the rug in the living room. The jungle juice interwoven with the beige carpet fibers had turned from red to green to blue to purple during various stages of scrubbing, leaving the contaminated sections of the carpet dark and sparse. The color of Joe's face had also changed during each scrubbing phase: hangover gray to panic red to sweaty orange to surrendering white.

In hopes of a temporary solution, furniture had been rearranged to cover the stain, and the living room had a feng shui meltdown. The sofa and chairs were returned to their former divots. Carpeting installers were contacted, and estimates had been handed down like prison sentences. In the end, the cost was too high and the time too short. Joe's parents had returned that night, and they could be heard screaming at him in Spanish from three houses down. The punishment was a doozy. The Valdivias laid off their landscapers for six months and forced Joe to spend every weekend mowing and grooming his yard.

Members of the football team had cruised by Joe's house on Saturday afternoons tossing catcalls while he pushed the lawnmower or pruned the shrubbery. Oliver ducked and didn't make a sound during these drive-bys. He knew Joe's humiliation far outweighed the punishment. He also saw a darkness in Joe that hid behind his eyes. Joe never forgot those taunts, never forgot the mouths that threw them.

Joe never hosted another party. And if alcohol was consumed on his property, it was forbidden indoors. Oliver was only allowed inside to use the bathroom or get a glass of water. Even then, he was required to remove his shoes before entering. Joe's fear of his parents ran deep. Six months of caretaking the grounds of his home had taught him to take zero risk when it came to illicit behavior. Oliver admired this relationship. If he had more fear of his own parents, would it have shaped him differently? Would he wade through life more carefully, with more forethought, with more cunning? Would he have figured out who and what he wanted to be? The grass was always greener, just ask Joe. The guy was shockingly knowledgeable in eco-friendly fertilizer.

Oliver sipped his third beer, sitting on a lawn chair flanked by Mitch and Joe. "Do you guys remember that girl at one of the football games? The one who was waiting by the fence for me?"

"Emily Bowman's little sister. The one that blew you off on New Year's." Mitch sneered.

Oliver winced. Had it been that obvious? Even Mitch had picked up on it, so that question was answered.

"Daphne." Joe wasn't playing the pronoun game.

"Yeah, her." He wanted to know how Joe knew her name. Maybe Mitch told him. Or maybe Oliver had slipped and mentioned her. Asking would make him look guilty of some crime he hadn't committed. "What did you think of her?"

"Ball buster." Mitch laughed.

"Kind of hot, in that scary, goth sort of way," Joe smirked.

Oliver was surprised by their positive reactions. "Really?"

"She might bite your dick off, but it would be really good up 'til that point," Mitch said, matter-of-factly.

"She asked me to prom." Oliver expected this confession to be peppered with more embarrassment.

"You like those firecrackers," Mitch said.

"I didn't say I liked her."

"You didn't say you *didn't* like her," Mitch said.

Oliver opened his mouth to defend his omission, but Joe cut him off. "So, you're going with her?"

"No." Oliver was amazed that Joe considered his going to prom with Daphne an option. Not that Oliver needed or wanted either Mitch or Joe's approval. "I'm already going with someone else."

"Pussy," Mitch teased.

"And you regret it." There was no hint of question in Joe's words. They hit Oliver with the potency of smelling salts.

Oliver tread carefully. "Regret what?"

"Going with whoever prom-queen-cheerleader-student-council-president you're going with."

"It's Penny Layton."

Mitch brightened in recognition. "From the spring break party?"

Oliver nodded.

"And the New Year's party," Joe added.

"She's hot," Mitch continued his singular thought without pause or breath, "You should've been at that party, man. It was awesome."

"So I've heard," Oliver sighed.

"Yeah, why weren't you there?" Joe trained his eyes on Oliver.

Oliver met his challenge. "If Daphne asked you to prom, would you have said yes?"

Joe shifted in his lawn chair and the hinges squeaked. "I don't know. It's something different, man. Something different." Joe tossed his empty beer across the room, aiming for the garbage can. The bottle hit the rim and bounced off, shattering on the cement floor.

Mitch rolled off his chair in a fit of laughter, prompting Oliver to laugh at Mitch's muscular body floundering on the ground. Joe joined in, laughing at his own misfortune while simultaneously sulking to the broom and dustpan resting in the corner.

Maybe Mitch and Joe weren't so bad after all. But they weren't serving their desired purpose of making him feel smarter, wiser, and more evolved as a human being. He hunched at Neanderthal level, barely upright, and drew another long swig of beer.

NIAGARA FALLS

Janine shifted on her stool at the Sweetie's counter, nearly falling off. "Holy shit! You went to Joshua Tree and found a pair of cojones on a cactus." She frothed at the mouth. "So, on a scale of one to ten…"

Daphne paused from washing the scooper in the sink. "An eight."

"An eight? That sounds horrific."

"I initiated. If he would've kissed me, it would've been a nine."

"A nine? It should be an eleven!"

"It can't be more than one hundred percent. It's statistically unsound and makes the whole rating system irrelevant."

"Why not a ten?" Janine planted her cheek into her fist.

Daphne continued scrubbing the scooper, the metal lever jangling in defiance. "I've kissed three people in my life. I don't want to set the bar at perfection with someone

I'll never kiss again. That's madness. And, actually, since I don't give out tens, nine is ten. I'm downgrading it to seven and a half. A seven-and-a-half kiss, ladies and gentlemen, nothing to daydream about here."

Janine shook her head slowly. "Poor puppy."

Lumping the three kisses together further diminished the shining glory of the Oliver kiss. Putting Janine's stupid cousin, Oliver, and Andrew Taylor in the same sentence tallied a dispiriting average on human lips.

Andrew (still revered for taking down the class bully in fifth grade with his accidentally perfect dodgeball launch) had been her first kiss. His kiss was only engraved in her mind forever because of the happenstance of it being the first. The Andrew kiss wasn't worth expanding on because it wasn't good (even to a girl who fiercely wanted to be kissed, who had an open mind and nothing to compare it to), and it was done on a dare. The dare had not been Daphne's, and Andrew had publicized his disgrace after its fulfillment. Douche.

Daphne stopped torturing the scooper and set it on a towel to dry. "So want to go stag to prom with me?"

"I don't even want to go." Janine swallowed. She'd dialed down the usual volume in her voice to barely a whisper. "I got turned down."

Daphne was equally surprised and sympathetic. "You asked someone?"

The words tumbled out against Janine's will. "Mel Jennings."

"Mel? She's hot. I love her hair."

Now it was Janine's turn to be surprised. She sat up

but kept her words low. "We've been hooking up since New Year's."

"The closet at Penny's." It all made sense. Janine hadn't been getting high, she'd been getting some.

Janine hung her head, torn between guilt and delight in her mischief.

"You literally fell out of a closet with Mel!" Daphne folded over laughing.

"I'm glad you find my coming out so funny."

Daphne cackled. "And you closed the door! You left her in there."

"She's still in there."

Daphne dug into the freezer, scooping out a cone. "Well, there's something sexy in a secret. Until it would be sexier if it wasn't a secret."

Janine's mouth twitched with the hint of a smile. "How long have you known?"

"I don't know. A while. I knew you'd talk about it when you were ready. Talking is kind of your thing."

Janine nodded.

Daphne handed her a cone with a scoop of mint chip. "You look like you could use this. Sexual liberation ice cream on the house."

"You da best."

"So, on a scale of one to ten, what's kissing Mel?"

"A ten!"

"Not even a 9.9, like gymnastics before they messed it up?"

"You know me. It's a ten or nothing."

Daphne laughed with her whole body, the oxygen of

a thousand trees filling her blood. For a few minutes, she forgot all about Oliver Pagano.

• • •

In the three weeks since the Jimmy Choo blowout, Daphne had come to terms with not seeing Oliver again until prom. She hadn't visited the chapel after school, nor dropped off any notes anywhere else. He hadn't called or texted, probably didn't miss her at all, which was particularly infuriating. A nerve in her left eyelid would twitch if she thought about it for more than five minutes. By this point, the twitch was commonplace.

She was leaving Sweetie's after her shift when she spotted someone leaning against the side of the building.

The shadow spoke, "Hey."

She didn't look at him because she didn't want to smile. She didn't want to cry. "Hi, Oliver."

"I found a trail that has a waterfall. For Niagara Falls."

She shook her head, "I don't know…"

"We've come this far. We're almost done. It's crazy to quit now." Desperation overwhelmed the enthusiasm in his voice.

She remained uninspired. "Maybe the crazy part was starting in the first place."

He ignored her negativity and kept buzzing like a salesman. "We could go tomorrow morning."

"I'm working tomorrow morning."

"I know, I called and asked Jed which shifts you were working this week."

Daphne glanced inside. Behind the counter, the freckles

on Jed's cheeks rose with pride. She swung the door open. Paired with the glare on her face, the bell clanging against the door frame didn't have a welcoming effect. "Jed, from now on, never give out my shift information."

Jed's cheer faded into failure. She started to let the door close and swung it open again, attempting to remove the bullet she'd lodged in the messenger. "Please."

"I asked him to switch shifts with you tomorrow and he said he would," Oliver explained.

She swung the door open again. "Jed, from now on, please don't switch shifts with me unless I ask you to."

Jed nodded, beaten by the day.

"I also told him to cover for you if your mom calls," Oliver added.

Daphne swung the door open again. "Jed, if my mom calls, please cover for me. Cleaning the bathroom, you know the drill." The door fell to a close and she tugged it back open. "Thanks, Jed."

Jed beamed, redeemed.

"He likes you," Oliver stated the obvious.

"Who doesn't?" Passive aggression was her current superpower.

"Let me give you a ride home."

"I want to walk. I'll see you tomorrow at ten." She hastened without glancing behind her. However long he'd lingered or watched her, she was five blocks closer to not caring.

The next morning came sooner than she'd expected. She knew getting in Oliver's car was a mistake before he'd even pulled up to the curb. She wasn't in the mood to socialize, to swallow her feelings, to be the bigger person, to be an adult. Yes, she was being petty, but she didn't care. She'd been an adult for the last seven years. It was someone else's turn.

Upon arrival, Oliver was his usual, considerate self. He'd packed them lunches, brought enough water for two camels, and carried it all in his own bookbag, leaving nothing for Daphne to bear except the weight of her mind.

They started out on the wooded, secluded trail. Ten minutes away from civilization and they were in the middle of nowhere. That was the magic of the L.A. foothills.

"What are you doing after prom?" Oliver asked.

Daphne heard the same reluctance in his voice that she felt in her own stomach. Yet, they'd both been compelled against their better judgment to make this day work. "Norae bong," she said.

"What's that?"

She wasn't in the mental state to play this game. Prom would always be a spot that was sore to his touch, afterparty included. "It's karaoke, but better. Why are you asking? It's not like you care."

"I wouldn't ask if I didn't care."

Daphne responded with a huff. She had only bitterness to expel and he didn't deserve it, so she stopped there.

Oliver accepted the olive branch. "Fine, we won't talk. Let's enjoy nature."

Waves of nausea rolled through Daphne. Spending time with Oliver used to make her feel queasy in a good way. Now the movement of her innards felt like E. coli consumption. There was such a fine line between elation and lethal bacteria.

The awkward hike stretched for miles. They got to the

waterfall, a sad excuse for a stream that happened to be flowing in a downward motion. Under normal circumstances, she would have ooed and aahed at the sight of trickling water in the Los Angeles metropolitan area. But with prom looming and the tension of the delayed arrival of her Berkeley acceptance, Daphne was not romanced by small quantities of dihydrogen monoxide.

"This is it?" she muttered.

"You were expecting Niagara Falls?"

"I was at least expecting something pretty."

"It's pretty. Kind of."

"You could stand at the top and pee and it would have the same effect."

"I'd have to consume a lot of beers."

"Anything is possible if you put your mind to it."

Oliver couldn't tell if they were tossing jokes or hurling insults. "You must think very little of how I spend my time." He smiled.

"Who even wants to go to Niagara Falls, anyway? What's the big deal?"

"Well, it's huge. The photos probably don't do it justice."

Daphne's face burned. "It's a suicide hot spot."

"Don't go there, Daph."

"They probably made elaborate plans to jump off together holding hands."

"You're making this ugly when it was probably innocent." He scratched his neck. "You know there's always a rainbow at the bottom of the falls, where the mist hangs in the air?"

"Too bad they'd never see past the rain. And when did you become a 'there's a rainbow at the end of everything' type of person? It's trickery of light. You're resting your laurels in illusions, now?"

"I never would've brought you here if I thought it would upset you."

"What did you hope to accomplish?" She asked as an emotionless, blank slate so he'd have to give a real answer.

"I wanted to check something off the list." He took a breath, knowing he needed to reveal more. "I wanted to talk to you. I wanted things to feel normal again."

"Maybe this is the new normal."

"You want that?"

"I can't change it. Neither can you."

They turned together and began the long walk back to the car. Birdsong grated against her eardrums. Oliver kicked a pinecone into the dense trees, playing games.

"Why are we doing the list?" she snapped. "Emily and Jason aren't watching us. We aren't learning anything about them. And whatever I've learned about you and myself, I wish I didn't know."

"You mean that?" He sounded like he'd been punched in the face, rubbing his sore cheek in disbelief.

"No. But I wish I did." She searched the sky for clouds but found only blue and smog.

He spoke with pauses, giving her chances to cut him off. "Then we should stop. Hanging out. The list. Everything. Finito."

Daphne nodded, not out of anger or exhaustion or grief. She nodded because she wanted it to end. He was right. She wanted more from him than she was ever going to get. It was time to let go, even if that meant letting go of Emily, too. It wasn't worth finding Emily if it meant losing herself.

"Whatever we're doing, it's important. It means something." He glanced down, unwilling to beg to her face. Oliver wasn't ready to let go, but he wasn't ready to hold on.

"I think I've gotten everything I can get from the list. It's been…" She didn't owe him absolution or contempt. "You know what it's been." She looked straight at him, neither happy nor sad, but no longer bitter. It was the least she could do for Oliver, Emily, Jason, and herself.

"Give me some more time. To figure things out." His eyes were still in the dirt.

"What things?"

"About dating…seeing…you."

"Oliver, I'm not big on ultimatums, but if you wanted to be with me, you'd already know. I've accepted that. It's time to move on. For both of us."

"I'm complicated."

"You're not that complicated." She smirked at him, a smirk from the past with no subtext, all in good humor.

He craned his neck, acknowledging one of his many flaws.

The ride home was quiet, but it wasn't the airtight seal of recent car rides. The air between them blew mild amidst the melancholy wafts of uncertainty coming from the vents. The list was over. Something new had to begin for both of them, and neither of them knew what that would be.

Daphne received the answer when she emptied her mailbox that evening. One of the items was a fat packet addressed to her from The University of California, Berkeley. It should have been the happiest moment in her life. Instead, all of her energy, positive and negative, had been exhausted on Oliver Pagano: trying not to be angry with him or upset at herself for giving up on him, stamping down the warm dust that fluttered through her whenever the sound of his voice crossed her mind, trying to prepare for the devastation of seeing him with Penny at prom.

As Daphne reached her front door, she recouped a piece of her joy. Berkeley was her ticket out. No more parents, no more Oliver, no more L.A. desert masquerading as an oasis. In four months, she would be in a land of redwoods and bridges and rain and seasons.

The sound of her parents' muffled arguing from their bedroom further validated her future relocation. In response to her mother's condescending *Of courses* and *Typicals*, Daphne's dad said phrases that included *Can't afford it* and *Debt* and *Mortgage*.

"What about Daphne?" her dad asked.

"What about her? She'll be fine," her mom snapped.

The rest of the argument was too garbled for Daphne to hear. She closed her bedroom door and buried herself under the covers with Elliott Smith. She would take out every student loan herself if it meant escaping out from under the roof that held together these miserable rooms, the ghost of Emily around every corner.

• • •

Daphne zipped up her prom dress, a purchase made based on the best sale price to lack-of-hideousness ratio. In the end, a simple blue-silver sheath had been the standout. In certain lighting scenarios, it matched her eyes. Daphne liked how different it made her feel, elegant and sophisticated, two words her usual style never evoked. She paired the dress with nude heels and a carefully curated assortment of chunky necklaces that would make Iris Apfel proud.

She applied a more natural version of makeup than she normally wore and tried to convince herself that it wasn't for Oliver. It was for a change. Lots of photos would be snapped tonight, and it would be good to show off her *natural beauty*, though she still doubted its existence.

While meticulously blending her eyeshadow and highlighting her cheeks, Daphne saw Emily through her reflection. Her sister never made it to senior prom. The rational part of Daphne's brain told her that she was far more fortunate than Emily. She wasn't tortured in the same way. The parts of Emily's neurology that dangled like a broken rope bridge were (mostly) connected in Daphne's brain. Her thoughts could safely cross back and forth in her mind. Even though her life wasn't going to follow the scenic hike that flashed through her daydreams, there was a calm voice somewhere deep inside telling her that it was going to be okay. She never felt any temptation to end it all. The only times she never wanted to wake up were the nights she cried herself to sleep. But she always awoke refreshed and ashamed of her morbid wish. If a night's dreams could wipe a day away, she could only imagine what a couple years at Berkeley would do.

Still, there was that irrational part of her brain, the part that ran on passion and jealousy. The part that saw *Romeo and Juliet* as fifty percent romance and fifty percent tragedy. It casually whispered how lucky Emily had been in high school. She'd had a boyfriend who'd spent every moment beyond sleep and school with her.

Emily and Jason watch a movie on the couch. The white-

blue light from the screen flashes on their faces. Jason's arm wraps around her; she doesn't need a blanket. She nestles her head into the crook of his shoulder and he rests his chin on her head.

In the end, they had loved each other so much, their illness so in sync, that they'd chosen to die together. Why did Emily get to have that love, but she didn't?

The sun caught the edge of the 2006 nickel on the right side of her dresser. White light lasered into the mirror and blinded her. Daphne slid the nickel to the left. The sound of smooth metal against lacquered wood was satisfying on this dismal day. She propped the nickel against the mirror, Jefferson at ninety degrees. Above him, her face looking back from the mirror was incomplete.

Oh, fuck it.

She blotted on the oxblood lipstick and felt like herself.

The moment Daphne climbed in the limo bus and saw The Drama Crew and Janine, her dread melted away. Holly, Macy, Anna, Danielle, and Janine looked like different, more enhanced versions of themselves in colorful dresses and prim up-dos, and Kyle was dapper in a tux. The group cheered her entrance and adorned her with a tiara before she could refuse.

Prom was like any other dance—not so different from any other day at school, really. Removed from the classroom, the class clowns still carried on with their attention-seeking antics, the jocks were still jocks, the geeks still geeks. Fancy clothes changed nothing.

The first thing Daphne did was search for Oliver and Penny under the guise of dancing with The Drama Crew. They were easy to spot in the middle of the dance floor.

Daphne took a moment to soak them in, admire the flawless fit of Oliver's tux, the crisp edges of his bowtie, his jawline catching the glow of the disco ball.

Janine brushed up against Daphne. "You're torturing yourself."

"No, I'm facing my torture and accepting it, so it won't be torture. There, it's done." She turned to Janine. "How about you?"

"I don't think Mel's coming. She's not so far in the back of the closet that she'd come with a guy for cover. Would she? Man, I didn't even think about that. Thanks."

"That's what friends are for," Daphne apologized.

Janine twirled her around. As Daphne spun away she tripped over a pair of feet, stumbled, and was steadied by a firm pair of hands gripping her arms. Oliver's face beamed down at her.

"Two left feet," she conceded.

"Bad for dancing."

"And Jimmy Choos." She winced after saying it. The last thing she wanted was to ruin her own night by picking a fight with her nondate.

His face took on a serious tone, but he hadn't come to fight, either. "Daphne Bowman, quickest tongue in the West. You look…stunning."

Her skin went hot and bright red.

"You like how I ignored the Jimmy Choo comment?" he teased.

"Like how I ignored your fake compliment?" She smiled.

"Not fake. And not generic," he reprimanded her.

"You didn't wear the chicken suit. Big miss." She shook her head. "You look hideous."

Penny slid up to Oliver and snaked her arm around him. "I think he looks pretty damn handsome."

"There, it's decided." Daphne winked at Oliver, the same wink she tossed him when she snuck out of work. The wink from slippery shrimp and Thanksgiving, a lifetime ago. The spark of recognition in his eyes made Daphne's stomach bubble, a sensation that cued her exit. With a bizarre combination of the sprinkler and the moonwalk, Daphne shimmied over to Janine.

"That was hot." Janine snickered. "The dancing, not the weird ménage à trois."

"That was my Patronus dancing. Watch all the boys come flocking. Wait for it…"

"They'll get here. Just might not be tonight."

"Maybe they'll be waiting when I get back from the bathroom." Daphne did more of her sprinkler-moonwalk while scooting off the dance floor. She could still hear Janine snort from twenty feet away.

In the restroom, Daphne found herself hurrying, anxious to get back out on the floor. Despite being dateless, the night was shaping up to be fun, and Oliver was simply another body, another faceless penguin blurred by music. When she exited the stall, ready to repel whatever the dance floor might throw at her, a figure in red waited near the door. It took Daphne a couple seconds to notice that all the stalls were open. She was alone in the bathroom with Penny Layton.

Penny laid menacing eyes on Daphne. "You said there was nothing between you and Oliver."

Daphne washed her hands. This conversation was so fun the first time, it must be had again! Daphne punched the soap dispenser as though it had wronged her. "No, I said we weren't hooking up. Whatever is between us, is between *us*."

Daphne shook the excess water off her hands and stepped toward the door. Penny lurched sideways to block her exit. "Oly told me about the list."

The betrayal cut Daphne to the core. She hadn't even told Janine about the list in any detail. Wasn't it enough that Oliver and Penny were sucking face and probably much more? Now Oliver had given away the only part of him that Daphne possessed.

"What did he say?" Daphne didn't mean to ask the question out loud. It was supposed to remain between her ears, pounding back and forth to the beat of injustice.

"That's between *us*." Defensiveness trembled through Penny's voice, a frailty Daphne could easily identify because she'd heard it in her own voice so many times. It was all so ironic. Daphne couldn't keep herself from laughing, a full, rough cackle.

"What's wrong with you?" Penny tried to sound superior, but intimidation tinged her question.

Penny's doubt only fueled Daphne's laughter. Here she was, spending her prom cornered in a bathroom by the dance captain. Penny's prettiness and popularity had unraveled, her insecurity laid bare. This is what Oliver Pagano did to girls without even trying. Daphne's own emotional threads from Oliver were still frayed.

"He's here with you. What more do you want? You're Penny freaking Layton." Daphne pushed past Penny, not hard enough to knock her over, but hard enough to let her know that the conversation was finished, and Penny's pom-poms couldn't save her.

Daphne raced out onto the dance floor and lost herself in her circle of friends, jumping up and down to the beat of the bass, one song dissolving into the next. She was jarred into the present time and space when the percussion dropped out and the music slowed to a romantic sway. The Drama Crew grumbled to each other and crept off the dance floor, making space for the couples of the night.

At the edge of the dance floor, out of the corner of Daphne's eye, a set of fingers tapped on Janine's shoulder. Daphne and Janine turned around to see Mel, a vision in white, the crown of her blonde hair and bangs swept into a pompadour. She nervously scratched the lower half of her head, which was shaved.

"Wanna dance?" Mel's face was a diorama of emotions. Awe tightened her forehead, wonder glittered in her eyes, her cheeks glowed with three shades of embarrassment, and her lips pursed in anxiety. Janine might say no.

Daphne watched Janine's face. She thought of ten wise-cracks Janine would make if she saw this romantic display happening to someone else. Presently, Janine's brain was in emotional overload. Her entire body froze. All that came out was a sluggish nod. It was enough. Janine took Mel's hand and they moved to the dance floor, the slow song pushing them together and holding them tightly.

Janine's triumph warmed Daphne. The other girls and Kyle cooed, and for ten seconds all was right with the world. Holly leaned over to Daphne. "Best prom ever."

The description was accurate. For all her erroneous, silly, and masochistic notions about romance, Daphne still had the ability to be pleasantly surprised. Just then, an even larger surprise stepped in front of her. Oliver held out his hand. "May I have this dance?"

She examined his face, thinking she might have imagined his words. His eyes held that tarnished glimmer that only shone when he told the dark, absolute truth.

"I don't know, I have to check my card. It's pretty full." She should have said *yes*. Simple, direct, easily translatable. Every cell in her body screamed *yes* at a rate five times her heartbeat. Instead, she'd blurted out the usual sarcasm like an asshole Jane Austen. Noticing Penny's red silhouette looming in the distance, she corrected herself. "Okay, I think I'm available."

Oliver led her to the middle of the floor. She clasped her hands around his neck and rested her cheek against his chest. Where she belonged. He wrapped his arms around her waist and they swayed like this until the final chorus.

Oliver loosened his hold and Daphne lifted her face from the pectoral pillow. The disco ball cast colorful trapezoids on his face. His mouth struggled in an effort to smile or speak or kiss her, Daphne couldn't tell. The slow music bled into "Jump Around" and the bodies around them multiplied and flailed up and down. The door to the moment was closing. Daphne looked up at Oliver and pled for him to hold it open. Do something, anything.

But the door was heavy, and he crumpled against its weight. "Song's over." The last of his fingers lifted off her hips. He began to shift with the current around him. "It's not about the song." The dullness in his eyes cleared to amber, and he devolved into another meathead jumping up and down to a song that was older than all of them. "Come on, jump!"

She took a step back and he touched her arm. His jumping didn't miss a beat. "No, stay. Come on."

She yelled over the music. "Maybe it is about the song."

"Daph…" Oliver stopped. He didn't know what to say.

Daphne read the small lines in his forehead. He knew what he should say, and he knew what he wanted to say. Floating around behind his skull were two conflicting statements, so he said nothing. His unspoken lie and truth whipped around her until the notions of each were evaporated by the shrill bleating of the song. Daphne's pulse rattled in her chest. She was furious for allowing herself to be sucked into the Oliver vortex yet again.

Meanwhile, Penny put her dance skills to good use and bounced through the crowd. She appeared at Oliver's side like a magic trick, the big reveal. The dance floor was all smoke and mirrors. Now Daphne could see all the illusions crystal clear. The reflecting light of the disco ball illuminated the truth. "My card's full. So is yours." She turned on her heel.

Daphne bobbed with the music through the crowd to Janine, Mel, and the rest of her group of thrashing kangaroos. She wasn't ready to headbang yet, but their vitality was infectious and welcome. With each hop, her heart calmed. With each push off the ground, she pumped air into her deflated self.

RUN WITH THE BULLS

OLIVER KEPT JUMPING. HE HOPED BY REMAINING IN CONstant motion, he wouldn't feel Daphne's rejection twisting against his ribs. With each landing, the shame that accompanied whatever he'd been trying to accomplish on the dance floor eased a bit more off his shoulders.

Maybe he wanted a girlfriend, wanted an Emily.

Oliver jumped higher to knock the thought away. He wasn't Jason. He never wanted an Emily. But his mind countered itself like a kung fu master, blocking his best attacks. Daphne wasn't Emily. It was ridiculous to compare the two. One was alive, and one was buried with his brother.

Oliver's remorse also stemmed from the extinguished glimmer in Daphne's eyes, from understanding that he'd failed her yet again. Maybe she didn't want to be with him anymore. He'd done nothing but try to drive her away, and he'd succeeded. Besides baseball, it was the only sport he'd ever been good at.

He didn't have to dwell for long. Penny maneuvered herself into him. Their bodies brushed against each other as gravity pulled them to the ground. Their shared rhythm softened his knees so he couldn't jump as high, but Penny continued to jump higher, propelling herself upwards. He couldn't tell if she was a skilled jumper or if it was a power play designed to make him feel inferior. He'd practically ditched Penny at her own prom. This whole night was making Oliver question his standing as a decent human being.

"You like her," Penny shouted over the music, neither teasing nor accusing, a statement mixed with a question, delivered with an air of sexiness. Oliver got the sense that Penny had played these romantic games before. She might even be better at them than him, and he felt an odd sense of security.

"I'm not gonna lie, I like a lot of things." He cringed at his own statement. He'd turned into one of those smarmy guys who said smarmy things to salvage smarmy situations.

The smarminess passed through Penny without evoking any decipherable expression. Perhaps she was immune. "It doesn't look like she's interested. And I like a lot of things, too. The things that are jumping right in front of me."

Oliver appreciated her confidence. It reminded him of his own—bold and slightly false. "Do you want to get out of here?" he asked.

"More than anything." The line sounded like she pulled it out of her back pocket every time the opportunity presented itself, which was too often. Without thinking more deeply into it, Oliver took Penny's hand and led her to the nearest exit. He refused to turn and see if Daphne caught them leaving. He didn't want to be pelted with her smugness from across the room, nor did he want to witness her not noticing.

A black hole in place of the Pacific Ocean amassed outside Oliver's driver window. He was afraid that if he looked outside for too long, it would swallow him up. Penny had taken control of the radio, and EDM wasn't his favorite. He appreciated the crescendo of composition, but he wanted lyrics, something to sing along with. As long as it wasn't Elliott Smith.

"You dropped this."

Penny was holding out her hand. He recognized the paper, its even folds and bent edges, from the corner of his eye. Shit.

"When we were doing all those funny poses for the group photo," she said.

Bringing the list to prom had been stupid, reckless. It had been a last-minute decision, based on some half-baked rationalization that maybe Oliver could give Jason the chance to experience the prom, too. Ridiculous. Jason hadn't been there, hadn't experienced anything.

Oliver was driving to forget. Daphne Bowman and the numbers on the list were disappearing with each bend in the Pacific Coast Highway, and now Penny would have ten thousand questions. Clever of her to wait until he was trapped in the driver's seat.

He took the list and dropped it into the cup holder, done with it for tonight. He wasn't going to offer any information. She would have to ask.

"Daphne told me about the list. When we were in the bathroom."

Something invisible punched Oliver in his Adam's apple. "What did she say?"

"What do you think she said?"

Oliver smiled because he knew. He could bet his car, his parents' house, his entire future on Daphne Bowman's response. "Nothing."

Penny smirked back, caught in her half-truth. "You both say you're not hooking up—"

"We're not."

"Is that list why you were at Joshua Tree?"

"Yeah." He didn't want to talk about it. But if he said he didn't want to talk about it, she'd want to talk about it even more.

"You're finding closure?"

Closure. A word only used by people who weren't searching for it.

"Something like that," he said.

"I hope you find it. Both of you." She looked out her window into the black hills dotted with house lights.

"Thanks." Oliver kept his eyes on the road. Maybe Penny and Daphne *had* been close friends, once upon a time, odd as it seemed. He flipped on his blinker. "This is it."

Mitch's aunt was out of town and through a month-long onslaught of white lies, he'd been granted a key to her beachfront Malibu home. The plan was to camp on the beach because the whole Joe-beige-carpet ordeal still had everyone on guard against indoor spillage. The party was exclusive, so the volume could be controlled—Mitch, Joe, and the Ies. Penny and Oliver were the last to arrive.

"Can you imagine living here?" Penny asked as she took in the bonfire and three small tents set up on the beach. Music rolled in with the smell of burning wood and salt air.

"No, I can't." Oliver was well aware of his upper middle-class status. He'd been born to well-off parents who were hardworking and sensible with their money. He'd gotten every possession he'd ever asked for from them, yet they'd managed to keep him from feeling entitled. Even with all of his blessings, the idea of a house in Malibu felt unattainable. The luxury of the waves only the rich could afford.

As he surveyed the fire and three tents, the numbers popped into his head from the defunct list. Four and five— skydiving and the Sahara. Biking in Venice and finding the Sphinx. Dancing in the sand and making s'mores. Wishing up to the faint stars and the kiss. The kiss. Time stretched and compressed so the memories were near and distant at the same time.

"You guys made it!" Mitch greeted Oliver at the cooler.

Oliver landed back on Malibu at this campfire, these tents, Penny. "Thanks for having us. Mitch, you remember Penny."

"Hi, Penny." Mitch grinned at Oliver a little too widely.

Penny pretended not to notice and browsed the cooler. After surveying the impending damage, she became picky in the way only girls who know they're pretty can. "Do you have any liquor? I'm not a beer fan."

"Ask and you shall receive." Mitch thrust his hand through the ice to the bottom of the cooler and surfaced with the cheapest bottle of vodka money could buy. She kissed him on the cheek, and he flushed the same shade of red as the label on the plastic bottle.

A quarter of a bottle and four beers later, Oliver and Penny sat on beach towels, facing the black roar of the ocean. The conversation when she'd given him back the list, vague as it was, hadn't been terrible. Maybe he could talk to her like he did with Da—that other person he was trying not to think about. "Penny, what's your bad?"

"What's my bad? What do you mean?"

His words slurred, "My brother killed himself seven years ago and—"

She interrupted him, "I'm so sorry, Oly—"

"There's nothing to be sorry about. The sad part is that since he died I've been so angry at him, and I tried to be so unlike him that I don't know who I am. That's my bad."

Penny debated for a moment. "I don't have a bad. I'm all good."

"Everyone has a bad."

She spoke to the endless void in front of her. "I kissed someone I shouldn't have. Messed up everything."

"What?" This wasn't the direction Oliver had antici-pated, but he couldn't judge confessions after requesting them. "I mean, who?"

"Is this Truth or Dare?"

"No." He gritted his teeth. They were back to speaking different languages.

"Then I'm not telling," she teased.

"Okay, that's a good start. What else?"

"I like my skeletons in my closet." She took a serious swig from the bottle.

"I'm not asking about skeletons."

"I shoplifted once when I was seven. I never got caught."

The hesitation in her words might have ceased the

compassionate from pressing further, but the earlier events of the evening and the licking fire behind him fueled his curiosity.

"What are you most afraid of?" he asked.

"I'm afraid you're not drinking enough." She tilted the vodka bottle in his direction, a peace offering. The fire's shadows highlighted the worry in her face.

If he disrupted the sediment lining her soul again she would ask for a ride home. Kicking up her inner dirt wouldn't save him, anyway. He took the bottle and gulped, grateful for the burn in his throat.

Enough guzzles later that the questions about the meaning of life no longer seemed pressing, Oliver leaned into Penny's waiting lips. He was reminded of the temporary greatness in the good-enough-for-now. The kiss was serenaded with the splashing of Mitch and Joe running naked into the ocean. After a flurry of profanities and speculation that their genitalia may never recover, they chanted at the Ies, trying to lure them into following.

"I think I could use another skeleton in my closet." Penny unzipped her dress and it fell to the sand at her feet. "Are you coming?"

His eyes fell with the dress and stopped at her red undergarments. "Uh-huh," he managed.

She ran into the water, screaming before the cold took her breath away. Oliver stripped down to his boxers and chased after her.

Where Penny harbored a skeleton, Oliver washed himself clean. In water over their heads, they wrapped their arms and legs around each other for warmth, skin prickled with goose bumps, kicking to stay afloat, kissing to breathe. The waves pushed them in and pulled them out. The current drifted them back to waist-high water. Mitch, Joe, and the Ies catcalled at Oliver and Penny's exposed upper halves. Penny sank down into the water to hide her now sheer bra, and Oliver kneeled with her. They either needed to move out further or leave the water altogether.

"I'm cold." Penny shivered with purple lips.

"Me, too."

"Will you hide me?"

Oliver sashayed up the beach, using his body to screen Penny's. Mitch and Joe booed across the beach, and the Ies smacked and punched their chest and arms.

In the tent, Oliver and Penny wrapped each other in towels. She took another hefty swig of vodka and poured a little glug on his neck. He jumped.

"What the…"

She attacked his neck with her tongue, giggling.

"Oh, okay. That's kind of wasteful. But for a good cause. It would probably work better with tequila. You know, with the ocean salt."

Penny drizzled a glug on her own neck.

"I get it. You're trying to shut me up." He licked her neck.

She eased to the ground and sat on the sleeping bag like a cheerleader, legs folded to the side in two triangles. All that was missing were the pom-poms. And her clothes. She reached up and took Oliver's hands, pulling him down.

"I'm really drunk," he said. It wasn't a lie. However, he'd been drunker in previous social situations and never needed to announce it.

"Me, too." Penny kissed him. Her fingers ran along the band on his boxers.

He envisioned the future. He could close his eyes and let it happen. It would feel so good, so warm, so close. He opened his eyes, expecting to see Daphne. He jerked his head when Penny's almond eyes leveled with his. Maybe he was drunker than he thought.

"Are you okay?" Her real question was *Did I do something wrong?*

"No." He'd answered the wrong question. "I mean, yes."

Oliver read the impending conversation in the crystal balls of her heavy eyes.

Let's not do this, he'd say.

Why? Is it me? she'd ask.

It's the opposite of you, he'd reassure, unsuccessfully.

She kissed him, and he tried kiss Daphne away, but she wasn't leaving. Visions of their adventures in Joshua Tree, and Venice Beach, and Chinatown swirled in his closed eyes. His best friend was gone, and for a terrifying five seconds he had a lump in his throat that he couldn't swallow around. He couldn't even move his tongue to keep kissing Penny. Tears weren't far behind. He needed to end the Daphne montages by ending the night, and he had two options—have sex with Penny or keep his proverbial pants on and try to spoon away her insecurity until sleep put them both out of their misery. The easier, former option pulled at him with astounding force.

"Oly?" Penny had noticed that his jaw had stopped moving.

"Yeah, I feel kind of woozy." It was more of a croak than a sentence. He reclined onto the sleeping bag.

"Oh." Surprise, failure, annoyance, relief, so many emotions rolled off of one syllable, a single vowel.

"I think I need to sleep." He closed his eyes.

"Look who can't handle their liquor," she scoffed.

Tonight, he wasn't handling anything particularly well. The evening deserved to end with him sleeping in the cold puddle of a lie. "I'm a lightweight."

"Can I get you anything? Water?"

"No, just lay your beautiful self next to me."

She rested her head on his chest. "You better not puke on me."

"Oh, you're not into that?" he laughed.

"Ew!" She jabbed her fist into the fleshy part of his side.

He closed his eyes and pulled her close. Her breath tickled his cheeks, and he could feel her eyes, closer than her mouth, questioning everything. He relaxed his arms, turned his head, and pretended to be asleep. After a few minutes, she settled against his ribs and his breathing fell into sync with hers.

The next morning, they woke to the chorus of the surf. Penny leaned onto Oliver's bare chest and propped up her chin with her elbows. "I had a great time last night."

This was the moment when Oliver should have climbed through the hangover déjà vu and gotten out of the tent.

I can't do this.

I'm sorry, I think we should just be friends.

It's the opposite of you. Really.

But Oliver was still trying to piece together where the ocean ended and last night's dreams started. Penny had one foot in each. "Me, too."

● ● ●

The day at Disneyland was a blur, as intended. Joe had borrowed his mom's SUV so they could ride together and save gas money. Oliver tried to drive separately, but Joe gave him a glare that threatened their friendship, and Joe didn't bluff. Fortunately, the Ies and Penny slept the whole way, and Oliver made a playlist that would keep Joe awake. Upon arrival, the crew chugged the leftover cooler contents, loaded up on gum and mints, and made their way into the park. Penny marked her territory with Oliver on each ride, holding his hand in line, kissing him to celebrate each passing minute, pulling him behind a bush and sucking on his ear. It was claustrophobic and, appropriately, Oliver's world felt small (after all). He hadn't had the *we should just be friends* talk. It was a difficult conversation to strike up when constantly surrounded by Mitch and Joe and the Ies. Every moment they were alone Penny countered by attaching her face to him.

Oliver bought her cotton candy as a distraction. "If the roller coaster got stuck upside down, what would be your biggest regret?" He wanted her to respond by asking him the same question.

"Uh, nothing, because they would get us down and we'd be fine." She tore from the blue cloud of woven sugar.

"What if they could only save one of us, and you had to sacrifice your life to save mine?" He chuckled to soften the hypothetical. "Not that you owe me your life or anything."

She groaned off the question. "Why are you a sad drunk, Oly?"

"I'm this sad sober, too." He flashed her a somber smile that she refused to believe.

She tapped the inside of his knee with hers. "No, that isn't who you are."

Her words summoned the wind. The fog of uncertainty that had been surrounding Oliver dissipated into the immaculately cultivated grounds in every direction. The answer was clear, probably always had been, but he was finally able to see it. He wanted to be seen, wanted someone who wasn't afraid to lift up his dark corners and dance in the soot. "All the good and all the bad."

"What?" Penny was losing patience.

He didn't have time to explain. "I have to go."

"To the bathroom?" Worry flooded her eyes.

"Home. I'll take a cab. I'll pay for it, if you want to come. Please, come."

Penny's face blistered at his proposition. "You're going to ditch me here?"

The fury in her voice pinched the nerves in his neck. He took a deep breath. "Penny, I'm so sorry. I can't date you right now." *I didn't realize, but there's someone else,* edited for cruelty.

"What?" Penny wasn't used to rejection. Her undeveloped skill of hiding hurt, anger, and dismay allowed her emotions to take over the landscapes of her face.

The pain in his neck doubled. "I'm a huge asshole, I know. I hope we can be friends."

"Seriously?"

"You can beat me with your cotton candy if you want." He hoped suggesting physical harm upon himself would prove his sincerity. He was not expecting the empty gesture to fill his eyes with blue fluff and the edge of the cardboard cone to dig into his nose.

"We're in the happiest place on Earth!" Her exasperation cried up to the sky.

He scraped the sugary cobweb off his face. "Well played. But, I mean it, Penny. I think you're a cool person, and I'd like to be your friend." The top layer of fibers had already melted onto his skin, staining his face with sugar. When he opened his eyes, Penny was gone. All the children and adults in his vicinity stared at him, the unexpected attraction of the day. They were unsure whether to laugh or show concern.

Oliver took off and weaved through the horde of sweating, sunburnt people, joyful barriers between him and the future. Through her irony, perhaps Penny was right about this being the happiest place on Earth. It all depended on who was standing next to you.

During the long ride home, Oliver tried to doze to pass the time, but his heart was in his stomach. The stickiness coating his face wasn't helping. The cab pulled up to the Bowman residence. As usual, the empty driveway and yard offered no clues as to who was inside. Oliver stepped up to the door and rang the bell. He waited for Daphne to answer. After that, he didn't know, didn't care.

Instead, Daphne's dad opened the door and the excitement circulating in Oliver's chest dissipated. Tim looked nothing like Oliver had imagined, appearing both older and younger than his preconception. His forehead was etched with lines, but his eyes held the same blue youth as Daphne's.

Tim's face lit up in recognition and dimmed in correction, knowing and not knowing the face before him.

"I'm Oliver…Pagano." Oliver cleared his throat. "I'd like to date your daughter. Please. Sir."

Tim nodded, affirming his own sanity. He did know this face. "Jason's brother. You look like him."

The inevitable resemblance romanticized by memory. Oliver tucked his chin, his reflex at the mention of this curse that time couldn't break. His eyes and bone structure would always be a mirror for Jason. Oliver's reflection was the living remains.

"Both good-looking boys," Tim continued.

"Thank you. But, I'm not much like Jason." The theme of the last seven years bore repeating.

"You want to date my daughter. That makes you more like him than anything can make you unlike him."

Oliver's shoulders sagged. The Bowmans sure knew how to prove him wrong when it came to Jason.

Tim picked up on Oliver's body language. "But, I understand what you're saying. Would you like to come in?"

"No, I'm going to loiter on your doorstep, if you don't mind."

"Her mother and I will have to talk about her dating. It's a contentious matter. As I'm sure you're aware."

Oliver nodded.

"You gave Daphne that drawing, with the mask and the knife?"

"She showed you that?"

"Her mom looks through her stuff," Tim admitted.

Daphne hadn't exaggerated the police state of her household.

Tim brushed off his remorse in parental fashion, as

though it hadn't existed. "You're talented. Is that what you want to do after college? Work in art or design?"

The suggestion caught Oliver off guard. "I don't know. I hadn't considered it. Maybe."

"Well, it was a great gift. She's a fighter, that one. Stronger than any of us."

"Yes, she is."

"When Daphne was little and first started dressing herself, she would wait…" Tim paused, determining the least masochistic way to tell his story. He swallowed, but somehow his throat sounded drier than before. "She would wait until Emily ate breakfast to see what Emily was wearing and find the closest thing to it. Daphne marched up with her cereal bowl in her matching outfit and Emily would act so annoyed. But her mom and I saw right through it. Emily was flattered. She knew she was Daphne's hero."

Oliver smiled, thinking of the Emily-approved outfits Daphne still wore.

"Even now, I can't believe how Emily knew that, and still…" Tim's sympathetic glance fell on Oliver. "Well, you know better than anyone."

Oliver hadn't been placing himself in the context of Tim's story. Jason hadn't been his hero. He'd never dressed like Jason. They'd played video games together, but Oliver had adjusted to one-player games without sentimentality. Oliver only missed a few of the comic book titles he'd stopped buying after his brother's death. And Jason had been a wrestler, a sport Oliver had no interest in.

Suddenly, the realization struck him. Baseball. Oliver had buried it. Something painful now radiated in the afternoon light.

Oliver had devoted his summers to baseball in grade school. He'd been an outstanding player, winning scholarships to various camps. Though baseball wasn't Jason's sport, he'd played catch with Oliver every time he'd asked, which had been virtually every day from March through October. Even on the dark days and the summer before the end, Jason had never protested. After Jason died, Oliver had continued to play for a while, but it wasn't fun anymore. He stopped improving, stopped caring. His teammates caught up and surpassed his skill.

Oliver had always attributed this loss of interest to finding greater appeal in football and basketball—sports with cheerleaders. But it had all stemmed from Jason, from Jason's absence in the backyard, Jason's baseball mitt tucked away in a closet, collecting moths. The realization yanked Oliver's breath from his throat.

"Daphne needed a hero..." The man in the doorway housed a monster of regret.

Oliver pretended not to notice that Tim was tearing up. The effort revived Oliver's lungs. *You could still be her hero.* Oliver drove the words from his mind to his mouth but couldn't get them out.

Tim bowed out as gracefully as the haunted can. "I don't know when she'll be home. But if you change your mind, the door's open."

"Thank you." At that moment, Oliver was thankful for countless things, one of them being Jason.

Tim closed the door and left Oliver alone on the doorstep. He stared out into the front yard, never checking his phone, willing time to pass, judging the hours by the lowering of the sun in the sky, the yellow flame melding to orange and pink and purple.

The limo bus pulled into the driveway at the last shades of sunset. Daphne's bare feet stepped down onto the concrete, her heels dangling by the straps clutched in her hand. Her blue-gray sheath bore the wrinkles of a fun night and a long day. A chorus of goodbyes spilled onto the driveway behind her. She laughed and waved at the bus, her shoes flopping around like puppets on strings.

Oliver clambered to his feet with stiff knees and a belly full of firecrackers. The movement on her porch caught Daphne's eye. She didn't pause or speed up en route to the front door. The fire under his ribs compelled him toward her.

As the bus backed out of the driveway, Janine's voice shot through the cracked window and rolled across the lawn. "Stop!"

The limo bus screeched to a halt. Janine demanded with utmost seriousness, "Do not move this bus."

The bus lurched on its wheels, shifting into park. Behind Daphne's head, Oliver noticed the shadows of dark faces against the window, a captive audience for his lawn theater. Daphne kept a safe distance between the two of them. Oliver estimated the space to be the length of her arm plus the length of the shoes and their straps, should she be tempted to use them as weapons like Penny had.

In the hours spent waiting on her doorstep, Oliver had come up with three things he could say. With each step toward her, he'd left them behind, one by one, flattened beneath his shoes crunching on the grass. If she wanted an explanation, he could supply it later. "Can I be your boyfriend?"

The comeback flashed across her forehead: *I don't know, can you?* She searched his eyes for the truth, waiting for him to rescind his words, erase the mistake, as he'd done so many times before. Before she could question any longer or louder with her bright eyes, he closed them by stepping into her with a kiss. Their mouths pressed and pulled. With each movement, the weight from the last seven years lifted off his shoulders. His hand reached to her face and caressed her jawline. Her shoes clattered on the driveway as her hands moved to his chest, her body fitted against his.

The kiss ended on its own terms, her soft lips brushing against his one final time. Excessive whooping filled the bus, to the point where the driver had to open the door to let the noise escape into the evening breeze. Oliver hung his head, a deep blush conquering his cheeks. Daphne flashed ten fingers behind her, wiggling them against her tailbone. He knew it meant something good.

"That's right, baby. Nothing less!" Janine yelled from the bus doorway. Behind her, Mel laughed. She looped her arms around Janine's waist and kissed her neck. The door closed, leaving them in silhouette as the bus eased onto the street and into the sunset.

Daphne stood still. She and Oliver looked at each other like they were new people. "Your eyebrows and eyelashes are blue," she said.

"I got what I deserved."

She stuck out her lower lip but decided against further questioning.

"Want to go for a walk?" he asked.

The enthusiasm in Daphne's nod suggested that if he'd asked her to trek to the nearest landfill and dig for pennies, she'd have the same reaction.

"Let me change." She went inside.

"I'll be here."

Oliver waited for half an hour before Daphne reappeared in a T-shirt, jeans, and the Emily boots.

"High maintenance," he quipped.

"I had to call my mom, make sure we're all on the same page about me going for a stroll with someone of the opposite sex. I don't even remember what I had to sign away to be standing here right now."

"But you're here."

"I'm here."

He took her hand. Their fingers fit together as though they were designed for this very moment.

• • •

Oliver prepped in the mirror for his first real date with Daphne—dinner and a movie on a school night, another step into adulthood. His lungs prickled in a good way, like he was grabbing the world and holding on for the ride. He celebrated the special occasion by working extra texturizer through his hair.

As Oliver crossed Daphne's yard, the static in his chest hardened to lead. The front door floated ajar, creaking with the draft. Oliver stepped back and gave the house a once-over. All the windows, and the garage door, were closed. Everything appeared normal. He pushed the front door open and poked his head inside. "Hello?"

The sound of shuffling feet and the hiss of running water came from the kitchen, but he couldn't see anything. He tiptoed through the living room. Only a sliver of the kitchen was visible through the crack of the doorway, but he made out reddish, syrupy splotches on the floor. With each step, they grew redder. Blood. A butcher's knife rested beside the sink. Daphne was the pair of feet, darting across the doorway.

He charged over, too scared to call out her name. When he reached the doorway, the sight of blood stopped him in his tracks. The larger-than-expected quantity of it was drizzled all over the floor, the counter, and the sink. Against the blue-red, the tile brightened to avalanche white.

Daphne opened and slammed drawers, leaving bloody smears on the wood. Her T-shirt quivered between her shoulder blades, and her breath sounded as though it was being wrenched from her throat. Oliver stepped straight through the chaos to reach her. He grabbed her arms and turned up her wrists. The skin was unscathed, blue veins under blood-crusted skin. His relief came out in a curt exhalation, the first time his lungs had worked since discovering the open front door.

Daphne's eyes shot up to meet his. "It's from my dad." She shook off Oliver's hands. "He's in the garage." She grabbed a stack of dish towels from the drawer.

"I didn't...I saw all the blood, the knife..."

She turned off the faucet. "A knife in a kitchen. Imagine." It sounded more like spitting than words.

The scream of the approaching siren startled them both.

"Stay here." She bolted out the door connecting the house to the garage.

Voices murmured through the wall and Oliver heard the garage door grind up. He lingered in the kitchen for a few minutes. He thought he might be sick. To distract himself, he moved to a clean patch of tile, streaking it crimson with the bottoms of his shoes.

Oliver had never been good at following instructions, and he needed air. He removed his shoes, crossed the carpet, and waited on the driveway. It occurred to him that he was watching this gruesome scene play out mere feet from where his brother had died. He kneeled and hung his head to keep from vomiting.

Under the fluorescent lights in the garage, Tim's pale face was ghoulish green. His blue eyes lost all resemblance to Daphne's as they drifted around the room. Blotches of pink emerged through the bandages on the underside of his left forearm and in the crease of his palm. He wobbled on his feet and made strange sounds that never took the shape of words. The paramedics struggled to load him on the gurney.

"No, don't try to walk, Dad. Sit down." Daphne was the adult, as usual, injecting normalcy into the situation. Tim protested with incoherent babble but resigned himself to the gurney. The metal creaked in acceptance.

Daphne's face pulled taut, ready to snap when no one was looking. She followed the gurney into the sundown spectacle. Neighbors gathered where the base of the driveway met the road. Their whispers crept over the boundary of the street. Oliver met Daphne halfway down the driveway, watching the gurney legs lurch up and slide into the ambulance. He doubted that in the past five minutes she'd forgiven him for insinuating that she was suicidal and/or accident prone, so he didn't try to hold her hand. He brushed her arm so she would know he was there. Her stillness hinted that she'd already discerned his presence.

"It's just like that night. I was right here. The ambulance." Her voice was simultaneously thick and light. She almost sounded drunk.

He wanted to say the thing that she would say to him if their worlds were reversed. He scrambled through the sage ridges of his intellect, empty and out of time. His response was inadequate but necessary. "He's going to be fine, Daph."

His words mended no wounds and her eyes pitied him. She climbed into the ambulance. Oliver wasn't sure what he'd failed at, but he was determined to fail better. "I'll be waiting at the hospital."

The ambulance doors closed on her distraught face. The vehicle pulled away, graciously waiting a block before igniting its siren. Oliver dragged a garden hose from the side of the house and sprayed down the garage and driveway. The neighbors scattered, nothing to see lest their toes be stained with blood.

He knew which hospital to go to; he'd been there before. Oliver sat in the waiting room for an hour listening to the squeak of shoes on the never-quite-clean floor. The last time he'd sat in this room was the night Jason died. Oliver had rushed to the hospital in a similar manner. It was the only time that he'd ridden in his parents' car without wearing a seatbelt. Not comprehending the severity of the situation, his mom and dad downplaying expertly, Oliver had relished the rogue adrenaline of avoiding the belt and buckle. They hadn't noticed his liberated shoulders jostling against the backseat, his body open and susceptible to injury. The price of freedom.

At the hospital, his parents had been quiet. They had cried, but not overtly. They must have sensed Jason was gone before getting confirmation and held it together for Oliver so as to not upset him. He loved and hated them for this. In one sense, he hadn't been scarred by their cries for the rest of his days. On the other hand, for the duration of his parents' lives, he would have to hold his wits about him under terrible circumstances when all he wanted to do was crumble and let them sweep up his wreckage.

When he spotted Daphne walking down the hall, he jogged to meet her arms. The way they clamped onto his back before he came to a full stop restored his faith in himself.

"I'm sorry." *For your deadbeat dad, and for accidentally thinking you were trying to off yourself.* He squeezed her tighter.

"My mom's here. We're only all together if something bad happens."

"Want to get out of here for a few?" It was a well-intentioned, yet selfish, request.

"I can't leave."

"Maybe some food?"

She nodded, and her chin dug into where his neck met his shoulder.

In the hospital cafeteria, they each took a tray and shuffled through the long, eclectic line: bereaved visitors ceding to sustenance, staff wishing they'd packed a dinner, and patients proving they could feed themselves in hopes of release.

Oliver hadn't eaten a cafeteria lunch since sophomore year. If he put on blinders and didn't breathe through his nose, he could pretend they'd travelled back in time and he and Daphne were in the school lunch line. He settled on a chicken cutlet, mashed potatoes, and corn. But not just any corn—magical cafeteria corn that's bathed in a top secret substance so it tastes unlike corn or anything else on Earth. His nostalgia was quickly overpowered by the scent of bleach.

Daphne played it safe and plopped a premade tuna salad sandwich on her tray. "He lost a lot of blood, but he'll be okay. Maybe some nerve damage in his hand."

They were nearly to the cashier when Daphne stopped moving with the pull of the line. Her lips quivered, and the trembling spread to her jaw and downward. The silverware clattered on her tray. Oliver didn't hug her, fearful that he might break a seal that needed to stay intact. She was on the brink but still holding together.

"Hey, it's okay. You'll feel better after you eat." He dumped the contents of her tray onto his and pushed against her so she slid the final few steps to the cashier. The seal broke. Her hands sprang to her face, sobs leaking through the seam where her pinkies met. The cashier gave Oliver a concerned look while she counted his change.

He wrapped his free arm around Daphne and led her to a table near a window so she could face outside. He moved his chair close to hers, and she lowered her shield. The capillaries under her eyes and around her nose looked like they'd been drawn on by a spider with a red pen at the end of each of its legs. And there was black makeup everywhere.

He'd seen her cry before, been the cause of the tears.

Those tears had tumbled down her cheeks with grace, as effortless as drawing breath. These tears possessed her, unwilling to relent until they had all been cried out. He knew it was partially his fault. There was nothing he could do to make it better, to make it go away. He was just as helpless now as he'd been at eleven years old, in this same hospital. History was repeating itself, and it wasn't easier the second time around. Seven years' worth of tears were building in his eyes, too.

His instinct was to resist, hold his eyes open to dry them out, but it wasn't working. He wanted to appreciate the breakthrough, the fete of experiencing something that moved him to tears. The truth was he hated himself for crying at this moment. He hadn't cried since Tricia's breakup letter, head buried in his pillow. Now, in public, in front of the one person he needed to be strong for, he was falling apart.

"I thought you knew me." She looked straight through him.

"I know you." A tear licked against his cheek and the sensation was so foreign it startled him.

"You thought I'd slashed my wrists. You thought I was like them. Because I told you I was scared of becoming mentally ill. I never should've told you that."

"No. You were standing in all the blood. There was so much blood. I lost my mind." A goatee of tears collected on his chin.

Daphne grabbed his hand, which meant his face looked more discombobulated than hers. With her touch, he let go. The embarrassment washed away with the deluge of tears. Empty and full and free.

"You don't want this. Tears in a hospital cafeteria." Her self-deprecation couldn't camouflage the fear. She thought he was going to break up with her.

He did his best to not sound insulted. "Daph, this wet face I'm sporting, it's been a long time coming and it feels kind of amazing."

"I don't know if I believe you."

"Why would I lie?" he asked.

"Why would you tell the truth?" Daphne responded.

"Because it's what we do, you and me. We're slayers of the truth."

Her eyes sparked with something he couldn't identify, another mystery for another day.

"This isn't a breakup meal." He wiped his nose.

"You do that? Breakup meals?" She took a bite of her sandwich as an excuse not to hold his hand or look at him.

"It's happened. Usually unintentionally."

"Usually." Daphne rolled her eyes.

"Is this how we fight? You lift a word or phrase that I've said and roll your eyes?"

She caught herself rolling her eyes again and almost smiled.

He smirked. "I like it. And you've mastered it."

"We're not fighting."

"And I'm not breaking up with you."

"Okay." Even if she believed him, she still couldn't look at him. "My dad decided to prune the shrubs with the electric trimmer. While wasted."

"Shit."

"He slashed his wrist and nearly lost a finger. He says it was an accident, but you can form your own conclusions.

And he's blaming it on poor gardening skills." Her eyes were dry, but she was inconsolable. At least her sandwich was gone.

"Look, you'll be out of here soon. One more summer, and you'll be away from them all." *And from me.* It was almost enough to send another tear down his face. He swallowed against it.

Daphne's gaze met his. She'd added the *from me* as well. Maybe this whole meltdown was equal parts pruning incident and their own severed nerves. Daphne didn't have it all figured out anymore.

He welcomed her to his world with a wistful grin and a shrug. "And your parents only have so many limbs they can cut off, so there's a light at the end of the bloody tunnel."

Daphne smiled, nearly laughed. Every piece of Oliver went warm.

"Can I have some of your corn?" she asked.

"I don't know. Maybe you should be punished for ordering poorly."

She dug her fork into his plate. "What do you want for ordering wisely?"

"Nothing I don't already have."

"I'm sure you can come up with something." She winked, and his heart leapt. He had a few ideas, but he kept them to himself while he let her eat all of his corn.

The fatigue of the evening set in and smothered the playfulness between them. They cleared their trays and an empty elevator whisked them downstairs. The fantasy of time travel to a shared school cafeteria dissipated when the elevator doors opened to real life. Daphne dropped his hand in the waiting room.

"Do you want me to go in with you?" he asked.

"No. Thanks. I'm sorry you had to see him like that. It's him, but it's not him. But it's him. I wish you would've known him...before."

"You wouldn't be nearly as interesting. I probably wouldn't like you at all. I know you wouldn't like me."

"I barely like you now." Her mouth tilted slyly.

"Exactly." He'd said all the right things and meant every word. He was learning. She kissed him goodbye and it was better than the sidewalk after Joshua Tree or the driveway after prom.

Oliver went home and sought out his parents. They were combing through design books in bed.

"Goodnight."

He could tell by their incredulous expressions that they questioned his motives. His dad recovered, not wanting to scare off the rare sighting of their son after dark. "Goodnight, Oly."

"How was the date?" His mom asked.

"Fine." Oliver took a step to walk away but turned back. "No, it was great."

His parents both smiled, sharing his excitement.

"Goodnight." He headed to his room.

"Sweet dreams," his mom called down the hall.

Oliver followed her advice.

• • •

While Tim healed, at least superficially, a full calendar of social activities distracted both Oliver and Daphne from the present and the future. They also gave Oliver the opportunity to earn Janine's approval. Daphne's best friend made little attempt to hide her skepticism. Janine was as friendly as she needed to be, and he would have to prove the rest. He finally won her heart with the suggestion of a norae bong outing. She even punched him in the shoulder, a little too hard. And Daphne was impressed at his attempt to make a positive memory out of the prom miss. The sore shoulder was worth it.

Singing in the small, dark room, Oliver was endeared to The Drama Crew for life. Or at least until the end of the summer, but he was trying not to think about that. He focused on the dancing faces surrounding him, the best one with her face next to his, matching his volume into the microphone. He and Daphne Bowman were an entity forged by depth and time, a shared tragedy and a quest to make sense out of the misunderstood. Now they were also bound by bad pop music.

The list resumed. Daphne pointed out with disdain that running with the bulls had been a Jason contribution, and Oliver couldn't disagree.

Daphne scowled. "Cows freak me out. I don't like looking something in the eye before I eat or wear it. I couldn't even look at the chicken suit without a pang of guilt."

"The running of the bulls is their chance to eat you back."

"I'm a girl, I'm not allowed to run with them. Sexist bulls."

"Let's have a different Spanish celebration," he said. His lips spread to a wide, devious grin.

"That look in your eye scares me."

"It should."

That Saturday, Oliver's enclosed backyard became a warzone, and Daphne the first victim. He delivered the shot quickly and accurately. She moaned and touched the gash beneath her ribcage, squinting down at the smattering of orange-red coating her fingers. Blood and seedy guts oozed from her shirt, dripping down her leg. When her eyes rolled up to him, for a split second, he was actually afraid.

"You're going to pay for that Oliver Pagano," she growled.

Daphne tightened her grip on the weapon and launched the tomato with a piercing war cry. The intimidation worked. His knees locked when they couldn't decide which way to run. The tomato pegged him square in the shoulder, the entrails squirting his face.

"Ah, my eye!"

The impact jolted the contents of his brain, making space for today's date. It thudded against his skull: April 28th. He'd forgotten Jason's birthday, the one day of the year he allowed happy memories of his brother and Emily.

Jason hasn't made it through the front door before Oliver bounces into his personal space.

"Can we play catch?" Oliver steps on Jason's toes.

"Ow! Dude, stop. Maybe later."

"Please!"

"I have to take a shower." Jason pulls the soaking wet Quickee Car Wash T-shirt away from his stomach. When he lets go, the fabric sucks back against his skin.

"Now! Pleasepleasepleasepleasepleasepleasepleaseplease…"

"Fine," Jason says.

Oliver grabs his hand and leads him to the backyard.

"Surprise!" The backyard ignites. Thirty bodies spring to life. Party hats and streamers catch the sun's glare. The entire wrestling team turns "Happy Birthday" into a raucous fight song, cheering after every line. Oliver's parents join in. They

light sparklers and make yellow magic against the evening sky. Emily stands front and center, a sheepish swivel in her hips.

Jason smiles, genuinely surprised. Oliver looks up to him, expecting acknowledgment for his pivotal role, but Jason only sees Emily.

"The look on your face," she laughs. "Happy birthday to me."

"You did this?" Jason asks.

She shrugs, nods, blushes.

"I hate you," he says, but his voice speaks the opposite.

"I hate you, too." She wraps her arms around him, he squeezes her tight. She whispers into his ear.

Daphne's whisper from New Year's tickled Oliver's ear drum. *"You're afraid of falling in love with me."*

He stood in the midst of a different celebration, holding a tomato. Daphne crept toward him, a fierce creature, seething, ready to kill him with love. Countering her steps, he let the fear pass over him in the shadow of a cloud. Today wouldn't be about Jason. Or Emily. Maybe next year.

"It stings!" Oliver blinked like a demented flirt and massaged his eye socket.

Daphne granted him no mercy and pelted Oliver with three more tomatoes when he turned his back to clean out his stinging eye. Janine nailed him with one on the ass for good measure before hurdling over lawn furniture like an Amazon warrior. She charged toward Mitch, Joe, and the Ies, stunned in a huddle against the fence after witnessing Daphne and Oliver's gore. Behind Janine, Mel and The Drama Crew followed, armed with heirlooms.

Mitch and Joe reciprocated, hurling a few tomatoes at the advance with glancing wounds. Mitch and Joe scattered and drew The Drama Crew after them, leaving Janine to prey on the weak. The Ies shrieked and ducked, but it was too late. Red grenades blasted against their bowed heads, dyeing their hair red. They whimpered and groaned in a fabricated way that sounded more like achievement than pain. Janine punished them for lying with two more tomatoes to the back.

"Don't be victims! Throw your damn tomatoes!" drill sergeant Janine screamed at them. Mandie grunted and threw a tomato. It floated five feet to Janine's right and nearly took out a sparrow on the bird bath.

"You will never survive the zombie apocalypse," Janine shouted.

Thunk! The left half of Janine's face oozed red. No one was more surprised than Jamie, who beheld her empty hand in wonder. In their smartest move yet, the giggling Ies retreated to the other side of the yard before Janine could retaliate. She scraped the seedy muck off her hair and flung it to the ground.

"Baby birdie's learned to fly," Janine snarled, a proud predator. She raised her arm, ready to attack the nearest running body, which happened to be Mel. They blasted each other at the same time, all is fair in love and war.

Coral streaks arched over the backyard, bloody rainbows ending in sickening splats. Red-splotched bodies staggered across the lawn in the warped game of tag. Howls of laughter called up to the sky, a prayer and an answer.

GO TO OUTER SPACE

THE MINUTES TICKED AWAY IN A DREAMY BRUME DURING the last school days. At the sound of each bell, Daphne treaded a different hallway, parked herself at another desk, and waited for the next hour to pass. She'd completed her final projects a month ago. The orientation package from Berkeley had already arrived in the mail. The envelope hadn't held the excitement she'd imagined. The present had transformed from a string of misguided events into a moment to prolong. Summer approached, only a quick series of sunsets away from fall. She would move to San Francisco. Oliver would go to Montana.

Daphne acknowledged the tail chasing brought on by the near future. Obsession changed nothing. She did her best to hold her ground in the present, kiss Oliver like there was no tomorrow. But the future, once the brightest star in the night sky, was now a threatening storm. When the wind whipped her face, she took shelter in Emily's empty bedroom.

Within weeks of her death, Emily's room had been stripped, her belongings packed and sent to storage. The canopy bed and shabby chic dressers that Daphne dreamed would belong to her once Emily went away to college were donated. The bright blue walls that Emily had painted herself were unsaturated with three coats of white. In one month, any evidence of Emily's existence in the Bowman household was erased without discussion.

There was no one Daphne could appeal to, no one to whom she could explain how whenever Emily was over at Jason's, Daphne would sit on the floor of Emily's bedroom, too afraid to sit on the bed and disturb the sheets. She would admire the blue walls, mulling over what color she should paint her own room, but she could never come up with a better color than that bright blue, the color of the sky on a sunny day after rain. Daphne looked up from the ground and imagined it was her own room for as long as she could, until she grew fearful of Emily's return.

Now Daphne sat on the same piece of floor as she had when she was ten. She flipped through color swatches in her mind, trying to find that perfect blue. Her eyes darted from corner to corner of the room until she found a remnant. An inch-long streak of sunshine blue on the ceiling had been missed by the whitewash. Emily was still here, even if she was just a sliver. Daphne pointed her phone at the speck of blue and snapped a photo. A room in her future would be painted this color.

· · ·

"Happy birthday." Oliver presented Daphne with a cupcake. A single candle burned at a catastrophic rate, wax threatening frosting. "I think the candle company is running a scam."

"They had one job!" Daphne exclaimed before she blew out the candle. In her haste, she forgot to make a wish. She saw her oversight in the snake of gray smoke curling up towards the sky. For a few moments, her stomach ached with the missed opportunity, until she remembered—she'd survived.

Eighteen. She had survived the lethal year that had loomed over her for six years and followed through on its prophecy. Seventeen had begun as the best year of her life, morphed into the worst, and molded into something even better than the best. Now that her eighteenth birthday had arrived, she rolled her eyes inwardly at the notion that making it past one specific day in May could change the trajectory of her future. Yet, it was accurate. Eighteen held no stigma, only promise.

Daphne tore into Oliver's clumsily wrapped present and popped open the black velvet box. A necklace with a silver pendant of a bull gleamed at her, dainty and sophisticated for a farm animal. The bull's knee was bent, its head down, charging at the world.

Anxiety reverberated in Oliver's voice. "I know you're not a horoscope enthusiast, but it seemed appropriate, since we didn't attempt to run with any bulls. Now you can have one running with you whenever you want. But you don't have to wear it. I won't be offended. Only if you—"

She'd let him suffer long enough. "I love it."

He heaved a sigh of relief. "You do?"

"Put it on me."

His jittery fingers steadied to attach the clasp behind her neck. She ran her finger across the smooth curves of the pendant, over the small bumps of detail, and remembered running her finger across the 2006 nickel in the car on that Tuesday. She just as quickly stomped Jefferson away. That Tuesday had no place here, amongst the Crayola-scented candle smoke and utter bliss—but she traced the entire perimeter of the pendant for good measure. The pendant's weight would soon become familiar, making the necklace indiscernible when worn, a piece of her. Oxblood lipstick and a Taurus pendant, her two bovine signatures.

• • •

Daphne found herself sitting in the same chapel pew she sat in on weekdays, even though it was Sunday morning. Oliver had asked her to attend a service with him. She said yes without asking why. Hymns from half a lifetime ago sang to her. Father George's sermon on brotherly love was brief and inspired. It was refreshing to hear Leviticus used as a love letter to all mankind instead of a stepping stone for intolerance.

When she stood at the end of the service, her spirit was warm and full. Father George shook her hand on the way out with a twinkle in his eye. When he shook Oliver's hand, they shared the same twinkle. They knew something she didn't. It was a rare mystery of the universe where she rejoiced in not seeking out the answer.

Another mystery waited for her when she unlocked the

front door, one she'd been trying to figure out for eighteen years. Her parents.

"How was church?"

Daphne jumped at her dad's voice, at the sight of both of her parents seated on the couch next to each other. The scene was a ghost of Christmas past arriving in late spring.

"Good. New Testament-esque Leviticus." Daphne sat on the floor instead of taking the only open seat on her dad's La-Z-Boy. She noticed the twitchy way her parents were casting glances at each other. This conversation wasn't about church.

Her mom bowed her forehead toward her dad in a gesture of fierce encouragement. Clearly, they'd discussed the course of action prior to Daphne's arrival, and her dad was meant to lead the conversation. Daphne bowed her head, anticipating another abstinence-promoting sex lecture, this one delivered to her in her Sunday best.

Her dad cleared his dry throat and scratched the bandages that still wrapped his left arm and hand. "I think I need help."

"You do," Daphne said.

"I do need help. Yes. I do." He understood the words as he spoke them. Their repercussion beat against his temples.

"It's nice to hear you say that." Daphne meant it. Even if it had taken the better part of a decade for him to say it, even though she didn't trust a word of it.

"There's a clinic that has an opening, but it will fill soon, so I'd need to leave tomorrow," her dad continued.

Daphne nodded but remained stoic. She'd been burned by him more times than she could count on her fingers and toes. She refused to display optimism.

"If I leave now, I'll miss your graduation…" At the bottom of his voice he was still searching for a way out.

Daphne would never be his excuse. "Go. It's a bunch of idiots wearing matching robes."

"Well, I know how much it means to the idiot sitting in front of me."

He remembered. When Daphne had been little, when most girls dressed up as princesses and pranced around the house on an imaginary horse, Daphne had paraded around in her dad's bathrobe pretending she was at graduation. She had balanced a magazine on her head and tossed it into the air, cheering.

"You need this," she said. "We all need this. It would be the best graduation gift I could get."

He rushed over and pulled her up into an awkward hug with the strength of the dad from long ago. His arms were safe and warm. She felt like a little girl again, in the best way.

"There's something else." Her mom drew in a long breath.

Daphne didn't want to make her mom say it. "I know you can't pay anything for college. It's fine. I'll take out loans."

Her mom bristled. "No, that's not…what…"

"When I got my acceptance letter, I heard you and dad fighting. Saying you couldn't afford it."

Her mom shook her head. "No, never. We were probably fighting about your dad going to a treatment facility. I've been…encouraging him for a long time."

It made sense. The snippets she'd heard could've been about rehab and not college.

"Your future is more important to us than anything," her dad said.

"So we're going to sell the house and downsize to an apartment. That way, we can help you out with tuition as much as possible." Her mom reached for her dad's hand.

He squeezed his fingers around her palm. "And also afford rehab."

"Okay, wow. Thank you," Daphne said. Her parents were finally behaving like adults.

She couldn't help feeling a little sad. No longer coming home to this house would be strange. So much of her life had been shaped between these walls. Now it was another thing to let go of forever.

Her mom spared no sentimentality. "So when you pack for school, you need to pack everything you want us to take or put into storage."

"I will," Daphne matched her mother's businesslike tone.

"We're going to miss you." Her mom's throat stalled.

"I'm going to miss you, too." After all, there was a certain amount of comfort in familiar dysfunction.

All three broke into sloppy tears at the same time, huddling against each other in the center of the room. Something had changed. When Daphne came home for winter break, Casa Bowman wouldn't be fixed, but things might be better. The gaping holes that had been eroding for years could be filled, stone by stone.

• • •

Under the fluorescent lights of the school hallway, Daphne's face tingled as though she had a sunburn. Oliver's unshaven face had pressed against hers throughout the weekend's vacuum of time. Her mind was wide awake even though she'd been up until 2:00 a.m. talking to him on the phone. She had no memory of what they'd talked about. Even after two hours of constant chatter, they'd both ended the conversation reluctantly, though it gifted Daphne with pleasant dreams. This is what love did—woke you up.

A draft grazed her cheeks when she closed her locker door, revealing Penny behind it, ready to pounce. Daphne jumped at the sight of her.

"Don't you look smug," Penny said.

"I think you have the wrong locker."

Daphne strutted down the hall, unwilling to shift her mood for whatever drama Penny was serving. Penny chased after her, sandaled feet pattering to catch up.

"I let you and Janine come to my New Year's party. You owe me."

"I'm not breaking up with Oliver." Daphne threw the first punch.

"Oliver who?" Penny tried to smooth the bitterness, but the jagged edges poked through her voice.

Daphne didn't respond. She slowed her steps as a sign of compassion.

Penny said, "I need you to write my English essay on *Lord of the Flies.*"

"Are you serious?"

"You're the only person I know who's…smart."

"You're smart, Penny. Stop making excuses and read the stupid book."

"I can't read it. You know how bugs freak me out."

"That's not…" Daphne sighed.

Penny's nose twitched, and her lip quivered. She willed her voice to remain strong. "I'm failing English and might lose my early acceptance to UCSD."

It had been a long year for everyone, and a book about the dark forces ingrained in humanity might hurl Penny into despair. "Okay, I'll help you write your essay. The key word being *help*."

"Thank you," Penny muttered, expressing no gratitude. Instead, her thanks begrudgingly accepted forgiveness from someone who'd wronged her.

"But you need to read the CliffsNotes. There won't be any flies in there," Daphne said.

"Fine. Let me know when you're…free. It's due Tuesday." The deal sealed, Penny veered right and disappeared down a staircase, the clapping of her sandals applauding behind her.

• • •

Sweetie's became a purgatory between the present and future where Daphne could spend time with Oliver but multitask enough to not think about the fall. Fall. She worried it would feel like hanging off the rock at Joshua Tree without Oliver there to save her. She couldn't yet accept the fact that he would be in another state in just a few short months.

The Sweetie's haven was quashed one Saturday when the owner, Paul, dropped by unexpectedly. Oliver had been leaning against the counter, his face an inch away from Daphne's, their lips about to meet. Paul began ranting about health code violations and business ethics. A new no-significatant-others-allowed-unless-they-bring-at-least-two-friends-and-each-spend-over-five-dollars-and-no-touching policy was instituted.

Daphne saw this as unfair, but Paul had always been kind to her and had granted her every day off she'd ever requested. Luckily, there was still no policy on best friends, perhaps due to the lack of touching. Janine's weekend visits dwindled, most of her spare time sucked up by Mel. But Mel had track after school, so Janine dropped by during Daphne's weekday shifts. It was the only time they socialized outside of school anymore.

"You agreed to write her paper? Schmuck," Janine said.

"I'm helping her. She was desperate. It was unsettling. You would've enjoyed it."

Janine squirmed, small movements against solidarity.

"What? A chance to rag on Penny and you're not taking it?" Daphne asked.

"She's not so bad," Janine admitted quietly.

Daphne's confusion grew louder. "She's been your personal Satan for years."

Janine took a breath. "We made out."

Daphne abhorred double punctuation. Choose a question mark or exclamation point, but you can't have both. This, however, was a moment where multiple question marks and exclamation points were not only encouraged, but necessary. "What?!"

"It just happened. She was experimenting. And I was crushing on her."

"When?!" Again, multiple punctuation.

"When my dumbass cousin that you were hooking up with was in town."

Daphne's mouth fell open. "Ah. So?"

"Sew buttons."

"What was it like? I don't know. What am I supposed to ask? My two best friends were making out behind my back."

"She said she didn't want it to happen again, and I got pissed. I thought she was like me. I was so relieved. And when she wasn't, I kind of lost it. I hated her. And I was afraid she'd tell everyone."

"But you had it over her, too."

"Yeah, but it was my truth. Not hers."

Daphne nodded.

Janine still fidgeted in her seat. "She promised she wouldn't tell. And I don't think she ever did."

"Why didn't you tell me?" Janine had never kept a secret from Daphne for longer than a day or two, except Mel. Daphne didn't like this pattern.

"I was the reason Penny left us. I thought you might leave with her. I couldn't lose both of you."

Daphne placed her hand on Janine's forearm. "You weren't the reason. We grew apart, no one's fault."

"You're breaking the no touching rule," Janine said.

"Fire me."

Janine gasped. "No! How will I get free ice cream?"

"Okay, but, seriously, how did it happen?" Daphne asked.

Janine hung her head.

Daphne giggled. "You're blushing! You're blushing over Penny Layton!"

"She kissed me. I swear." Janine was still dumbfounded by it after all these years.

"I don't doubt it. The girl goes after what she wants. It's terrifying to be on the other side of it."

Janine's head bobbed in agreement. "No shit. Put it up." Janine raised her arm and Daphne high-wristed her.

The bumping of those delicate bones was Daphne's constant. Seeing Janine once a week, once a month, once a year, Daphne going to Berkeley, Janine going to SC, nothing would change between them. She was as sure of this as she was of rainbow sherbet being the least popular flavor in the freezer.

"Okay, I need some mint chip, stat!"

Daphne jumped at the crack of the whip and plunged the scoop into the freezer.

• • •

The dread that usually accompanied Daphne as she stood on the Laytons' welcome mat was partially quelled by Janine's Penny revelation. Still, it wasn't entirely gone. Given the intangible power Penny wielded, Daphne knew why Janine had been afraid for so long.

Daphne rang the doorbell and hoped Mrs. Layton wouldn't answer the door. Daphne didn't want lemonade, or mocktails, or whatever bougie drink Mrs. Layton would be presenting on a matching platter. Daphne wanted to write this essay as quickly as possible and deflect any barbs thrown by Penny with minimal injury. Hydration would only slow the process and heighten the torture.

But the lemonade gods were listening; it was Penny who opened the door holding the CliffsNotes. Shrouded in the glow of her allegiance to Janine, Daphne had expected to view Penny in a new light. But Penny's ashen face cast too large of a shadow. Her eyes counted down to meltdown: 5, 4, 3, 2, 1 and the tears flowed.

"They killed Piggy," she sobbed.

Sometimes the world was perfectly unfair. All of a sudden, they were twelve again and dying each other's hair and promising to keep secrets. Daphne hugged Penny and Penny squeezed her, crying into her shoulder. Something in the universe had fallen back in line, if only for the duration of a *Lord of the Flies* essay.

• • •

In a tent in Oliver's backyard, Daphne and Oliver made out, every inch of their skin creating an irresistible friction between them.

"I forgot. I have a graduation present for you." He didn't bother putting his shirt back on when he unzipped the tent.

She cringed and called after him. "I didn't get you anything."

He reappeared with a black, globe-sized box with pentagonal panels. "It's okay. This is kind of a joint gift. Well, I hope it is."

"Best kind of gift for you."

"Well, Thoughtless, it's the only kind of gift for me," Oliver teased. He clicked on the contraption and it clanged to life. Purple and green-tinged galaxies lit up all sides of the tent.

"Whoa." Daphne marveled at the outer space surrounding her.

"Number nine. And some mumbo jumbo about always

being under the same stars even if we're not together. Yada, yada, yada."

"So eloquent." She didn't wait until he was fully on the ground before she kissed him. He playfully pulled her on top of him and helped her tug off her shirt. Only crickets and their laughter played in the quiet night.

She hovered over him, peering down into his eyes, his irises dulled with pleasure. "I want to," she whispered.

"I didn't get the star projector to get in your pants."

"Well, it worked." She sucked on his ear and groped his fly.

They both removed their pants. He reached into his discarded jeans pocket for his wallet and pulled out a condom. "Not saying we're going to, but just in case."

While she appreciated him giving her the chance to back out, she had always been a woman who knew what she wanted. Tonight was no different, and she bristled at the suggestion. "Take off your boxers," she said.

Reassured by her annoyance, Oliver obeyed. She slipped out of her bra and panties and they lay on their sides studying each other's bodies, hot and cold in all the right places.

"Are you scared?" he asked.

"A little. More excited."

"Me, too," he confessed.

"Why are you scared? You've done this before."

"Not with someone I loved."

She scooted over, grabbed the hair on the base of his skull, and kissed the fear out of him. The condom unwrapping and placement survived fumbling fingers and nervous laughter.

Maybe it was from the avid biking in her childhood or

using tampons for five years, but nothing hurt. Awkward, yes. Uncomfortable, maybe. Painful, nothing of the sort. He moved slow, so slowly she wanted to tell him he could go faster, but she worried the instruction would be mistaken for critique. *Next time.* She was already an addict.

The twisting of Oliver's face was the most erotic part of losing her virginity. Between kisses, his face transformed from worry into hope into lust into worship. When he collapsed with the final shudder, she held him to her heart and wrapped her legs around his. This was the closest she'd ever been to someone, ever would be.

After a few deep breaths, he came back to life, kissing her neck, moving his lips down—across her heart, over her stomach, down until her sharp inhale told him where to stay. With every passing second, little pieces broke apart from her body and floated up to the stars, until there were so many cracks, too many holes, there was nothing left to do but shatter and let the universe put her back together again.

"You're amazing," he said, kissing his way back up to her lips. He pulled a blanket over them, and she curled into his spoon. The sleep in his breath floated across her ear.

"By the way, I love you, too," she said.

He tightened his arms around her. This was how she would sleep. Until her curfew, which was in an hour.

• • •

Elliott Smith accompanied the hum of the projector. Daphne lay in her dark bedroom, the previous night replaying against the stars that adorned her bedroom walls. The urge to call Janine and recap wasn't bold enough to move her fingers to her phone. She wanted to talk to someone, though, and that person was Emily.

Clink-crrrrrrrr. The metallic zing came from the dresser. The 2006 nickel propped against the mirror had slipped down to sleep flat on its side. The vibration from its sudden movement faded into the thickness of the late afternoon. A sign or well-timed gravity? Both emboldened her feeble bond with her sister.

She wondered if Emily would like Oliver. He was inherently like Jason, try as he might to rage against it. Would Emily even like her? Daphne had let their mom find the list—perhaps that was unforgivable. When it came to Emily, Daphne would always be ten years old, sitting at her desk, guarding her words.

Her questions were rational and deductive, but emotion crept in and tears poured down her face. These were important questions, and they deserved answers.

Daphne hated Emily for a few sniffling breaths and forgave her before she finished wiping her eyes. She remembered that last conversation with Emily, her wink at the list. Daphne concluded that gushing to Emily about how madly in love she was with Oliver Pagano would elicit that same wink. Without speaking, Emily would congratulate her. *You made it. I knew you would. I love those boots.*

NUMBER 10

TIME CLOSED IN ON OLIVER. THE PASSING DAYS FELL AWAY like a cliff crumbling under his feet. A job at the car wash and its summer tips had been tempting. Opposite Possum wasn't as formidable as it once was, but Oliver wasn't ready to step into the shoes of Jason's old job. Instead, he'd gotten a less lucrative job at a movie theater and spent his days shoveling popcorn into cups only to sweep half of it up from the stadium floors. He didn't mind the sweeping part because he was never alone and had befriended even his most timid coworkers. He was able to coax conversation from the most resistant with little pressure, and the hours passed quickly from theater to theater.

It was the shoveling part he tried to dodge. The length of conversations behind the concession stand amounted to someone grumbling under their breath, *[Insert Manager] is such a(n) [insert expletive]*. Popcorn and soda cursed him with time to think about Montana, fast approaching with its vast plains and rocky glaciers. Lost in a trance of ice cubes and carbonated beverages, he had a recurring vision of a bison pawing the tundra and charging at him. The cold burn of soda overflow on his hand snapped him back to California.

The opposite of his life had sounded so melodic when he mailed the lone application. He'd been blindsided in the best way possible, but he was still reeling, unsure where to land. He knew one thing. He didn't want to follow his girlfriend to college. That kind of codependence was pathetic. He was also sure of another thing. He loved Daphne Bowman. He didn't want to be apart from her. It seemed impossible.

The only perk of employment was that Oliver's curfew was erased. After his evening shifts ended, he drove for hours just to drive, lost in contemplation, windows down, night air rapping against his face. He turned home and toppled into bed when the edges of the sky glowed white-blue with the day to come.

• • •

The time of departure had arrived. Oliver resisted his dad's help with loading his car. Nonetheless, his dad made all of the trips up and down the stairs with him. After the last packed box had been stuffed in the trunk, after Oliver sat on the box because its nook was too small for its volume, after the box cracked and bulged in protest, and after he slammed the trunk door closed with satisfaction, his dad spoke for the first and last time.

"You're a man. A good man, Oliver. I'm…"

He trailed off and Jason's shadow receded from Oliver, leaving the late summer sun to blaze down upon only him. The warmth was overwhelming, and the tears in his dad's eyes added to the heat.

"It's because of my masterful trunk packing skills, isn't it?" Oliver grinned.

His dad snickered through a sniffle, and Oliver wrapped his arms around his dad's back.

His dad squeezed him tight and patted his shoulder blade. "I'm so proud of you."

After that day in the driveway, Oliver also packed away his resentment for the company name, Pagano and Sons. The dark cloud over the plural was gone.

• • •

The remains of eighteen years littered the floors of Oliver's disaster area bedroom. The walls were untouched, like the single house still standing after a tornado. The blank walls of his Montana dorm room called to him, and they would display nothing from the past. His mom waded through the discard piles on the floor as he dropped a basketball into the final box for the backseat.

"Starting to look very empty in here."

"I'm leaving as much as possible, and I'll be back in December." Oliver was distraught enough without his parents' help. "Dad got me in the driveway. Are you guys tag teaming me?"

She sat down on the bed, which meant she had something to say and wouldn't leave until she was done. "Did you know your great-grandfather built all the furniture he used to sell with his own hands?"

Oliver shook his head and stopped loading the box. He knew his great-grandfather had started the family business, but this was a new revelation in his lineage.

"Beautiful pieces. A true craftsman. He was an artist who made a living selling his art. It became a business when your grandfather took over, because he had no art to give. And your dad and I happened to love the furniture business."

"I know."

"But we're lucky. It was chance that worked out, and we feel blessed." She took a breath. "The business will be there for you. But if you're not there for it…" She shrugged. "We'll sell when we retire. It will all end happily as it arrived."

Oliver nodded. He wished he could give a more detailed answer, but he didn't want to accidentally make any promises. His parents deserved better than that, and so did he.

"Montana is awfully far away," his mom mused.

"So is San Francisco, if that's what you're hinting at." He regretted mentioning San Francisco, giving her a window to pull open the curtains and discuss Daphne. If his mom encouraged him to move to San Francisco, he would further resist doing so. And he didn't want to resist it.

"No." She paused and sucked the insides of her teeth. "Oliver, you're alive. You're allowed to make mistakes. You're allowed to change your mind."

His mom hugged him. It was a preparatory goodbye for the actual goodbye hug in two days. But this one was better because his mom had just forgiven him—for everything. The long hug would stick with him while he drove north to Montana through the rocky hills of wine country, the Pacific at his side. In his mom's embrace, the tension in Oliver broke apart. He had his answer in the form of a non-answer. There wasn't a right or wrong choice. His future wasn't a fork in the road, it was a winding path for him to pave. He might even sign up for an art class. Or graphic design.

• • •

That night, Jason tiptoed into Oliver's mind, the memory that Oliver always pushed the furthest away, burying it deep within him. Tonight, Oliver let it move, stretch its legs, dance around the insides of his skull.

"Bet you can't hit it over the fence," Jason says.

In the backyard, Jason drops his mitt as home plate and takes ten reaching strides in front of it.

"Bet I can." Oliver touches the mitt with the bat, measures his sweet spot, sets his stance, and hoists the bat over his right shoulder.

Jason winds up and throws. The ball flies at Oliver in slow motion. His swing is swift, and CRACK!

The sound still shakes his bones.

The ball sails over the fence.

"Home run!" Jason chants, throwing his arms over his head. "Better hurry and grow up. The Dodgers need you."

Seeing his brother's joy, Oliver's chest is so full of so many things, ready to explode.

Jason picks up another ball. "Come on. Hit me right here."

He taunts Oliver with a mischievous grin and taps the bridge of his nose.

Oliver tightens his grip on the bat and the ball comes at him, closer, closer, closer.

Swing.

Oliver marched into Jason's bedroom. He pulled Jason's mitt from the back of the closet and brushed off the dust. He removed the basketball from the final box and replaced it with the mitt. His chest was half full, half empty with the pride and anguish from the memory. A new force also pushed against his sternum. Empathy.

His brother had suffered, had lost to the darkness. But in whatever capacity, he'd had Emily. Oliver hoped that Jason had the privilege of loving Emily. Loving her with all of his light, however dim. The light that had led Oliver to Daphne.

For the first time, Jason and Emily were a comforting image. They calmed his own trepidation while he waited for the doorbell to ring. It was the last night. The night that had given Oliver a summer of insomnia.

Oliver flung open the door, kissing and lifting Daphne into the air, taking her by surprise. He returned her feet to the porch.

"I'm lucky it was you." He breathed into her hair, smelling her scent.

"I'm lucky it was me." Her flush was the best compliment.

"Coffee?" he suggested.

"Sugar and dairy disguising itself as caffeine? Sure."

Oliver and Daphne sat across from each other at Frank's Diner, coffee and donuts in front of them. This time, Oliver faced the door.

"Old-fashioned. That says something about your personality." Oliver creamed and sugared his coffee.

Daphne dipped her old-fashioned into her coffee. "Do tell."

"You're a purist. No cream. No sugar. No icing. Just coffee and cake donut. You're like vanilla: timeless."

She smiled while chewing. "Tell me that in ten years."

"I will." He took a bite of his glazed with sprinkles. "What does my donut say about me?"

"You like sugar and flavorless dyed particles."

"Essence of my being." He grinned and took another bite. The same waitress from months ago refilled his mug.

After the tinkling of spoon against ceramic, sweetness dissolving into brew, Oliver pulled out his copy of the list and laid it in front of him. The piece of paper bore the markings of a true adventure, bent at the corners, rumpled in the middle, small tears in the side edges. Everything was accounted for except the blank number ten.

He rapidly jotted on the worn paper and pushed it to the center of the table. New numbers in sharp, black ink trickled down the margin. The list continued, eleven through twenty.

Daphne tossed him her feisty look, the glint in her eyes that made him want to dive across the table and kiss her until his lips were raw, hold her until the sun came up. He wanted to be forever lost in those eyes.

She pulled the list over and scribbled down her number ten. With a flourish, she dropped the pen on the list and sat back in the booth, waiting for him to meet her challenge.

Oliver slid the paper back in front of him and read. He met her gaze with a checkmate grin.

"That's exactly what I was thinking," he said. "Let's go."

"Right now?" She chugged her coffee.

"Right now."

He took her hand, and they went.

RESOURCES

If you or someone you know is struggling with depression or suicidal thoughts, please know that there is help. You matter.

For depression, please get help right now.

National Alliance on Mental Illness (NAMI)
nami.org
Call 1-800-950-6264 (NAMI)
Text "NAMI" to 741741

Substance Abuse and Mental Health Services Administration (SAMHSA)
samhsa.gov
Call 1-800-662-4357 (HELP)

Teen Mental Health
teenmentalhealth.org

If you are suicidal, please get help right now.

National Suicide Prevention Lifeline
Chat at suicidepreventionlifeline.org
Call 1-800-273-8255 (TALK)

ACKNOWLEDGMENTS

This book and I have been on a journey. We wouldn't have made it here without the guidance of many wonderful, talented people. A very special thank you to my agent, Aimee Ashcraft. You were the first person to love this book as much as I do (sometimes more), and you've been a true champion for SGTMY every step of the way. Also, thank you to Kimberly Brower and Brower Literary for all of your expertise.

I've been blessed having Lia Ottaviano as my editor. You understood this book from the beginning and made it cleaner and sharper than I ever dreamed. I stand on the shoulders of the entire team at Diversion Books: Sarah Masterson Hally and her beautiful cover, Erin Mitchell, Angela Man, and Eliza Kirby.

Publishing is a slow whirlwind, but I've connected with so many lovely people who've helped me weather the storm. Brenda Drake and everyone involved in Pitch Wars have built the most supportive community an aspiring author could ask for. The awesome writers of Team32 helped me survive being out on submission. The brilliant

Electric Eighteens carried me through 2018 and beyond. I love you all.

Thank you to Beth Ontrop for being my family for the last twenty years and for always giving stellar reading recommendations. And thank you to Mariel Conry for being excited about this book when I needed the encouragement.

Thank you to Amy and Duane Brown for being the best in-laws someone could hope for. Thank you to my sister, Kim Montgomery, for always listening to me yammer on about writing and life, in general. Thank you to my mom, Claudia Morrison, for being a lifelong reader, and for always buying me books when I asked for them. We never made a trip to the mall without going to a bookstore. And thanks for buying the *Good Will Hunting* soundtrack.

The two women to whom this book is dedicated would've been thrilled for SGTMY and me. My Grandma Super was an octogenarian who frequently went polka-dancing with her girlfriends. Without you, my move to L.A. wouldn't have been possible, and I'm forever grateful. And my Grandma McCarter, who was a difficult woman, born before her time. But you were always my biggest fan. Thank you. I miss you every day.

I wouldn't have wanted to write YA without the gifted teachers I had in Morris, IL. I thank everyone whose classrooms I sat in from Franklin to Garfield to Center to MCHS. I was learning even if I didn't know it at the time.

A special thank you to a few teachers who instilled lessons I've used long after graduation: Sharon Morris, who taught me that people are not always what they seem (for the better). Sharon Marizza, who gave a quiet girl some confidence. And David Rice, who I'm truly honored to call my mentor and my friend. You taught me how to find meaning in words so that I might write words with meaning.

And I've saved my largest thank you for last because it will never be big enough. Thank you, Nathan Brown. So many hats are piled on your head, and you look dashing in all of them: first editor (he gives very thorough notes), head cheerleader, and life partner. I love that every day I get to look at you and ask, *Where are we going next?*

LISA SUPER is a brunch enthusiast based in Los Angeles. She's worked on a number of TV shows ranging from pop culture phenomenons (*Flavor of Love*) to traumedy gold (*One Mississippi*). While every day in LA is an adventure, traveling with her husband across the globe is her favorite hobby. *So Glad to Meet You* is her first novel.